Springhee[l]
The[...]

HARBINGER

E.J. Davies

ArdArt
PUBLISHING

Springheeled Jack: The Harbinger
is a ArdArt Publishing book

First published in Great Britian in 2019
by ArdArt Publishing

978-1-9162207-1-3

Set in 12/18pt Garamond by Amy Carr & Wayne Noble

A CIP catalogue record for this book will be
available from the British Library.

Printed and bound in Great Britain by Clays Ltd, Elcograf S.p.A.

JOCELYN

THANKS

FOR

COMING

I would like to dedicate this novel to my Dad.
Upon his knee I sat as a child listening enthralled
to his tall tales of 'Springheeled Jack'.
The seed was planted deep in my mind.

I would like to thank my friend John for
being there at the start, also, my wife
Caroline for being there at the end.

Also to Debbie, Wayne and Amy
for their support, encouragement and patience.

The End?
London, the year of our Lord 1402.

They had at last managed to capture it, the harbinger, the cause of all the chaos and devastation brought upon the city and its unfortunate inhabitants. Bloated blackened bodies floated in the Thames, homes and businesses burned along its shore. Many had left once the fires began, those that had remained were consumed by a madness, killing and mutilating all they found whether it be man or beast. However now, after all hope had been thought lost, they finally had the cause of it.

The six men pushed and heaved their way through empty streets, struggling with the large cumbersome cart. They had all questioned why the use of animals had been forbidden, but the Priest had spoken to each of them, warning against the weaker minds of both horse and oxen. "If they are strong enough to move this cart," he had told them, "then they are strong enough to kill. The Beast could easily control the mind of any cattle we use. We cannot take any chances once the Beast has been captured. The strength of man's body and mind will suffice, if you be pure of heart."

A cage had been roughly constructed by the Blacksmith, under instruction from the Priest. He had fixed large iron plates to a cart creating a shell-like prison for the Beast, the Priest had performed a blessing over each part as the Blacksmith worked. It was heavy and it was solid. It had to be.

Imprisoned within, the Beast ripped at the plates, it released a piercing haunting sound, half scream, half hiss as its flesh burned each time it made contact with the metal. Its grey skin blistered and pulsed, puss began to build on the edge of the iron, thick and yellow. The plates became slippery. Not wanting to touch the foul slime the men had to find other places upon which they could exert their force.

The Beast thrust its long arms out through the gaps attempting to grab its tormentors, dragging its flesh against the metal as it withdrew back into its prison when the pain became too much. It sat squat, its long naked body barely contained within the cramped area, its limbs twisted unnaturally, waiting for the chance to lash out at its captors.

Each time it did, the men leaped away from the iron cart fearing the grasp of the Beast and its long black broken talons. They had all seen the results of being held within its dark embrace. Each man had lost family members to its influence, had witnessed the madness it caused to those around it, the evil it induced and the death that it revelled upon. They feared it and that fear sustained it.

It was slow going. Up ahead of them their destination and the Priest. He waited anxiously for them outside the churchyard, his figure illuminated by fire, his silhouette black against the large oak doors upon which his shadow danced. He wanted to help them, to share in their burden, but he knew he could not. He had explained to them that his leading of their party would have ensured they had no hope of capturing the Beast. It would have sensed God's power within him, would have realized its possible fate and fought more vehemently. Its escape could not be facilitated.

Half their number had been lost in its capture and a further two in the short distance they had come. Its mere presence enraged those who were weak minded, it possessed them, caused a blind evil bloodlust that compelled them to kill anything or anyone. The only way to stop them was to kill them. Not doing so would ensure your own demise.

The six remaining men held onto the amulets the Priest had given them when they had agreed to participate in its capture. Strange figures cast in iron hung from a leather strap, some hung them around their necks, others tied them to their wrists. Although all were offered, those now left had been the only ones to take them. The only ones that had found a new faith in the old magic, the old forgotten Gods.

Lightning filled the sky; a loud crack of thunder overhead announced the coming of heavy rain. The Beast thrust its arms through the gaps between the iron plates welcoming the cool water. Rivulets ran off its darkened waxy skin mixing with the puss to form a slippery mass. It slid down the plates pooling around the hands of its captors. With no place left for them to move their hands to, they held on as it covered their skin, the touch of it sickening them.

Rain soaked the earth; the path became muddy. Each of the four wheels carved deep trenches into the softened ground. The carts back wheels began to slide towards the burning houses that lined the street. Desperately the men pushed, attempting to manoeuvre it back into the centre of the path. Each of them knowing that the Beast's presence could possess any unfortunates still residing in the tumbled down buildings.

The rain became heavier, the mud thicker. Their strength waning the men cried out as they strained to move the cart nearer to the church "Please Lord, help us!" one screamed at the sky. The Lord answered with a deafening thunder clap.

The Beast's long arm reached out to the man as he cowered from the sound, its fingers grasping for his exposed throat. Just in time he had glimpsed its movement and stepped out of reach, holding out his amulet.

The front wheel of the cart jammed against a rock causing its back wheels to turn to the right and slide. Once again, they tried to stop it, but to no avail, the carts back edge crashed into a wall.

The men looked up at the dark house it had rested against. The burnt and broken door was no longer attached but had been left to lean against the space it had once occupied. The boarded-up windows black with the heat of the fire that had consumed it.

Lightning lit up the street, to the men staring up at the derelict home the windows took on the appearance of hollow blinded eyes, they looked back at the cart and began to heave it away from the house. None of them had been aware of the blank bloodied face of a woman peering at them from behind the burnt broken doorway.

She burst from the darkness pushing the broken door aside, screaming at the men as they freed the cart and began to slowly push it towards the church. Leaping at the nearest man she grasped at his neck, but he had seen her. Turning his head out of reach, he grabbed at the ripped clothes she wore and pulled her across his body. Using her own weight, he forced her to the ground and pushed her face hard into the mud. The Beast screamed at her, with renewed strength she slipped the man's grip and scrambled on all fours towards the cart. Another, seeing her crawling towards him stamped on her head as she neared hoping to crush her skull. Each man knew she was capable of killing them if allowed the opportunity, evil now resided within her, the screams of the Beast enraged her.

The man held his foot down on her head as long as he could, she squirmed under the pressure forcing her own face deeper into the soft mud. The Beast screamed and rocked the cart. He glanced around looking for a weapon, hoping that the others could keep the cart moving until he had dealt with her. He spied a large piece of wood, broken and burnt but small enough for him to handle. It meant letting loose of the woman. He looked down at her. She was forcing her fists into the ground in a desperate attempt to lift her body, her legs slipping in the mud as she did. It was his only option. He gave one last push down on her head hoping to hear the sound of her skull cracking. Nothing, the mud was too soft. He jumped at his potential weapon, grasping it he turned holding it in both hands ready to smash it into her.

The instant his pressure had been released she leapt up, but instead of attacking him she had turned and was now scrambling towards the group pushing the cart. The screams of the Beast called to her. She managed to slip between the men and onto the cart clutching at the iron plates, she heaved at them her whole body straining, hoping to break them apart.

"She's trying to free it, stop her. Stop her."

The cart slid to a stop as they tried to prize her from it. The Beast held onto her arms, its long black talons ripping deep into her flesh. They pulled her back, flesh tore from her arms. She neither noticed nor felt pain. Her sole purpose now was to release the Beast, doing so would stop the tormenting screams in her head, her whole body burned with the pain they caused.

Slipping their grip, she leapt back onto the plates, long flaps of her skin slapped against the iron with a sickening sound, her blood smeared black across the metal.

The large wooden beam came down upon the nape of her neck with such force that it snapped her spine. Her broken body fell slumped against the plates, the Beast pulled at her in a desperate attempt to keep hold as she slipped down and into the mud. The woman breathed a rasping final breath but that was all. She died, her body and mind broken.

Lightning lit up the rest of the street and seeing that the Priest was still waiting for them, the men took to their task once more. One last effort and they would be at the church gates, they all prayed the Priest could fulfil the promises he had made.

The Priest had seen the woman attack them from the shadows and had fought desperately with his conscious. Wanting to help them he had stepped from the doorway, but he knew he could not leave the protection of the church. He was already risking the influence of the Beast by waiting at the entrance to the grounds, but he had waited inside long enough, his will had weakened when no news of its capture had reached him.

He had instructed the men to send word so that he could be ready, but no one had returned. Now, looking at the small number of men struggling with the heavy cart he realised why. They could not have hoped to bring the cart and let one return alone with the news.

'*So many killed,*' he thought.

He had prayed that he had convinced enough of his congregation to go, to ensure their success. Now it seemed he had underestimated the Beast, and so luck also had been their ally.

He thanked God that his calculations had been correct and that the Beast had indeed been caught in this part of the city. He had realized, too late for many, that there had been a pattern within the madness and the murders that had recently taken over the city. There were of course killings occurring every day in every area, but he had rightly suspected, that the newly deranged population could not be blamed for them all.

It was the reported mutilation of a few of the bodies that had intrigued him enough to investigate, they had been killed by something different. He felt he had found a connection. A definite pattern made by the Beast, he had gambled the lives of his remaining flock on that calculation.

He eased with a sigh as the woman was brought down and the men continued with their unenviable task. He could now hear the cry of the Beast from where he stood, hoping to bring those under its influence too its aid, to escape, to finish its work. It seemed to him, that thankfully there was now no one in the area left to hear its cry.

The men looked towards him as they maneuverer the cart along the track. One man shouted, but his voice was lost as thunder clapped overhead. The storm was worsening, lightening criss-crossed the sky, the Priest now no longer believed it was all natures doing.

The doors to the churchyard behind him shook with the force of another thunder clap, reminding him that they were still closed. He turned and with all his might, pushed them open.

'Had they had become heavier?' he thought, struggling.

Another shout from the men. Once again, he didn't hear but resisted the urge to step forward onto the street.

'Could it be the Beasts influence deadening even the sound? Did it want him to step out from the protection of this holy place? Become a victim of its evil?' "The mask," he cried towards them, "did you fix the mask to it?"

"We did Father," replied the man nearest to him, they had almost reached the gate. The cart would only just fit through, so the men grasped it where best they could and pushed with their remaining strength. With no one to guide it the Priest prayed that it would not become jammed against the stone wall. If that happened, all would be lost. The few that were left had neither the strength nor the will to begin heaving it back and forth attempting to release it.

The edge of the iron plates scraped the stone on each side of the gate but instead of jamming, it easily slipped through. Each of the men would later swear that they felt the cart pull away from them, as if dragged from the front. It passed through the gateway and onto the hallowed earth of the church.

The men were left standing at the mouth of the gate watching as the cart came to a halt a few meters into the churchyard. All were puzzled and frightened. The Priest had also witnessed the movement of the cart, he sensed some presence had taken possession and dragged the Beast onto sacred ground, towards the church, towards Gods vengeance and away from the unwelcoming chaotic world it had created.

He walked over to the cart, the Beast was now silent. It sensed where it was. A power emanated from the land around it, for the first time it felt something new, something unknown. It felt fear.

Although a church now stood there, the land below it had seen many religions and many ceremonies.

The Priest had researched as best he could the history of the land. He had found text dating back hundreds of years in the church crypt, documenting the strange draw this site had had on the religious leaders of old. He knew this place was special, the only place within which the Beast could be imprisoned.

The heavy rain ran down his arms and onto the metal as he placed his palms on the cold iron. The Priest peered within, bringing his face closer and closer to the darkness. He could neither see nor hear anything. The darkness within was all consuming. Lightning illuminated the churchyard, thunder clapped and the Priest screamed leaping away from the cart. The men at the gate gasped and all subconsciously moved a step back.

Two flat black holes appeared just inches from the priest's face. A gaping maw opened and closed beneath and the foulest stench filled his nostrils. The sight of it had startled him, his heart pumped fiercely in his chest. He quickly realized that they were not its eyes, it was the mask he had instructed them to place over its head. Made from leather and iron it would restrict its power and cause it much pain as it burned and blistered the skin beneath. He had ensured the Beast could not remove the mask by having the edge of the leather straps fixed with an iron rim, the Blacksmith then locked them with an iron clasp. The power of iron had been known for millennia.

He once again moved towards the cart and peered into

it. Once his eyes had become accustomed to the darkness within, he stared at the Beast, its mouth open, its tongue flicking against sharp broken teeth. "We have you. We have you now. Let God bring justice upon you, as easily as you brought death to others," he spat at it.

The men at the gate stood motionless watching as the priest leaned over and spat down at the Beast. He looked up and walked over to them. "You have done all you can, but you cannot stay."

The men protested. They wanted it dead. They themselves wanted to bring death upon it.

"You have all paid dearly for what you have done this night, I cannot ask you to do more. You few are the last of the believers, you must take hope to those that remain," he said to them holding his arms wide, herding them out of the churchyard. "God will remember you all for what you have done. Now please, you cannot help me in what I must do." The priest took hold of the large oak doors and shut them on the men and the broken world outside.

They stood in the rain, tired, wet and close to collapse. "We cannot forsake him, we must help," the speaker moved amongst them. "Many men died bringing that thing here. What can one man do against so much power? So much hate?"

One looked away. "We have done what was asked, I have no more left to give," he said, as he turned to walk slowly back along the muddy street, exhaustion overwhelmed him, they all felt it. More followed until only one remained standing at the gate. He glanced back at the huge wooden doors listening, hoping that some sound, a cry for help from the Priest would bring them running back. Hearing nothing, he turned and followed his companions. Their figures black against the fires that raged for as far as they could see. The whole city burned. Their whole world had burned.

The Priest waited with his back against the doors, he hoped that they would leave. Death would be their only reward for remaining to help. The churchyard seemed darker, as if the presence of the Beast had affected what little light there was.

Through the rain he looked at the cart, its iron plates weighing it down. The wheels sunken into the mud.

'How did they ever get it here?' he wondered.

He walked past the cart towards the church doors. He had placed a large cross, also made by the Blacksmith, against them. Like the cage, it too was made from iron.

Retrieving it, he made his way back to where the cart had come to rest. The rain was relentless and the ground sodden. The Priest felt around the rim of the plates for the hidden clasp he had instructed the Blacksmith to build into it.

He had designed it so that once it was closed, it would self-lock and could not be opened unless you knew about the secret release. He hadn't dared tell the men about the clasp, he couldn't risk the Beast probing their minds and finding of its existence, nor did he mention as they set out on their hazardous task that if they closed the cage without the Beast first being trapped inside it, it was all over, no second chance.

He tried to imagine how they had captured it, how they must have struggled to secure the mask over its head. Overcoming it as it ripped at them, clawing at their flesh and minds until finally it had been imprisoned. Many of their own lying dead around them.

Finding the clasp, he released it. The top half of the cage sprung up slightly. Standing back, the Priest watched as long black fingers felt their way along the edge, it made no sound, but the Priest knew that even this lightest touch was causing it pain. It gripped the heavy top and easily lifted it open. The cart shifted with the change in weight, leaning over as the heavy iron top dropped to the side.

The Priest held onto the cross with both hands waiting for the Beast. He could see movement within the darkness as it began to emerge. Its long slender limbs sliding over the edge. Its thin emaciated body scrapping the side as it managed to heave itself from the cart. It slumped to the floor motionless.

'Was this a trick?' thought the Priest.

He held his breath waiting.

'It was a trick, it had to be.' He considered moving over to it, willing his body to move forward, but something

wasn't right. He felt it waiting for him. Moments passed, no sound, no movement, just the cool rain on his face. Suddenly he realized that he had taken a few steps towards it, he was almost within reach of its long arms. He jumped back as the Beasts arm shot out at him, its talons passing only inches from his robes. It held its head up and emitted a high-pitched scream.

The Priest shook himself and holding the iron cross in both hands forced it into the ground. It went deep into the softened earth. Immediately there was a thunder clap and lightning struck the cross. The whole churchyard lit up with a blinding white light, the Priest was thrown back, coming to rest against a gravestone.

Feeling the cold wet stone against his back, he held his hands up, pain causing him to shake uncontrollably. He looked down at his hands, they had been burnt black, his fingers bent into his palms, he couldn't move them. Slowly he shuffled himself forward onto his knees and looked for the Beast.

It too was on its knees screaming, its whole body writhed as a light surrounded it. It came from the cross, a divine power reaching out binding the Beast with a blinding white light, burning its flesh. It tried to stand.

"*O pater, pater*," the Priest chanted, raising himself up, moving towards it. Static charges whipped from the ground at his feet as he walked "*Ego, servus tuus ignorans, portem tuam iram contra hune serpentem humilem.*" He had never had cause to use words like these and he desperately hoped that they were correct.

The Beast struggled to its full stature. Thunder sounded. The rain fell harder. The Priest shouted to be heard above the weather. *"Te iacio in lucem amatam, o serpens plutonis."* Lightning once again struck the cross, its white power engulfed the Beast, its screams echoed through the churchyard.

It was forced back to the earth hard enough for its body to leave an impression in the soft grass. The Priest crossed himself, *"Amoris calorem dei tibi porto,"* he said, stumbling against a gravestone unable to use his hands to steady himself, he felt his life ebbing away.

The stone he found himself leaning against and those around him began to glow with a powerful charge. *"Te capio captivum in casa dei."*

The Beast began to rise above the ground, lifting, it was held in place by the power that now surrounded it. Bright blue light sparked between its body and the wet earth. The Priest, holding up his burnt hands shouted at the storm, *"Pater noster in animam tuam veniet et cordem malam capiet."*

Lightning struck the church twice, carving two long scars diagonally across its tower. Huge static bolts began to pound the Beast, it tried desperately to turn away but was held fast by the power surrounding it.

The Priest turned looking for the source of this new power. He was encircled in a white light. It was coming from the gravestones around him. He could feel them vibrating as each bolt fired at the Beast.

"Cor molesta capiatur, abeat anima mala," he cried. The churchyard became as of day. The powerful light illuminating every corner, no shadows remained. *"Veniat deus ipse in corpus tuum,"* he shouted and cupped his burnt hands around the white-hot cross, no longer feeling the heat.

Prizing it from the ground he staggered towards the now blinding light that surrounded the Beast. The flesh on his face began to blister, his hair singed and burnt away. With his last few breaths he screamed the final line of the ancient ritual, *"Abi, abi, abi o malum!!!"* before forcing the cross deep into the centre of the light, feeling it strike the Beast.

The explosion threw him back, taking his sight before melting what is left of his eyes. The Beast dropped to the ground as the surrounding light disappeared, for a moment there was nothing but silence and darkness. Its flesh burnt, its power gone.

Impaled to the ground by the cross, the Beast screamed and writhed. Seeing the Priest crawling blindly, sensing his weakness it clawed at the earth in a vain attempt to get at him. The blinding light returned holding it firmly to the ground, bolts once again arced between the gravestones and the cross. Large cracks opened in the earth below the Beast, the ground shuddered as it ripped apart, a light exploded from the earth throwing a beam high into the night sky.

The Priest could no longer hear nor see any of this, his mind gone, his body trying desperately to save itself from the tremors he felt shaking the ground below him. He felt a wind begin to blow, stronger, cooling his burned face.

The Beast screamed twisting in the air as it was slowly brought down towards the open earth. Bolts of light strike its body in a constant stream from all directions. It griped at the soft mud as it passed below the surface, its long sharp talons doing nothing but scrape the soft earth away.

With a loud crack the hole closed around it and the light extinguished. The churchyard once again becomes silent, except for the soft patter of falling rain.

The Priest sensing that it has ended feels a calm pass over him, he lays his face to the cool moist grass.

He is dead.

Chapter 1
London, the year of our Lord 1892.

It had lain dormant for many years, surrounded by darkness, pain its only companion. Its own physicality, its own being had been forgotten, it had been forced by the blinding light into the dark safe recesses of its mind. There it fought its own demons, those that had tormented it with whispers of failure. However, now it was aware of something different, a forgotten sense, a lost sensation, one that now silenced those that whispered to it in the dark, one that it had not felt in a long time.

It hadn't noticed exactly when the sensation had started, only that it was now getting stronger. Its surroundings were changing. The earth that had imprisoned it was the same, the pressure it exerted on its body the same. Although something had definitely changed, it now knew that the power that bound it was beginning to weaken. It sensed a release was coming. Its body, from which it had become detached so long ago was becoming strong again. It sensed a second chance. It sensed freedom.

Chapter 2

The Church of St John was now a ruin. A haunted relic from a more innocent time. The world had grown cynical in the years following the battle between the Priest and the Beast. In an attempt to hide its past a decision had been made to change its name, but even as St Augustine's Church, the people had not forgotten its horrific past. They no longer came to its services, families felt uneasy sitting in the dilapidated hall, whilst the walls crumbled around them.

The church itself had begun to decay soon after the Priest had been found dead. It was said that a strange presence lingered there and had kept most of the parishioners away. Work to repair the church had coincided with the change of name, but that had soon ended with the lack of both money and interest, the speed of its decay accelerating over time.

The city didn't care, a new place of worship had been erected nearby, one that reflected the wealth of the families that had moved in, over time the city expanded way beyond the confines of the old roman wall and engulfed the small rural area.

The church had stood abandoned for a hundred years. The last of its parishioners' dead, the Beast forgotten. A tall tale told by adults to frighten children on dark cold nights. "Springheel Jack'll get you!"

Men had now begun demolition of the church. They climbed over all of it desperately trying to bring as much of the stonework down as possible in as little time. The Gaffer, a huge fat man puffed and panted, as he walked red faced around the building shouting at anyone he could see and sometimes at those he couldn't.

He never knew when his Boss would appear so in his mind he was to keep himself busy at all times, if he was busy then he made damn sure everyone was.

The fat man jumped back as a large slate landed in front of him, smashing on the stone path. "Hey, hey you on the roof," he shouted looking up.

A smiling face appeared over the edge, "Did you shout up at me?" the face asked innocently.

"Yes, I bloody did," shouted the Gaffer, waiving bits of the broken slate he had picked up from the ground, the red of his face deepened. "Look what your bloody doing will you! I've told you before. The more we save the more we can sell on."

The man on the roof shrugged his shoulders and disappeared back from the edge. The Gaffer fumed at the despondency displayed, but the man had gone. He looked around for someone else upon which to vent his anger.

Noah and Alfred had thought that the spot they had chosen to work from, was secluded enough that the Gaffer couldn't really see what they were doing. They were still under this misconception as a piece of the broken slate whizzed past them. Alf turned, seeing the red-faced Gaffer bounding towards them he grabbed his pick and began work on the churchyard wall.

"What's up Alf?" said Noah, noticing his friend's sudden interest in work.

Alf looked at his colleague and nodded towards the church. "Gaffer," he whispered from the corner of his mouth.

The Gaffer was storming towards them, his huge belly bouncing with each stride. "When did I say you two could have a break?" he bellowed.

"We weren't," came Noah's reply, as he jumped from his reclined position.

"Well what was you doing? It certainly wasn't what I'd specifically asked you to do."

The two men looked at each other, "We were looking at the footings, wasn't we Noah?" Alf answered nudging his workmate.

"Oh yeah," confirmed Noah, "that's right. We were inspecting the footings. Seeing how deep they went." Both men grinned up at their superior.

The Gaffer sighed, "Well now you've inspected them I expect you to be down to them by tonight, is that clear?"

Both men agreed that it was and began to pick at the wall. The Gaffer turned and putting his hands on his hips bellowed across the churchyard, "Listen, I don't want any more slacking. We've a few hours of daylight left and I want you to use all of them, understand?" he didn't expect a reply, just the sound of tools hitting stone. When he heard this, he resumed his walk around the church's perimeter, always keeping an extra sharp look out for his boss. He didn't want to be caught napping. He had every intention of collecting his full pay for this job and a little extra for whatever he could sell on.

Both Alfred and Noah kept slamming their picks into the wall, bringing it down stone by stone. "Why do you think nothing grows against this wall Noah?" Alf asked, noticing the Gaffer had gone he had stopped working and was once again leaning on the pick handle.

"Eh?" Noah looked up over the wall to ensure the coast was clear.

"This wall?" Alf gestured along its course, "nothing grows within a few feet of it, all the way round it goes."

Seeing that the coast was clear Noah had ceased work and was now also leaning on his pick, "That's the well-trodden path of the dammed that, it's a well-known fact. Souls of wrongdoers that can't enter a holy place."

Alf looked down at the bare earth below his feet and slowly took a step back. Noah burst into fits of laughter. Looking at him, Alf gave a little grin and began laughing himself, "You fool!" The men laughed as they broke the wall apart. By evening they had demolished a large section, piling the stone up ready for it to be loaded onto carts and sold. It was a good day's work and both men left happy. The Gaffer had had no more cause to reprimand them and they were sure they could talk him into buying a beer for each of them later.

Unfortunately for Noah and Alf, the Gaffer had had no intention of being in the pub that night, he had other plans for the stone they had so neatly piled.

Watching as the men left the site, he sat with his back against one of the gravestones, facing towards the west, he held his head up so as to feel the warmth of the last rays of sunlight before it disappeared.

Chapter 3

The Gaffer's bottom was cold and his back had begun to hurt when at last the sound of an approaching cart reached his ears. He stood and stretched. It had been giving him jip for some time now and he knew that he would eventually need to see a doctor.

He spied the men driving towards him and was relieved to see both his brothers. Waving at them he gave a brief whistle, his brothers acknowledged.

They halted outside the large churchyard gates and greeted each other. George jumped down and lifted a nosebag from the cart, he fixed it so that the horse could eat. "Right," he said walking round to join his brother waiting at the gates, "What's the plan?"

The Gaffer led them into the churchyard. "The stone and slate have all been piled around the grounds, so you'll have a bit of back work in moving it, but only take about a quarter from each pile. The Boss won't miss a little, but he isn't stupid and I think he's asked a Bobby to keep an eye on the place so let's get busy."

"What about the stuff from inside?" asked George.

"Most of the good stuff's gone," replied the Gaffer, "Just the pews and a few worthless things left now."

The three men set to their business, George and Hobart moving separately around the church collecting the stone. The Gaffer waiting beside the cart.

Soon they had moved enough stone for them to begin loading it onto the back of the cart. The three men carefully placed each piece onto the flat surface, the Gaffer climbed up onto the cart to stack the stones whilst his brothers collected more. He had hoped to achieve this quietly, but his size meant he couldn't reach down easily to pick them up, so he slid each stone to the centre with his foot, risking someone hearing them.

Suddenly there came the sound of stone crashing together followed by a muffled cry, the Gaffer turned towards the churchyard, he could hear one of his brothers cursing and quickly surveyed the surrounding area. Happy that no one else had heard them, he headed in through the gates. "What's going on?" he asked hoping to keep his voice from travelling, but with such a deep bellowing voice it was difficult. He could see his brothers, one leaning over the other. "What is it?" he asked again.

"George tripped over!!" Hobart said laughing.

"It's not bloody funny," said George looking round for the cause of his stumble. Spying something on the ground he pulled at it. It seemed to be a leather loop "This is it," he said, pulling it harder.

One side eventually gave and the loop slipped through his grip cutting his hand as the metal buckle caught his fingers. "Shit!!" he cried, holding his hand tight waiting for the pain to subside, once it had he grabbed at it again and began to pull.

The ground wasn't about to release whatever it was he had fallen over, pulling a small tool from his pocket he began to loosen the earth around the strap.

Both the Gaffer and Hobart bent over their brother watching as he worked to release the loop, "What is it?" they both asked.

"I'm not sure, give me a minute," replied George as he hacked away at the earth. They could all hear a scraping sound as the tool hit something solid, it was obvious that the strap was attached to something metal. Within minutes a black muddy piece stuck out of the ground, George pulled hard on it. With a snapping sound the thing came free. They could see that part of it was still in the ground, but George held the large piece he had freed, he tried to wipe the mud away. It was made of iron and leather, the rust colour had tainted the mud red.

"Is it some armour? Give me it here," Hobart tried to grab the dangling strap, but George moved his hand away.

"Hold on," said George holding the metal with both hands, "I think it's a mask, look, these holes look like eyes and I bet the other strap is what snapped off when I pulled it." He held it up to the setting sun, its light illuminated the two large eye holes. They all agreed that it was some sort of mask, "Funny looking thing though."

The ground beneath them gave a shudder. They all held their breath and listened. "Did you feel that?" George said, he stood, alarmed at the sudden shaking. The ground shuddered again. Each of the men took a step away from the small hole the mask had come from.

The ground beneath them erupted. All three men fell to their backs. Twisting over, they scrambled on hands and knees in an attempt to crawl away as fast as they could, they had never experienced anything that could cause the earth to move like that. In their panic they had failed to see the tall thin black shape emerge from the ground where the mask had been discovered.

George managed to get to his feet and was about to make a run for it when a long-emaciated hand gripped his head and twisted it, snapping his neck. He fell with no knowledge of what had killed him. His two brothers both watched horrified as he fell, each pausing in shock at the sight they had witnessed.

The Gaffer knelt facing the Beast as it moved towards him. It towered over him, bending until its face hung just a few inches above his own. Its huge lipless mouth open, pointed broken teeth bared. He tried to let out a scream but the fowl smelling breath of the Beast caught in his throat. It snapped its mouth shut on his face, sharp broken teeth ripping his flesh away. The Gaffer's huge body convulsed as his heart pounded within his chest. Subconsciously his hand gripped at his shirt attempting to release the pressure within. He felt his heart tear apart as it tried desperately to pump blood around his body. His final breath exited the torn flesh of his mouth as the beast moved slowly away.

Hobart now lay with his face to the ground praying that if he couldn't see the abomination that had sprung from the earth, it would ignore him. "No, no, no, no, no, no," he repeated.

The Beast turned towards him and spat the Gaffer's bloody ripped face down at him. It landed against his neck, he could feel his brother's warm skin against his own. His body leapt into action and he scrambled forward on all fours. The Beast's long arm shot out after him and its powerful grip held onto his ankle. Hobart screamed as he was pulled back, his shirt rode up to his chest, mud and grass filled his mouth as his face dragged along the ground.

The Beast turned him over and dropped to all fours. Its long arms and legs trapping Hobart as he lay under it, the iron cross forced into it by the priest pressed into his flesh as it closed the gap between them His large bare stomach touched that of the Beast, it felt cold and wet, bile rose to his throat. Leaning towards him, it let out a piercing cry.

Hobart felt its long fingers find his crotch, his bladder emptied as its needle like talons easily split his skin. With a single movement he was ripped to his ribcage. His innards spilling out and hanging down his sides. The Beast slipped its hand under his ribs and found his still beating heart. Surrounding it with its strong fingers it felt it as it pulsed against its palm, slowly it closed its grip and crushed his life away.

Looking down at Hobart's face it watched as he exhaled his final breath. It ripped the heart out through his chest cracking the sternum in two, Hobart's body briefly lifted from the ground with the force.

The Beast stared at the flesh it held, blood glistened black in the moonlight. Standing to its full stature it pulled the iron cross from its body, dropping it to the ground it released a deafening cry. It was once again free. Letting the steaming flesh fall from its fingers it leapt towards the nearby rooftops, a dark shadow silhouetted against the sky. Soon it had disappeared, the black cold night welcoming it.

Chapter 4

Lucy held the door open for her sister, Alice. "Come on," she urged, admittedly a little impatiently. The dark scared Lucy and the grounds around Bishop's Manor were very dark indeed. She would walk through the tree laden grounds all day if she was allowed to, but at night the trees twisted limbs took on sinister shapes and her imagination went wild.

Both sisters had gained employment at the manor as maids, Lucy, being the older by twelve months finding employment first and then her sister a few months later. Alice had visited the manor on a number of occasions once Lucy had acquired the job, it was during this time that she had been noticed by the head butler, Arthur Cooke. Not long after, it emerged that there was a vacancy and on one of her visits Alice was offered the position.

It was obvious to the rest of the staff the reason she had been offered the job. She was young and pretty, with long silky black hair. Arthur had been immediately taken with her and although Alice refused to say that she had noticed, he was always around her with a kind word and a compliment.

Alice hurried down the short corridor that led from the kitchen to the servant's entrance, both sisters emerged laughing into the night. "I'm not wrong," said Lucy linking arms with her sister, more through fear than sibling love. "Art's sweet on you, you're the only one who can't see it."

Alice giggled and if it had been light Lucy would have seen her sister blush bright red. "He isn't," she denied, "Art's the head butler, he wouldn't look at me!"

Lucy pulled at Alice's arm, stopping her on the path, "What! Wouldn't look at you? That's all he does."

Alice blushed even more, she was sure her sister could feel the heat from her red cheeks. "Stop it," she giggled. Both sisters laughed hard as they resumed their journey along the long gravel path that led to the manor gates.

Arthur had managed to catch the door moments before it closed and now stood in the doorway watching the girls as they walked away. He had wrestled with himself for days. He wanted to court Alice, was in love with her, but was unsure how to approach her. He had always taken his job very seriously, hadn't let his feelings for any girl interfere with it. But when Alice had visited her sister on that first occasion, he knew that she was right for him.

As head butler he could if he so wished, create a position for her and had dropped hints on many occasions that the manor could do with another girl. He hoped that Alice wouldn't suspected his motives, as he casually mentioned the position when she arrived one afternoon to walk home with Lucy. He had made light of the situation and commented that she should contact him if she was interested in employment, before walking off in the opposite direction trying to pretend that the offer, he had made her had been an off the cuff remark, secretly hoping though that she would accept it.

Lucy returned the following morning and seeking Arthur out, told him that her sister would be along later that day to talk about the position.

The two girls had almost disappeared from his view, with not as many windows lit this side of the house, the darkness almost had them. "Excuse me!" Arthur shouted after them, letting the door click shut behind him, "Alice, a word if you please." His heart was in his mouth as he walked after them.

The sisters had stopped, turned and waited as Arthur approached, Lucy nudged Alice in time with each of Arthur's steps. Both girls giggled.

As he approached they stood very erect and proper, showing the respect his position deserved. "Is there a problem Mr. Cooke?" Lucy asked, "We have finished for the day," she said, knowing he was squirming, she delighted in addressing him in the proper manner.

"No nothing wrong Miss Strong, just a word with Alice if she pleases."

Alice gripped her sister's arm tightly, "No that's fine Mr. Cooke. What word would you like?" Lucy giggled and tried to hide her face with her hand.

"Well," Arthur continued, "It's . . . of a personnel matter and one would hope to speak to Alice, Err, Miss Strong alone."

Lucy turned to her sister, "You speak with Mr. Cooke, and I'll wait for you at the gates," she said, then lightly touched Alice's hand. "Don't be too long, you know how I feel about the dark."

Lucy left them to talk. Her footsteps on the gravel sounded very loud, she became suddenly conscious that if there were to be someone lurking about within the grounds they could not fail to hear her approaching.

She stopped suddenly, *'was that a sound?'* she thought.

Lucy turned her head straining to hear anything. It was silent.

'Too silent?' her heart began to beat a little faster.

Turning back to face the house she was relieved to still see her sister and Art stood close to each other lit faintly by the dim light that shone from two small windows. Hearing them laugh Lucy let out her own breath, she hadn't realized she was holding it. "Fool!" she reprimanded herself, then began walking towards the gates once more.

She had hoped that she would be able to see them by now. The Lord himself had insisted that a lamp be always shining from them at night, but tonight for some reason it either hadn't been lit, or she had misjudged the distance of the path. Lucy hurried her step.

'A sound?' she thought.

Once again, she came to a stand, this time with such speed that the gravel moved beneath her feet. The sound of the small stones grinding together hung heavy in the air. She could not have been mistaken, they're had been a definite sound of movement and she feared it had come from somewhere ahead of her.

'Could it be someone on the path?' she caught herself thinking.

It didn't sound like someone walking, more a sliding, grinding of the gravel, then silence.

Her heart raced as Lucy spun around peering into the darkness, hoping now that one of her friends was playing a prank. She could no longer see Alice and Arthur, no longer hear their chatter. She turned to face the gates and prayed to see their protecting light.

There had been nothing in her short life that could have prepared her for what she faced. For a split second her brain could not comprehend why her view was restricted. There was something blocking it. It was almost black, yet she could see that it was moving slowly.

The Beast stood before her. It rose to its full height, towering above her, craning its neck, its face moved down towards hers. She could see its eyes, motes of light flickered across them. There was no light around but still they glinted.

Lucy breathed in hoping to force out a scream. Its arm reached out taking hold of her, its long fingers closed around her neck. They sickened her with their cold rancid touch, the scream died in her throat. It held her in its grasp, she felt its other arm move around her back and slowly it lifted her up towards its mouth. It caressed her neck, tapping each finger against her soft flesh. Its huge mouth now open wide, its black tongue flicking.

Deep from within its throat she perceived a blue glow. Like tiny flames, they caressed its mouth illuminating its broken teeth. Lucy tried to force herself back, her hands laid flat pushing against the pulsing skin of its chest. It sickened her to touch its cold flesh. The Beast was too strong for her, it closed the gap between them and laid its mouth over hers.

She felt the blue flame inside her, cold like ice on her tongue. Her chest heaved as it pulled her closer, her whole body crushed against it. Lucy's eyes became black, her mind dark.

She felt its tongue inside her, its blue flame reaching in, probing, wanting something from her. She sensed that whatever it sought, it had found, its body tensed and its hands closed tight around her. It breathed her in, taking her breath, her mind, her soul, her hope. Its mouth moved away from her lips. The blue flame flickered between them. An intense glow filled her mouth, so tangible it choked her. She felt her life ebbing away. Her body becoming limp. Losing consciousness.

Then she was free, falling. She hit the ground and lay for seconds staring up at the Beast before her body could react. Opening her mouth wide, Lucy let out a deep frightening scream. Again and again she screamed, hardly taking breath. The Beast crouched down over her watching. Its long fingers caressing her soft cheek.

Alice had just placed her hand on Arthur's chest when the first scream sounded stopping her playfulness, both stared into the darkness. With the second scream Alice reacted and set off at a run down the path towards the sound, "Lucy. Lucy," she cried.

By the time the third scream sounded Arthur was fast on her heals. They both came upon Lucy laying where she had fallen at the same time. Alice dropped to her knees laying Lucy's head in her lap, "What's wrong Lucy, what is it?" she pleaded. Lucy gripped Alice's coat and buried her face into it screaming, "Arthur," Alice demanded, "Get back to the house and raise the alarm."

Arthur looked down at them confused, "What? Oh. Yes. Yes of course," he looked around quickly, trying to work out what had happened.

Someone must have come upon her from the darkness, attacked her. His gaze fell upon the silhouette of the Beast.

It stood in the darkness the blue flame still flickering lighting its hideous face. Arthur gasped.

"What is it?" Alice asked hearing him.

Arthur couldn't answer, his eyes fixed on the flickering points of blue light, "What in God's name?" he uttered.

The Beast bound away towards the boundary wall and the darkness beyond. Arthur couldn't be sure of what he had seen, nothing he had ever seen nor in his imagination moved like that. Nothing that he knew of.

Lucy still had her face pressed firmly into Alice's bosom and thankfully it was suppressing the hideous sound she made. She had never heard someone screaming so loudly or without interruption. Alice held her, tears streaming down her cheeks, "Please Arthur, please help her!"

Arthur turned and ran back towards the manor. The glimpse he had had of the Beast still at the forefront of his mind.

Chapter 5

The black moonless night had given way to a bright blue sky, it seemed that even the inevitable smog of London that would by evening eventually creep over the city could not dampen the day.

William English was covering the protests in Trafalgar Square. A huge crowd had gathered to hear the police commissioner's speech and although it was going to be tight, William was sure that his report would make the paper's evening deadline. The newly formed Crime Investigation Department (CID) had not performed as the commissioner had promised. Since its inception it had been plagued with problems. So much money and time had been wasted on it that the whole city now demanded an explanation.

William looked around at the crowd, it filled the square and most of the streets that led into it. *'Most of the London must be in attendance!'* he thought.

The promised time for the commissioner's arrival had passed and the police were now struggling to keep order. Small fights had broken out and a sense that it would soon deteriorate into a riot could now be felt.

Pip darted through the crowd, his slender frame neatly dipping left and right avoiding contact with anyone. He had been tasked to "Find English!" by their editor and although the crowd was far larger than he had expected, the thought that he might not find him hadn't crossed his mind.

At fifteen he had now been employed by the 'London Evening Star' for two years, as a runner he seemed to have found his calling. His father had wanted Pip to be educated and find a good job, one that deserved his education. The family had made many sacrifices to ensure he had a better start in life than any of them had been privilege to.

Being tall for his age had helped him, he couldn't climb the chimneys of the rich, nor could he blend well into a crowd. The latter ensuring that he had not been noticed by the large number of men who had taken to forcibly employing small children for robbery.

His father had insisted on his schooling, when this was completed he had marched him into the office of the newspaper and demanded they employ him. Edward Kingsley, a large Scottish man and the editor of the newspaper, had laughed at the demand. Not with malice but with the sheer audacity of the man's request. He had employed Pip that day and neither of them had regretted it.

He headed towards the steps of the National Gallery. The commissioner was to make his speech f rom a platform erected there and he knew that Will would be stood as near to it as he could, so as to hear every word.

Pip swayed with the crowd as they surged, never losing his footing. Reaching the front, he dipped between two fat men, who were both surprised when he appeared before them and climbed one of the struts securing the platform. "Will," he shouted back at the sea of faces, "Will English?" his eyes searched the crowd for any sign of recognition.

A hand appeared to his right, "Here, over here," cried a voice as the hand waved.

Pip leapt back into the crowd and emerged facing Will like a pearl diver emerging from the depths, "Can't see much from here," he remarked, looking back at the platform.

"I don't need to see to make a report, just to hear," returned Will smiling, "Now what are you doing here?"

The crowd moved forward and Pip felt his arm grabbed and pulled. Will had taken hold of him and moved them to the side, away from the platform as those at the front were crushed against it. Pip caught his breath, "Getting a little crazy," he smiled turning to Will, "Kingsley wants your report, it's going in the evening edition."

Pulling out his pocket watch Will sighed when he read the time, it was getting late. The speech was meant to be over by now. He thought for a moment, "All right, let's go," he said.

Looking back over the crowd he assessed thelikely hood of them making it through the heaving mass of people, deciding against it and gripping Pip once more he began pushing his way across the front of the crowd to where he hoped it would thin out. "I have a fair idea of what he's going to say anyway," he shouted back at Pip, "he's really just a politician, nothing specific and nothing he can later be pinned down about."

The crowd surged forward once more and the grip Will had had on Pip's arm was lost. Turning back, he glimpsed the young boys face for a moment as the surge took him further away. "I'll meet you back at the office," Pip shouted, as he disappeared into the melee of bodies. Will left him knowing Pip was probably better off on his own, he doubted that even if he had been given a head start, he would beat the young lad back anyway. Pip had an uncanny knack about him, an inbuilt compass. Always taking the right turn, always finding the right street.

Will was glad to be leaving the growing sea of people, he sensed a fever within the crowd. One that he felt would not be eased by the commissioner's words.

Will climbed the two flights of stairs passing the printing office and the print makers until finally entering the smaller reporter's office. There were five desks placed along the side wall, each positioned beside a small window. Beyond the desks was a small office that had been constructed at the rear of the room.

Will sat at his desk and pulled a few sheets of paper from the drawer. Only one other desk was occupied. Charlie Lipton looked up at Will, "Pip found you then?" he commented.

Will sharpened his pencil with his pocketknife, "Yeah, still can't understand how he does it but he always manages too. Didn't think I'd beat him back here though."

Charlie laughed, "You didn't, he's been in, seen the boss then went out again," Both men laughed.

Will set about writing his report. It didn't take long, he knew the promises that had been made concerning the problems faced by the CID and that the speech made by the commissioner would only reiterate them. Any good reporter could have pre-empted his speech.

He did pause however ensuring that he chose the correct words for the feeling he had about the crowd. Something had changed in London, he had a feeling something sinister was beginning. He was sure of it.

"Have you a moment Will?" Kingsley spoke from his office doorway; his Scottish accent was still strong but there had been a cockney twang in it since his move south.

Will shifted in his chair turning to face him, "Of course."

Kingsley returned to his desk, waiting for Will to enter his office. As he did so he placed the completed report on his desk.

"You heard the speech then?" Kingsley asked picking it up.

"No, not really," replied Will, "but we all know what he's going to say, it's mostly about the feel of the crowd and the reason they were there. Its old news until parliament takes action and someone new takes charge."

Kingsley placed the papers back onto his desk and indicated for Will to take a seat. As he closed the door the editor began, "It's about parliament that I wished to talk to you, well a member of parliament to be precise." Will pulled the seat out from the desk and sat opposite, "Last night there was an attack at a Manor House in Victoria Park, north east of the city centre. Bishop's Manor to be precise." Kingsley said sitting back in his chair, "Now you know that the owner of Bishop's is Lord Sanderford, the Foreign Ambassador? What you might not know is that a large part of his wealth has come from mines he either owns, or part owns in Southern Africa. He and his partners have been raping the Dark Continent for many years. They have abused both local tribes and fellow settlers and now the military are involved."

Will opened a pad and pulling a pencil from his pocket began to write. Kinglsey immediately held his hand out staying the action, "No Will, I don't want any notes made about this yet, I might be wrong and if I am I'd like no knowledge of this conversation to leave this room."

Will pocketed his pencil and Kingsley relaxed back into his chair, "It's rumoured," he continued, "that there is so much money involved that parliament was instructed by her Majesty to intervene."

"Why would someone so high become involved?" questioned Will.

"To ensure that the British flag should never cease to fly over the continent," Kingsley answered, "her empire must stay fast. Sanderford has too much to lose, his position as the Foreign Ambassador is of course in jeopardy, but more so his business investments as Lord Sanderford."

Will mused over the words, "And you believe the Lord was attacked last night because of his involvement in Africa?"

Kingsley moved towards Will leaning onto the desk, his voice quieter, "The Lord wasn't attacked directly, it was a maid walking in the manor grounds, but I do believe that he was the intended target and this," he paused to pick up a scrap of paper, "Miss Lucy Strong," he read, "Happened to stumble into the attackers and foil their attempt. If they have not yet been discovered, then they may try again. This my friend, is where you come in. Snoop around, talk to Miss Strong, find out what she knows." Kingsley paused, slipping the name across to Will, "She must have seen them and something about them frightened her. Sent her mad with fear by all accounts. What would frighten a young girl so much?"

Will thought for a moment, "I don't know."

"I'm thinking," Kingsley continued, "that she would have never had reason to encounter the people of Africa before. Dark night last night, no moon, easy for a black to move unseen and who better to employ to avenge the tribes crushed by Lord Sanderford and his business associates, than one of those poor trampled souls, nothing to lose."

Will could see the logic in it. He picked up the scrap of paper and stood, "Where will I find Miss Strong?"

Kingsley grinned as he answered, "She's in St. Thomas's. Doctor's name is Henry Mortimer."

Will looked confused at him, "But that's for the insane! What's she doing there?"

"I told you, something frightened her, sent her mad apparently," he answered, unsuccessfully holding back laughter, "Worried that they'll keep you in?"

Will sighed and left the office, "St. Thomas's," he whispered to himself. He did not take any pleasure in visiting such a place. He may never have been there, but its reputation was known to all in London.

Looking up at the almost empty room he slipped the paper into his pocket. Charlie was still bent over writing,

"See you soon Charlie," he said pacing the distance to the door. By the time Charlie had looked up he was out of sight.

"Oh," he remarked to the empty room, "see you then."

Chapter 6

Will stepped out into the bright sunshine once again. It had not been an hour since he had returned to the office, but his mood had changed. It wasn't just about the trip to St Thomas's, it was true that he wasn't looking forward to it, there was something in the air, an anger.

The mood in Trafalgar Square had changed, he felt it happen as he and Pip left. That feeling had followed him, hung over him. He shook it off and stepped to the curb hailing a cab.

The street bustled with trolleys, cabs and carts. Nothing here was different to any other London street. The sounds, the sights, the shouts of sellers, the hustle and bustle of life. Will welcomed its familiarity.

Gloved hands from behind covered his eyes, he felt the soft material gently touching his face. "Guess who?" a voice asked.

Will didn't need to, he knew his wife's voice anywhere, "Why I do believe it to be Queen Victoria herself!" he joked with her placing his hands over hers.

"Silly," Sarah giggled behind him.

Will held onto her hands and twisted around.

"Then I know not who it is, for there is no other woman I would rather spend my time with," he smiled seeing her beautiful face. Pulling her towards him, he kissed her. She gently pushed him away.

"Please, William not in public!" her hand covered a gentle smile, her cheeks began to blush.

"Oh Sarah," he said, slipping a hand under her lowered chin and raising her face. He stared directly into her deep blue eyes, "You're my wife Sarah. If I cannot show how happy I am that you are, then this would truly be a sad world," he smiled at her, "Now please don't tell me that you walked the whole way here, not in your condition."

Sarah placed a hand on her very pregnant stomach, "It's because of my condition that I have to walk, no money spare to take cabs silly. We need all we have for this." Will looked down at her and placed both arms round her gently squeezing her into him.

"I am so in love with you, you know," he said, then kissed her again, this time Sarah didn't resist. "Now what brings you here?" he asked linking arms with her as they began to stroll along the street.

"Oh, it's silly really," she answered, "I woke feeling a little down, I just wanted to see you. Was that foolish?"

Will whistled for a passing cab, "No, my dear Sarah, you are never foolish. Now that you have seen me we'll have you on your way home."

A Hansom cab pulled up alongside them, "Oh Will," Sarah protested, "I thought we could walk in the park, spend a little of the day together."

Will opened the cab door, "I'd love to Sarah, but am afraid I've to be somewhere, if this cab wasn't taking you home it would be taking me to St. Thomas's."

Sarah gasped, "Why would you want to go to that God forbidden place?"

Ignoring the question, he eased her onto the step and into the cab, "Jubilee Street, Whitechapel please cabby," he said shutting the small door.

"But why must you go there?" asked Sarah, leaning from the window.

Will stood on the step and kissed her, "There's someone there I have to speak to, please don't worry I'm not going to be staying!" he smiled and winked. "Now you get off home," he said, passing a shilling up to the cabby, "I won't be long. Promise."

Sarah giggled as the cab set off. Will waved watching it mingle with the many other vehicles on the street, soon it was lost amongst them.

Will hailed another as it passed, "St. Thomas's hospital please," he shouted up to the cabby as he stepped in. Sitting straight backed against the leather of the Hansom, Will closed his eyes and took no notice of the world passing by.

Chapter 7

Lost within his own world, Will hadn't realised the cab had stopped, nor had he heard the cabbie announce their arrival. Two loud knocks on the cab roof did stir him though, "St. Thomas's sir," the cabbie once again informed him.

Will shook himself back to reality, he hadn't noticed himself dropping off, "Sorry," he called climbing out. Placing a few pennies into the cabbie's hand he turned to face the hospital behind him. The cab turned easily in the wide street and set off in the direction it had come.

The street seemed eerily quiet, compared to the normal everyday hustle and bustle of the city. Will looked up the short driveway to the imposing gate. On each side of it stood a wall six-foot-tall, curving away from the gate towards the street, it ran unbroken in both directions before disappearing out of view at each corner. Will knew that it circumnavigated both the building and its grounds without another point of access.

Walking the short distance to the gates he was immediately aware of how cold it became as he passed into the shadow cast by the wall. The heavy iron gates had at one time been painted white, but that paint was now peeling. Will doubted that neither the staff nor the inmates cared.

Up ahead he could see the imposing hospital building. Its facade, like the gates had at one time been white, its barred windows black. He had read that it had been originally built to house prisoners from the Napoleonic war, then later changed to a hospital. Slowly over time the hospital had become the asylum it now was. The look of the building suited its purpose.

To the left of the gate was a small security room, and from its wall hung a tiny bell that could be rung by reaching your arm through the gate. Cautiously Will placed his hand through the bars, conscious not to touch the peeling paint. He pulled the string and the bell sounded. Its pleasant ring seemed deadened by the oppressive building it faced.

A moment passed before a red-faced man appeared, "I'm Angus Broadbent, gate security. How may I be of assistance?" he announced looking passed Will towards the road, "admittance?"

Confused by the man's actions Will looked around, there was no one there. Suddenly, understanding his meaning, he answered. "No, no one to admit. I'd like to see Dr Henry Mortimer please?"

Angus Broadbent rubbed his chin with his hand, his day-old stubble sounding as he did. "Dr Mortimer eh? Have you an appointment?"

Kingsley hadn't mentioned if one had been made or not. "I'm not sure." he said truthfully. "I'm from the *London Evening Star* newspaper." Will paused waiting for a response. "William English, reporter." he added, hoping it would provide some strength to his request.

"Newspaper man eh?" Angus replied, still unsure. "Never read that one. I'll see if the doctor will see you." he eventually decided. Turning away from Will he walked quickly towards the front door.

"It's about Miss Lucy Strong, she was admitted last night!" Will shouted after him unsure if Angus had heard him, but he felt that a little more information may help his request.

Angus pushed open one side of the large double doors that served as the hospitals entrance and slipped inside. Will noticed that he had only opened the door wide enough for him to enter, imagining that he did so to stop any lurking inmates a chance of escape. He then reproached himself for such a stupid thought.

A few minutes later, Angus appeared at the still slightly opened front door, as he walked back towards the gate he gave a little wave. Will wondered at such a curious thing, *'Maybe the madness is contagious.'* he thought smiling, he hoped not.

"You're in luck," Angus announced, as he fumbled with the gates lock. "Dr Mortimer will see you sir, he'll meet you in his private quarters, to the right as you enter."

Angus swung the gates open easily, Will was amazed by this, expecting a god-awful squealing as he imagined the man tugging at the old decaying things. Stepping through them and into the grounds he made his way towards the open door.

"To the right as you enter." reminded Angus, closing the gates as soon as the reporter had passed. They closed as silently as they had opened.

Reaching the house Will looked back towards the gates, the scene was again calm and quiet. Angus Broadbent had secreted himself back into the small security room, Will imagined that he was once again busy with whatever it was that passed his day.

He pushed at the large wooden door hoping to open it further, it opened easily for a short distance then stopped, Will again pushed at it, but the door was stuck fast. *'No wonder Angus had slipped through the gap,'* he thought, *'it was all he could do.'* Turning his body Will slipped through the gap and entered a vast open hallway.

Inside, a marble floor led to a very elegant central pillared staircase. Will observed that there were four doors on the ground floor. One on either side of the staircase, another to Will's left, and the fourth to his right. All were closed.

Leaning back against the front door he pushed it closed, the latch echoed loudly through the open space.

As instructed, Will walked over to the door on his right, it was the same size and colour as the other three. Although he dared not try to open the others, he imagined that this one would be the only one of the four to be unlocked.

Turning the handle, he opened the door and entered a large well-lit room. Looking around at the contents it was obvious to Will that he had been asked to wait in the Doctor's study. Across from him before a wall of books was a desk and two chairs. To his left a large hearth, a fire had been lit and beside it stood a large comfortable looking arm chair. Will walked over to the fire, winter was coming and his short wait at the gates had given him a chill. He turned to warm his back.

Behind the desk stood a small stepladder leaning against the shelves giving access to the topmost books. Next to the door hung a large mirror and a portrait, of whom Will had no idea. The final wall housed two large barred windows looking out towards the gates. It seemed a lot nicer looking out than it did looking in.

The fire didn't give off much heat, it had been allowed to die down. Will thought about taking a few logs or some coal from the store next to it and getting it going again. He listened; the place was deathly silent. Concluding that he wasn't going to be joined for at least a few minutes, he lifted two logs and placed them on the dying embers.

'Dare I pull the chair closer and sit? Would that be bad manners?' he thought. Again, no sound from the hallway. "Oh, what the hell." Will spoke to the empty room as he pulled the chair closer. *'This was much cosier.'* he smiled, the logs had taken and the flames were now at a much better height.

Will felt content and would have been happy not to have be disturbed at all, *'At least,'* he thought. *'For a short time.'*

Unfortunately for Will, the door opened and a tall slim man with long flowing hair rushed in. He threw the apron he had been wearing towards the bookcase and within the same motion, was donning his suit jacket. "Ah Mr. English, you've made yourself comfortable I see." he said. Will coughed with surprise and jumped up. "Don't worry dear boy, its fine, wouldn't want the fire dying, now would we?"

Pulling the chair from behind the desk he dragged it over to where Will stood beside the fire. "I'm Henry Mortimer." he stated holding out his hand. Will shook it. "May as well join you here dear boy. Sit, sit." Releasing his hand, Will sat. "Now," continued the Doctor crossing his legs. "How can I be of help to you?"

Will felt a little confused and flustered, within a minute he had gone from sitting alone by the fire to being startled, assured, accompanied and finally questioned. He took a deep breath; the Doctors actions had been so fast that Will had forgotten to breath. "My name is William English," he began. "I'm a reporter for the *London Evening Star.*"

"A very entertaining publication." interjected the Doctor.

Smiling, Will continued "Last night a young woman was attacked and brought here, Lucy Strong I believe her name is." Will waited a moment hoping for some sign of recognition from Dr Mortimer. When none came he continued. "She was brought from Bishop's Manor. Near Victoria Park."

The doctor sat back in his chair, "Yes, yes, I wasn't on duty last night when the young lady in question was admitted, but I did get the chance to see her this morning. She is now much recovered and is resting."

Will was a little shocked by the statement, he had expected something far more serious. *'How could someone who was considered unstable enough as to be admitted into an asylum, be considered recovered a few hours later?'* he thought.

Dr Mortimer looked hard at Will suspecting what he was thinking. "Would you like to see her?" he asked.

Will had considered asking the question but was unsure if he would be allowed direct access to her. "Yes, yes that would be fantastic," he replied. "I have a few questions she may be able to answer."

The doctor rose and offered Will the door, "Although I am allowing you to see Miss Strong," he began. "I am quite certain that she will be of no help to you. I did say she was resting, but dear boy, it is an induced rest. She is very heavily sedated."

Both men left the room and returned to the large hallway. "This way." the doctor indicated towards the staircase, "Up the stairs and to the left Mr. English, she's housed in the Lavender ward."

As they reached the top of the stairs both men walked back around the balustrade to the left reaching a large door identical to those Will observed as he entered the building. He could now smell lavender, it was very faint, but he couldn't deny its unmistakable odour.

Dr Mortimer reached into his pocket and pulled out several keys, finding the correct one he fit it into the lock and turned. "Does the smell of the flowers help the patients?" asked Will.

The doctor turned and smiled as the door opened, "No dear boy. It's to help us. If one of our . . ." he paused for a moment choosing the correct words. "Patients becomes lost and makes it into the grounds, our nurses can immediately identify from which ward they belong. The strong smell permeates their clothes and given enough time it does the same to the skin. This ward lavender, another rosemary and so on. It was my father's idea, quite a good one I think."

With the door open wide Will felt overpowered by the smell of the lavender, it was sickeningly strong. They stepped into the corridor beyond and Dr Mortimer closed and locked the door behind them. Will listened, the corridor was eerily quiet. He could see several doors on his right-hand side, and on the left opposite each of the doors was a barred window.

"Miss Strong is in room six." the doctor said, moving swiftly along the corridor. Will followed as quickly as he could.

As they passed an open door, two large brutish men exited. Seeing the doctor, one spoke, "He'll give you no more trouble Doctor, his medicine has been administered."

Will investigated the room. He could see that at one time the walls had been white, but like the rest of the building had begun to decay, damp coloured the walls. A man cowered in the corner, he had been beaten badly and was struggling to move. He was wrapped in a jacket that held his arms tight to his body with large straps. Will had never seen such a restraint before. Dr Mortimer stepped in and closed the door.

"One of our more hysterical patients, he needs . . . a more dedicated form of nursing."

Will noticed a red mark across the observation hatch on the door, "What's that for?" he asked.

Dr Mortimer turned and leaning on the door next to the mark answered. "It indicates that the patient is violent and not to be approached unless at least two persons are present." he opened the observation hatch. "He doesn't look violent, such a small meek gentle soul really. However, he does have an obsession with glass." he said, moving aside to allow Will to see the patient, the man was still cowering against the wall.

"Does he collect it?" he asked.

"No," Dr Mortimer said closing the hatch, "He likes to smash it and stick the broken pieces into the faces of young women." he smiled at Will, "Shall we? Miss Strong is two doors further on."

Leaving the two nurses, Will heard them lock the door on the man. Glancing back, he was relieved to see that they were walking in the opposite direction to them, back towards the hallway door.

Dr Mortimer stopped upon reaching the door to room six, he turned and lent against it. Tapping the door gently, he said, "Here she is." he opened the small hatch in the door, moving aside to allow Will the chance to peer inside. He was relieved to see that there was no red mark on the door.

The room was exactly the same as the one he had seen occupied by the cowering man. Once white, now damp.

Lucy Strong was curled up on the single bed, her arms wrapped around her legs holding her knees up into her chest, she was led with her back to the door. The hospital had dressed her in a grey smock. She led silent, unmoving. Dr Mortimer had told him that she had been sedated but from his position Will couldn't even tell if she was alive. "Can I speak to her?" he asked.

Dr Mortimer had moved away from the door and was staring through the window at the grounds outside. He turned reaching for the keys. "If you wish, although I can't see how it will help you."

Once unlocked, Dr Mortimer pushed the door open, Will entered. He moved cautiously towards the woman on the bed. "Miss Strong?" he whispered "Miss Strong?" Will jumped as from behind him the doctor spoke.

"Dear boy she can't harm you. As I said she's sedated."

He moved towards her slowly, cautiously step by step. "I'm a reporter Miss Strong, it's about the attack you suffered last night. I was hoping you could describe your assailant. Explain what happened?" Will was now standing over her, his knees against the rusted metal bed. He turned to Dr Mortimer. The Doctor looked down at the bed and shrugged his shoulders. Deciding to reach out, Will slowly moved his hand towards her shoulder. "Miss Strong?" The grey material felt damp to his touch. He applied a small amount of pressure and gently shook her. "Lucy?"

The woman's body jerked and twisted. Both arms grasped at Will. One gripped his arm the other his trouser leg. Vice like, they tugged at him. Will jumped back startled, he almost fell as he dragged the woman off the bed. He stared down at her, bending with the weight of her body holding onto him.

Lucy's face no longer had the appearance of a young woman, she looked haggard, her eyes hounded. She opened her mouth wide; Will could see her throat straining. He looked back towards the Doctor.

"Nurses," Mortimer stepped back into the corridor. "Nurses, a little assistance in room six please." he shouted before re-entering the room. The doctor began calmly speaking to her whilst attempting to release the grip Lucy had on Will's arm. Will shook his arm desperately, his stare returned to her harrowing twisted face, her mouth still wide open, silent.

The two nurses arrived at the room, whilst one lifted Lucy the other dug his fingers into her wrists and managed to release Will from her grasp. They returned her to the bed and sat on her. Dr Mortimer held Will's shoulder and pushed him towards the open door. "If you please Mr. English, the nurses will deal with Miss Strong now."

They left the room and the door was closed. Dr Mortimer straightened his jacket. "I think a nice pot of tea would suit us both, if you wouldn't mind dear boy, I'll have it served in the reception room."

Will looked up at the doctor, he was shaking, "What? What happened to her?" he tried desperately to regain his composure. "What was she doing?" he asked.

Dr Mortimer put his arm around him and gently walked him away from the room, all was silent in the corridor and Will felt glad of the doctor's calming voice. "I'm afraid, as I said, she would be no help. That was a screaming fit. That's all she does."

Will stopped, "A screaming fit? She was silent."

Dr. Mortimer again put his arm around Will's shoulders and led him towards the door. "Yes, yes. That is true, her vocal chords have been cut, I performed the operation myself this morning. All patients on Lavender ward are silent. Think of the noise dear boy if it wasn't so?" Opening the door, he ushered Will through before closing and locking it behind them.

Sitting in the reception room Will was still shaking when Dr. Mortimer arrived with a tray. As promised, it had upon it a pot of tea and a small selection of sandwiches. "I do hope you don't mind but I rarely get a chance to eat." he said, placing the tray down. Dr. Mortimer took a small side dish and a sandwich. Will looked at the teapot, he knew that if he tried to pour himself a cup, he would spill it. He decided to wait for the doctor to finish his sandwich hoping he would then pour the tea.

Chapter 8

Will had listened very carefully to Dr. Mortimer as he read through his notes relating to Lucy's admission, jotting down anything he thought relevant. Finally, he had been given the address of her sister Alice and hoped she would be more able to give account of the incident. He himself was dumbfounded as to what she could have seen that would be so frightening as to cause Lucy's condition. Surmising that she would now be unlikely to ever see St Thomas's from the outside again, he wondered as he left, if the operation to sever her vocal cords was reversible. He doubted it.

Knowing that there was more chance of hailing a cab from the main road he set off in that direction. He walked on the cobbled road deliberately avoiding the cold shadow of the wall, as he reached the corner, he spotted one and called it over. Handing the cabby, the address given to him he sat back, hoping that a quick chat with the sister would end this and he'd be back home with Sarah by early evening.

The house the cabby dropped him at, if Will was being honest with himself, was just what he had expected. If you could count on one thing from the inhabitants of London, it was that if you had money you let everyone know it. And where you lived meant everything.

Lucy and Alice lived in a small grimy terrace on Belhaven Street, an insignificant abode, as far away from the fashionably rich as you could get and still be in London. He doubted they were the only family living in the house, it was common in these areas for landlords to rent a different floor to each family, Will had even heard of single men living in hallways.

A washing line hung from one top window, it stretched across the street to a window opposite, high enough to be clear of traffic but unfortunately not from the soot and smoke drifting from the chimneys. Children ran along the street, in and out of houses. Usually followed by an angered shout from those that lived there.

Stepping up to the door Will knocked. He was looking down at the diligently cleaned front step when he became aware of one of the children standing next to him. "What you doing mister?" the child asked. Will looked down at the child but didn't answer, he knocked again. "You here 'bout Springheel Jack mister?" the child insisted.

"No," answered Will, "I'm here to see Alice Strong, do you know if this is the right house?"

The child shuffled his feet. "Yeah, she lives here, her

whole family does. She's my aunty. Her and Lucy. It's been mad here since she seen Jack though, I've been told to keep out." Will watched as the child wiped his nose across his sleeve before continuing. "Mr. Cooke came this morning," he said, admiring the silvery line he had made. "And grandma chased me out, got to go to me own house if I need anything she said."

Will lowered himself to the eye level of the child. "Whose Mr. Cooke?" he asked.

"He's the one who told me about Springheel Jack," the child sighed becoming bored. "It's him that scared poor Aunt Lucy. Bound away as if he had springs on his heels so says Mr. Cooke, blue flames shooting out of his mouth."

Will was about to inquire further but as his mouth opened so did the front door and a middle-aged woman appeared, her hand swung out clipping the child across his head. "What have I told you? Get off and play."

The child didn't need any extra encouragement. Without looking up he ran off into the street. Seeing one of his friends leaving the house directly across the road, he ran up behind him and leapt onto his back. "Springheel Jack's here!" he shouted, both boys dropped to the floor, jumped up and ran off down the street. Will smiled as he watched. His smile disappeared as he turned back to face the woman standing in the doorway.

She looked straight at him, her strong-featured face stone like, "Well?" she asked, "if ya peddling anything I don't need it and if ya after anything I aint got it!"

Will was slightly taken aback at her brutish demeanour. "No, no," he finally blurted out. "I'm with the *London Evening Star*, a reporter. I wish to see Alice Strong if it's possible, I was given this address by Dr. Mortimer at St. Thomas's."

The woman folded her arms, a clear sign to Will that his request had fallen upon deaf ears. "I, she's 'ere." answered the woman. "Her and her fella. But neither of them is at home to guests."

Will stood for a moment stumped as to what he could say to her that might possibly change her mind, when from inside the house a scream so loud and piercing sounded that both of them flinched. A man's voice shouted from inside, "Mary, Alice has started again, quick Mary."

The woman looked back along the darkened hallway behind her and closed the door, "I'm sorry." Will heard as it slammed shut.

He stood for a moment, listening to the screaming, although muffled by the door it sounded to Will like it came from a room at the back. He left the house and the screaming and walked back the way the cabby had brought him.

The two children were now running down the street towards him. He caught hold of the one that had questioned him, "Hey kid?" he asked, once again kneeling to be on eye level with him. "What's up with your aunty Alice? I thought it was Lucy that was…" he thought how best to put it, "scared."

"Beats me." replied the child, "she's been acting strange since she got back last night. Looks like Springheel Jack'll put her in St. Thomas's too!" he laughed and began chasing his friend again. Will stood and watched them playing.

He was struggling to understand just what he'd been asked to report on. What seemed a simple story was now looking like anything but?

The streets around him were becoming busy with workers returning home, he was reminded of Sarah and the promise he made to himself that he would like to be home early, to spend the evening with her.

He decided he had enough time to walk home before it became too dark. It would give him time to think about exactly what he was going to write and what to tell Kingsley in the morning. It was obvious to Will that Kingsley's theory was wrong. But there was still a mystery to be investigated.

Chapter 9

Will entered his editor's office. He had been troubled all night as to exactly what the contents of his report should be. Kingsley himself had put forward the theory of an assassination attempt by persons acting as agents for either his disgruntled business partners, or the tribes whose land they had raped. But to Will that angle didn't make sense.

'But what did?' he thought.

There seemed no logical reason for the attack. And no clue as to who or what had attacked her. The original victim driven insane, the sister, who although didn't witness the attack, but who was first on the scene now seemed also to be affected by it.

Kingsley looked up from an article he was reading as Will entered. "Did you see her?" he enquired.

Will sat opposite him. "I did and I even spoke to her."

"And?" Kingsley edged forward in his seat, his interest piqued.

Seeing that he had his editor's attention Will let a playful smile pass over his lips. "Nothing," he said, seeing Kingsley's shoulders drop, he continued. "She was absolutely no use, Dr. Mortimer gave me the details of her admission and it was basically what you said. Attacked by an unknown assailant, left insane." Will crossed his legs and sat back in the chair. "But that's the part I don't understand. What could be so frightening as to do that to someone? She'll never leave there. You know she screamed so much that they operated on her and severed her vocal chords?"

Kingsley looked shocked, "Why would they do that?"

Will thought of her, the look of sheer horror on her face. "I don't think St. Thomas's is a place where they need any real reason to do things like that."

Both men sat silent for a moment. "Anyway, I took the address of her sister, she was the one that was with her when it happened and had her admitted. I hoped to see her. And you know what?" Kingsley shook his head. "It looks like she's going the same way too."

Will could see that his editor was puzzled. He explained to him what had happened on the doorstep, how their mother was adamant that he couldn't see Alice, then the blood curdling scream which he could still hear, even after the door had been shut on him. "But the funny thing is, I'd spoken to their nephew just before it happened and again after. He was the one who told me it was Alice that had let out the scream and that she had been like that all morning. Talkative little chap, he mentioned a nickname. Said she'd seen Springheel Jack. Ring any bells?"

Kingsley fingered his temples. "Can't say I've ever heard the name before. Who is he?"

"I'm not sure." Will continued, "A phantom, a myth. The kid kept repeating that it was Springheel Jack that Lucy had seen, that's who was responsible for her condition. The fella with Alice, a Mr Cooke had told him that whoever had attacked poor Lucy had bound away as if he had springs for heels, blue flame on his breath."

Kingsley looked passed Will, the fingers of his left hand tapping his desk. Neither of them had noticed Pip stood in the doorway. Pip thought Kingsley was about to reprimand him for listening when he noticed him, but instead he turned his attention back to Will. "Right, I want you to write something up. Nothing too long, the attack, where the victim ended up, even mention Springheel Jack." It was Will's turn to now look puzzled. "Get it done in time for this evenings print and then I want you to track down that joker Waterford. See what he's been up to, where he was at the time of the attack. It sounds to me like this is right up his street."

Will left the office, sat at his desk and began to compose his piece. Pip sidled over, "Who's Waterford?" he inquired.

As he wrote Will answered. "The Marquis of Waterford. He's one of those well to do bachelors out Richmond way. Loves to throw big parties. He also loves to play elaborate practical jokes on people. Tried to paint the town red once, police stopped that one. Then he rode through Richmond Park on a carriage with his cloak up over his head." Pip laughed out loud. "You might laugh." Will continued, "Scared some poor woman to death, she thought he was headless."

Pip laughed harder, "What, she died?"

Looking up at him Will answered, "Dropped dead on the spot. So, this could be just another of his little jokes, get himself into headlines again. But it's quite a way from Richmond."

Chapter 10

Maximillian Barr sat at his dining table whilst his butler, Clay finished serving him his evening meal. "I want you to contact the group." he told Clay, his voice a deep rasping whisper. "I want you to organise a meeting, midnight tomorrow."

Clay placed the empty plate on the sideboard and picking up the newspaper turned to hand it to his master, "Certainly Sir, I'll arrange it this evening." he said as he handed Barr the paper. "Your newspaper sir."

Barr took the paper and unfolded it over the dining table. Clay stepped back and stood at his shoulder, waiting to be dismissed. He watched as Barr slowly read through the headlines, skimming over the follow up to the piece about the Commissioner's speech in Trafalgar Square. Turning the page his eyes fell upon the piece Will had written relating to the attack on Lucy Strong.

He ran his finger along each line as he read, immediately re-reading the article once he had finished. Barr closed the newspaper without bothering to read any further.

Stepping back as Barr pushed his chair away from the table, Clay watched as his master stood and without a word left the dining room. He rushed through the hallway and into the library opposite. Clay followed. "Sir, is something wrong?"

Barr ignored him, crossing the library to a large bookcase he began feeling for the small catch under one of the shelves that would allow him access to a second secret bookshelf hidden behind. With a click, part of the bookcase slipped forward, Clay took hold of it and pulled it free, both men slid it along so that Barr had access to the hidden books.

"What is it Sir?" Clay enquired, securing the set of shelves.

Barr, still ignoring him scanned the exposed bookcase, his head tipped slightly making the reading of the spines easier. His fingers flicked across the books as he read, every book covered the same subject. The Dark Arts. Finally, he spied the book he was looking for. It was old, the gold lettering had almost faded to the point of invisibility, its spine was broken and tattered at the edges. Pulling it free Barr placed it onto the desk behind him.

Clay moved in close so that he could see over Barr's shoulder.

In matters of the Dark Arts, Clay was no longer a mere servant, he was Barr's right hand, his second. The two men depended on each other.

The handwritten title of the book read *Demons and Demonology*. Barr opened the cover, being mindful of its delicate yellowed pages. Clay stood silent, watching each page as Barr turned them. Although he read very well, the language of this book baffled him. It wasn't written in any that was known to him. It was some kind of cypher.

Over the years they had been together Clay's knowledge had grown, but the contents of this book had been deliberately kept from him. Barr understood it all too well. The occult was his life. Both his wealth and power had prospered because of his knowledge of it. People feared Barr. And Barr knew just how to exploit that fear. They both did.

Clay watched as Barr slowed his page turning and as he did when reading the newspaper, began to follow the words he was reading with his finger. "Sir, has something happened?"

Barr tapped the page with his finger, "I don't know Clay." he mused "I don't know . . . It could be nothing. Please organise the meeting."

Clay left the library and made his way to the kitchen leaving Barr staring from the window deep in thought. He knew that one of the group members he wanted to attend the meeting would be there. As he opened the door, he saw Mark sat at the large table eating a small meal.

He remembered finding the boy eight years ago stealing anything he could from a nearby market. Clay watched as the youth picked his way through the crowd towards him filling his pockets as he went, he knew then that he had found someone whose talents could be used. As the boy passed, he tried to pick Clay's pocket, but found himself instead gripped across the face by the man, a strange smell lingered on his fingers. Slowly the boy drifted into unconsciousness.

He awoke hours later sat in the same chair upon which he now sat. Seeing Clay enter the kitchen Mark stopped eating and stood. "Good evening Sir."

Clay smiled seeing his obedience. "Please Mark," he said. "Sit and finish your meal." As he did Clay slid the chair next to him out from under the table and also sat. "I've been instructed to organise a meeting for tomorrow night, I want you to attend."

"Sir," smiled Mark. "That would be a great honour."

"Nonsense," replied Clay gently touching Mark's cheek. "You've responded well to my tutoring, I believe your more than ready."

The door directly facing Clay burst open as Mrs Stott the cook exited the pantry carrying a large sack, instantly Clay's hand returned to his side as Mark jumped up and grabbed the sack from her. "Ooh . . . thanks Mark, you're such a dear," she puffed. "Just leave them on the table, Wendy will sort them out later. Oh, good evening Mr. Clay." she said nodding. "Didn't see you there."

Clay stood. "Good evening Mrs Stott," he replied as he turned to leave, "I trust your well?"

"That I am Mr. Clay."

Reaching the door Clay called back without turning, "That's pleasing to hear Mrs Stott. And Mark . . . don't forget the meeting."

"I won't Sir." But as the words left Mark's lips Clay had left the room.

Chapter 11

The Beast crouched close to the edge of the roof, its head bent so low that its elongated legs reached high above it. It scanned the dark streets below. It revelled in its position, moving freely across the rooftops it could see all, giving it easy access to its victims. From the rooftops it would wreak havoc on the city below.

It crawled crablike along the edge, its long fingers scraping against the guttering. With ease it leapt from one side of the street to the other, up over the apex of the roof then down the other side.

The rain and smog had kept the streets quiet. Through the day the Limehouse basin had been bustling with hundreds of manual workers, but with money in their pockets, there were far better places to be than a cold wet dock.

From a few streets away, the sounds from a busy pub echoed to it over the soft patter of the rain. Music, song and laughter. It waited patiently, knowing its time would come. The dark always attracted people. There were those who craved the dark and the unseen acts it enveloped. It wouldn't have to wait long.

Its predatory eyes had been fixed on the street corner long before the couple, whose drunken laughter it had singled out, appeared. They staggered across the cobbled street to almost the exact spot the Beast was staring down at them from.

Its tongue flicked saliva down at them, thick and stinking. Mixed with the rain it fell on them. Ignorant of their fate the couple took no notice.

It watched as the woman stood holding out her hand, the man grasped it as she disappeared into an alley leading from the street to the Basin. The man laughed as the woman whispered something to him, before he too disappeared into the darkness of the alley.

Sliding over the rooftop to the back of the building the Beast slipped down to the edge to observe the docks below. Cargo crates had been piled between the building edge and the water giving the couple several dark places in which to hide. It watched them as they exited the alleyway.

The woman glanced into the darkness ensuring their solitude before perching herself against one of the crates, rubbing his hands on his waistcoat the man began to fumble with his pants.

"See anything you like?" asked Ethel lifting her skirt, revealing to the man her lack of underwear.

She had spotted the drunk in her local. *'An easy few bob.'* She thought. Quick one in the docks, then back to 'The Grapes' and back on the game within the hour.

"Oh yes" the man replied without looking up, instead concentrating on popping his buttons. He hadn't expected this and the sight of her dark hairy sex wasn't helping him get them open.

"Oh come 'ere." said Ethel grabbing his waistband, she smiled as she pulled him closer. With her free hand she quickly popped his buttons open and slipped her hand into his pants gripping his flaccid cock.

The man's hips had already begun thrusting drunkenly back and forth. Ethel couldn't believe her luck, he was drunker than she had expected and with luck it would be over in a few moments.

She let her skirt slip back down covering her sex. She moaned, moving her hand back and forth in time with his thrusts.

The Beast watched from above, its slender body hanging unnaturally over the edge, it hissed down at them, its predatory eyes widened, focusing on nothing but its prey.

"Ere, what was that?" asked Ethel, holding his cock still, but the man continued thrusting himself at her, only one thought on his mind. Ethel slapped his back, hoping to move him away from her a little, giving her a chance to see around. "Hey, I asked you if you heard something."

The man looked up at her. "There's nothing . . ." his body began to shake. "I'm coming," he announced, "I'm coming!" Ethel closed her eyes and leaning her head back she began to rub his cock again wanting him to finish.

The Beast breathed in deeply filling its lungs, it could smell them, smell their fetid sex. Dropping down silently behind the man it landed crouched on all fours, hidden by the darkness. Without raising its body, the Beast reached out with its slender fingers, gripping the still thrusting man around the neck. With a slight flick it snapped his spine, flinging him easily into the cold black water below.

Ethel, feeling his weight lift from her believed for a moment that he had finished. The loud splash of his body hitting the water brought her back to her senses, lifting her head she opened her eyes.

The long black face of the Beast stared down at her, only inches away from her own. Its gaping mouth wide open revealing a thick black flicking tongue, its breath rank, the smell of it filled her lungs making her feel ill. Vomit caught in her throat.

Standing to its full height it towered above her. It gripped the crate she was still leaning against, its strong talons splinter the wood, its long arms either side of her, ensuring she couldn't escape.

Drawing breath, the Beast hissed at her, its broken teeth bared, saliva dripping onto her pounding bared chest, slowly running down into the now heaving valley of her breast.

Ethel let out an all mighty scream leaning back against the crate, with all her might she kicked out at its rancid chest. The Beast leapt back, leaving Ethel nothing to kick at but thin air. Realising she was free from it, she seized the opportunity and ran for the alley, the one from which she had only moments before entered by. The Beast beat her, leaping at the entrance to block her escape.

It gripped at her hair twisting her head, Ethel tried to force its long fingers away with her own, hoping to release herself. The Beasts grip tightened, her thin skin ripped as it lifted her feet clear of the cobbles, Ethel screamed as her flesh is tore away from her skull. Her weight aiding the ease at which she is scalped. Dropping her body to the floor the Beast stood holding her hair, licking at the blood dripping from the torn skin.

Her pain was overwhelming, all consuming. Crawling forward Ethel used the crate to get back to her feet and made for a small walkway that spanned the mouth of the small dock. Her body working independently of her mind. She screamed and ran, screamed and ran, until she eventually fell gasping for air, her chest heaving as she crawled on all fours towards the walkway. Her feet slipped on the wet wood, blood running into her eyes hindering her progress.

She tried to ignore the pain, focusing only on escape. She was unaware that her screams were bringing people running towards the docks. A small crowd had quickly gathered at the entrance to the alleyway, hesitant, no one wanting to be the first to step into the darkness, none of them wanting the responsibility of whatever they might find.

Ethel crawled onto the walkway, holding on to the wooden rail she managed to stand. Unsure where her attacker was she paused, wiping blood from her panicked eyes as they flicked from left to right, straining to see into the darkness searching for any sign of it. Sure, that any second it would pounce.

Moving to the centre of the walkway she let loose her grip on the rail. Still no sign of it. Taking another step back she screamed as her bottom touched the rail behind her.

The crowd, still deciding on who should be the first to enter the darkened alley, leaped into action upon hearing her scream, they bumbled through the alley, now all of them wanted to be first to see the cause of the commotion. They began to spill out of the alley and amongst the cargo crates stacked around the dock.

Ethel turned towards the sound and managed to speak her first coherent word "Help!" she screamed at them, blood exploding from her mouth as she did, "Help, help, I'm here!"

The group moved between the crates, making their way to the dockside. "She's there," one shouted. "On the walkway."

The Beast had leapt across the enclosed dock and made its way to the top of the building, from its vantage point it watched the crowd enter. Slipping silently from the roof it dropped onto the walkway next to where Ethel stood.

Sensing its presence, she turned. Its long limbs held the rail on each side of the walkway, one leg bent up behind it the other resting on the rail next to its right hand, its body twisted unnaturally. Standing, it reached out and pulled her closer, its body enveloping hers. It slipped its fingers easily into her soft white throat, its jagged talons puncturing her skin which in one movement ripped through both her clothes and her flesh. The wooden rail behind her splintered as its limb arced through the air ripping her open.

The crowd fell silent, each held mesmerized in shock.

Her torn clothes fell away. Her naked body exposed, her once pert breast flat against her ribs. Intestines spilled from the open wound and dangled over her legs, her blood, black against the white flesh.

Her ribcage shattered, the Beast pulled back the bone exposing her heart and lungs. Placing its mouth over hers it sucked at what little air she had left inside.

The crowd shouted and screamed at the Beast, but no one moved towards the walkway. Many turned to run, but finding their exit blocked they begin to push against those still trying to get onto the dockside.

Blue flames flickered around its mouth, its tongue lapping at Ethel's bloody torso, leaving tiny blue flames dancing across her organs. Reaching into her chest cavity it slipped its long fingers around her still warm heart, ripping it free from the rest of her body. Raising it to its mouth it bit down, its sharp broken teeth tearing into the flesh, blood smeared over its jaw.

It leaped from the walkway carrying the limp body of Ethel with it. The crowd watched as it easily reached the rooftops above.

Crouching on the edge it released its grip on her , watching as she fell to the water below.

The crowd moved as one to the edge of the dock, peering into the black water looking for the body. "It's here!" cried one, "fetch a pole."

The men busied themselves with the retrieval of the body, desperate not to mention to each other exactly what they had just witnessed, each man keeping a watchful eye on the rooftops above.

As they lifted Ethel's remains from the water her entrails dragged along the dockside edge. Realising they had laid her down on her stomach, they turned her over. Those nearest balk in horror at the brutal carnage that had befallen her.

Her body open, her skin, now drained of blood an unnatural white. The Beast observed the men below, its body trembling with excitement. It felt their fear from them rising, it breathed it in, feeding on it. In its hand it held what remained of Ethel's heart, lifting it to its face it again bit at the flesh before throwing what remained down at the people below. The crowd stared in disbelief as the half-eaten meat landed before them. Their screams filled the air as the Beast leapt away into the night.

Chapter 12

The streets seemed unusually quiet as Will strolled towards the office of the *London Evening Star*. He had almost reached the doorway when he heard Pip call to him from further along the street. "Will," he shouted, "Will, hold on a minute." He paused and stood watching as Pip jogged the short distance between them, several newspapers resting over his right arm.

Reaching him, Pip singled out a paper and folded it with his free hand. "There's a piece in there you might find interesting." he said passing it to him, he was through the doorway before Will had had a chance to reply.

Holding the paper up he scanned the front page. "Second page, fifth column." Pip shouted back as he began to climb the stairs. Will opened the paper and folded back the page, once again he scanned the headlines.

Just as Pip had stated the article on the second page, fifth column did indeed interest him.

The report was about the brutal killing of prostitute Ethel Jones, in the East End docks the previous night. Will assumed by the lack of description that the reporter had been instructed to produce a quickly written piece ensuring it could be printed in time for the morning edition he now held. The facts, although sketchy, did mention that witnesses had seen her assailant leap from the scene whilst carrying the victim and had made its escape by using the warehouse rooftops.

Looking up from the paper Will felt sure there was a connection between this attack and the one suffered by Lucy Strong. He read the rest of the article, taking note of the name of the Detective that had attended the scene.

Placing the paper into his jacket pocket he turned away from the office entrance and stepped directly into his colleague, Charlie Lipton. "Whoa Will." said Charlie lightly holding Will steady before stepping back. He had seen him stood outside the office reading. "What's got into you?"

Will looked up as he brushed passed. "Sorry Charlie. Someone I need to see." he rushed off shouting back, "Tell Kingsley I'm following up a lead."

Will crossed the street and had hailed a cab before he had reached the other side. Charlie watched it for a moment before stepping into the building.

Chapter 13

Will had to force his way into the Leman St. Police Station. Since the previous night's killing, a crowd had gathered outside the station wanting to know exactly what the police were going to do about it.

Some of those present were not concerned with neither the murder of a common prostitute, nor any plans the police had put in place for solving such a brutal crime. Anarchists, they had been present at the Trafalgar Square rally and since then had taken every opportunity presented to them to badger the police.

Their voices shouted the loudest, they demonstrated with a fever, each time the crowd quietened they began chanting and pushing those at the front towards the doors of the station. The police had finally responded, fearing the worst they had placed two officers at the station entrance to ensure no damage could be done. This act had only succeeded in enraging the protesters further, and by the time Will had arrived the crowd had doubled in size and arrests had been made.

Pushing through the crowd Will took full advantage of a forward surge. The two police officers fought against the surging crowd, but they were pushed from the doors. Will, noticing his opportunity slipped inside during the confusion.

Straightening his jacket, he calmly walked up to the front desk. Around him officers were still trying to deal with a number of protestors they had arrested and had managed to drag into the station.

Pushing one of the protestors from his slumped position against the desk, the Sergeant looked up and spoke to Will "Can I help you Sir?" he asked. Will watched as the protestor slowly slipped to a crumpled heap on the floor. "Can I help you sir?" the officer asked again.

Clearing his throat Will replied. "Yes, I would like to speak to Detective Rutherford."

The Sergeant leaned forward and placed both elbows on the desk. "As you can see Sir, at the moment we are quite busy." he waved his hand over the writhing heap of both police and protesters.

Looking around Will could see that some of the officers were now dragging semi-conscious bodies through a doorway behind the desk Sergeant, who was holding it open for them with his foot.

Will imagined that a lot of sore heads would soon awaken in holding cells. An officer gripped the legs of the man crumpled next to Will, he watched as he too disappeared through the doorway. "Yes, I can see you've got your hands full," said Will taking the paper Pip gave him from his pocket. "But it's concerning this." he continued, pointing at the article.

The Sergeant scanned the headline Will was pointing at. "Oh, I see." he said looking Will up and down. "If you take a seat I'll see if someone is available to see you."

Looking over his shoulder Will spied a large wooden bench, he crossed over to it and sat waiting. The Sergeant observed him for a moment before leaving via the same door the protestors had been dragged through.

Will sat and re-read the article, making notes with his pencil in the space around it.

The Sergeant re-entered the room followed by a tall slim man and pointed in Will's direction.

Standing Will stepped forward offering his hand. "Detective Rutherford?"

The tall slim man took Will's hand, his grip was tight.

Too tight!' Will thought.

Feeling uncomfortable Will released his grip allowing his hand to fall at his side, surreptitiously wiping his palm against his leg as he did.

"No, I'm Detective Bolton, I'm afraid Rutherford isn't available at the moment. But if you'll come this way, we'll see what we can do for you." Bolton held out his hand indicating Will should enter the door now held open by the Sergeant.

Opening a second door, Bolton lead him to a corridor with several doors on each side. Will hesitated. "Right to the end if you please, last door on the left." Bolton instructed him, before following Will down the corridor. Reaching the door indicated Will waited as Bolton unlocked it, both men entered.

The room was small, square and bright, except for a desk and two chairs it had no other furniture. Daylight from single barred window illuminated the area. Bolton, made his way to the opposite side of the desk and sat down. Offering Will the only other seat he took a few sheets of paper from the desk drawer and began to write.

"Now," he smiled looking up at Will. "If I could just take some details. Name?"

Chapter 14

Will was fuming by the time he had left the police station. Pushing his way passed the few remaining protestors on the steps, he disappeared into the hustle and bustle of the street, wanting to be as far from Leman Street as he could.

He had answered all the questions Bolton had asked. His name? Address? Profession? Relationship to the deceased! In fact, all the information that any suspect would have been asked.

Arriving at the station he had had every intention of helping the police. Allowing them the knowledge he had gained by investigating the case of Lucy Strong, the thoughts he had on the similarity between this and the murder of the prostitute the previous night. He had left feeling that he had been treated firstly as a suspect, then secondly as a time waster.

In Bolton's opinion there was no similarity, *'Lucy wasn't dead for a start'* he had almost shouted at Will when he had asked for an explanation. Bolton went on to list many reasons why he felt he would only be wasting police time investigating, what was at best, an unsuccessful robbery on an unstable individual.

Will had, in his opinion given a good argument, he could see the similarities between the two attacks and had told Bolton in no uncertain terms that if the police wouldn't do anything, then he himself was going to investigate the case. He would then walk into Bolton's office to demand an apology when it was proved that Will was right.

Bolton had sarcastically wished him well and left. Will sat silent for a few moments, when it became clear that not only was he alone and was probably going to remain so, he also got up and left.

He now walked through the streets of London, his mind buzzing with the details of not only the attack on Lucy Strong, but also the murder of Ethel Jones. Bolton had let one thing slip in his listing of the differences of the two cases. Ethel Jones had been mutilated! Her heart had been torn from her chest. It had not been found, although witnesses did say that it had been dropped. The opinion of the police, was that the rats had taken whatever had been left.

As Will walked he toyed with the idea of visiting the local morgue. He knew that the victim's body would be there and that the police would request a full report before releasing it to the family, or more likely to allow its internment in a pauper's grave when none could be found. He would still have time to see the remains.

Almost instantly he came to the conclusion that, given the severity of the crime even his quick talking and position with the newspaper would make it unlikely he would be allowed into the building, never mind speak with the Surgeon tasked with discovering what actually happened to Ethel Jones.

Will decided that his best cause of action would be to return to his office and dig a little deeper into the murder, he was sure that with Pip's help he could easily find a few of the witnesses mentioned and the offer of a few beers usually loosened tongues enough to get the information needed.

Feeling a little more positive he set off in the direction of the office.

Chapter 15

Barr sat silent as Clay drove his carriage through the dark streets of London. He had also read the account of the prostitute's murder that morning and was now convinced that some dark force had indeed taken up residence in the city. He had felt its presence in the mood of the common folk, those that had less resilience to the poverty and degradation brought down upon them, those that had no purpose, other than to work constantly for their very existence.

That morning Clay had been dispatched to the area around Bishop's Manor, he had been tasked with sniffing out any information appertaining to the attack, to look for some physical change in the area. He was to search both the canal and Victoria Park for any evidence of the attacker, however small that evidence might be.

Barr was convinced that whatever had been released upon the city originated from this area. It was known to him that the area had an ancient past, that the ghosts of the old religions resided there. The knights of St. John had used the area, had even built their first church on sacred pagan ground.

He was extremely interested in the information Clay had returned with. He had been right. Clay had spoken to many in the area, firstly about the attack at the Manor, then about the area's history.

It soon became apparent to him that the residents had more to say on the attack than had been reported. He soon heard about the three men attacked in the churchyard, an incident that had preceded the one Will had reported on.

Clay had eventually approached a group of workmen who had until recently been employed in the demolition of the local church, the very same church that had been built by the knights. It had stood in the area for hundreds of years. Dilapidated and derelict the land had been recently bought and it had been agreed that the ruin was to be razed to the ground, but their work had been suspended soon after it had begun.

They told Clay about how they had found the three bodies when they returned to work on the morning after the attack of Lucy Strong. The workmen spoke of the horrific way the bodies had been mutilated and of the insistence of their employer that no mention of what had happened was to leave their lips, Clay smiled as their loyalty waned the more they drank.

It had been made clear to them that it was a matter between the police and their employer. They had been paid handsomely for their time and asked to resume back at the site in seven days. The one condition on their continued employment, was that no report of the incident was to reach the newspapers.

Clay had left the men where he had found them, drunk in a local pub. He had walked the short distance to the church, there he found a policeman walking the area. As he approached the policeman shouted and motioned for Clay to turn and leave. He was pleased to confirm the workmen's story.

He had walked the circumference of the church and had found the place where the solid wall had been compromised, the workmen had not only broken down the wall, but had unknowingly broken down its holy seal.

The carriage swayed and slowed. Clay brought the horses to a halt within walking distance of the church. Inside, Barr was now very anxious to see the site. He was certain that the church contained the answer.

Clay had explained, that although the church had been abandoned many years before, work on its demolition had only just begun and was at an early stage. Superstition had kept the locals away, Barr hoped that the records he knew most churches kept in their crypt had not yet been removed.

He knew that something had been released upon the city, he felt it. The deaths of the three men and that of the prostitute were no coincidence. He felt that they had unwittingly exposed something, something that had been imprisoned in the church grounds for many years. Barr wanted to know exactly what that thing was.

Clay had brought the carriage to a halt a few yards from the church grounds. He peered into the darkness hoping to catch sight of the patrolling policeman he had seen earlier. A mist covered the ground between the perimeter wall and the back of the church. Its gravestones rising from it like broken teeth.

Once Clay was certain there was no movement, he leant over and tapped gently on the side of the carriage.

Barr had been waiting for his signal, he opened the door and stepped out into the street. He was dressed in black, removing his cloak he threw it onto the seat. "So, this is the Church?" he mused looking up at the dark derelict building.

"Yes," replied Clay, "Bishop's Manor is in that direction," he said lifting his arm and pointing into the darkness.

Barr closed the door and moved into the shadows, "You know what to do Clay?"

"Yes Sir," he replied, "good luck."

Barr crossed the narrow street and made his way to the church. Crouched by the wall he turned for a moment to watch as Clay maneuverer the carriage past him and on towards the front of the building. Following the line of the wall he made his way silently to the point where Clay had told him the boundary had been compromised.

He waited before entering the grounds. Clay had been instructed to either engage the police in conversation or, if he had left to signal to him that all was clear. A few moments later the sound of Clay's voice calling to someone drifted through the mist, holding his breath Barr waited for the other voice to answer.

When it finally did, he took this as his cue and crept into the graveyard.

The mist surrounded his feet making it difficult for him to see what was underfoot. Cautiously he stepped past the broken headstones, some moved slightly as he laid his weight against them, others he had to step over, they had fallen forward when the coffins below had collapsed in on themselves.

Barr reached the church and tried the handle of the small wooden door he found there, it was locked. Leaving it, he made his way forward through the shadows keeping his back to the wall as he did.

Reaching the front corner of the building he paused listening to the conversation Clay was having, he could see his servant and the ghostly outline of his carriage but not the owner of the other voice. Their plan was working.

Barr slid around the corner and although now exposed and on view to anyone who cared to look, he found himself with his back was against a large double door, using all his strength he cautiously pushed one side open and slipped inside.

The interior was pitch black, though surrounded on both sides by stained glass windows, they let in very little light. He imagined that even through the day, the dirt and grime on them would make it a gloomy place.

Slowly Barr stepped forward his hands held out before him, almost blindly he waved them about until he touched one of the pews. Running his hand along the smoothed wood he found the end and the aisle between them that ran through the nave towards the altar.

He was relieved that although work had begun on the outside, they had not yet removed all of the fittings inside.

As he walked towards what he assumed would be the altar, his eyes became more accustomed to the dark. He could now make out the shape of each pew, some had been moved and stacked against the wall. He could see neither the pulpit nor the lectern and realized that as he entered he had not passed the font. Some of the more valuable things had been removed, Barr hoped once again that the crypt had been left intact.

In the north corner of the nave he spied a door and made his way towards it, once there he pushed it open.

Barr stepped into to a small room. Closing the door, he took a candle from his pocket and lit it. The room was empty, he suspected that it had been so for some time. A door in the far wall had been left slightly ajar and with the limited light from the candle he could see steps leading down from the room, he descended them.

The steps mirrored the state of the church, they were decaying. He placed each foot carefully on each one, ensuring that it wouldn't crumble away from him before he put all his weight on it. The walls were wet with damp, trying his best not to touch them he continued down.

As he reached the bottom the area widened, in the gloom he could see broken pews and bits of stone he imagined that had at some time in the past fallen from the building, being stored here with the intention of replacing them.

Various religious artefacts lay on a large chest, Barr carefully took each one and placed them on the floor. He tried to lift the lid of the chest, but it stuck fast. Noticing a pew behind him he placed the candle on it and using both hands he managed to lift the lid a few inches. The hinges, rusted with age screamed as he did so.

Holding the candle to the gap he peered inside, in the dim light he could see the prize he sought. The parish records.

With a large candlestick he prized the lid open, its rusted hinges cracking after being unused for so long. He could now see the ledgers stacked up. Each one had two dates hand written on the cover, date begun and date ended.

Ignoring the first few he took out, he placed them on the floor behind him. They were too modern for what he was looking for. Studying the dates of those that remained he made his way through them, reaching back in time with each one. Through the seventeen hundred's, sixteen hundred's, the fifteen hundred's, each one he dismissed and placed behind him.

At the bottom of the chest were two bound books, he smiled realizing that he had found the volumes he had come for. Taking them out he turned them over in the candlelight, neither of them had been dated.

He knew that Parish records had not become compulsory until the fifteen hundred's but churches had always kept some form of record. The Priest was usually the only person in the area that could read and write, so felt obliged to record the lives of those around him.

Barr placed the ledgers on the pew along with the candle. Unlike the others, their pages were loose, each one had been placed in once it was written. Eagerly he studied the first few elegant hand-written documents before carefully closing the cover and making his way back up the steps to the small room.

Once there he blew out the candle and dropped it to the floor, it was of no use to him now. He quickly made his way across the nave and with his back flat against the wall he slowly opened the door a few inches and peered out.

The street outside was empty, it seemed the conversation Clay had been having had ended, and as instructed he had now moved the carriage back to where he had dropped Barr off.

He waited listening for the footsteps of the patrolling policeman. Eventually he heard them to his left getting louder, closer. Pulling the door closed he stepped back out of sight, just in case.

Backing into a table he hadn't noticed behind him, he felt something move. Quickly Barr placed his free hand on the object to stop it from falling, standing motionless as the footsteps passed.

He listened as they became quieter, before turning to see what he was holding. It felt out of place. It seemed to vibrate under his touch. In the darkness he could just make out the shape of a mask. A leather strap dangled from one side. Deciding it was worth investigating once he had returned home, Barr placed it under his arm alongside the books.

Stepping out from the church he made his way back around the building. Carefully he retraced his steps, pausing every few feet conscious that he was moving in the same direction the footsteps had taken.

Clay was waiting where he had been instructed too watching for his master, as Barr emerged from the churchyard he passed his cloak twice across the carriage lamp, indicating all was clear. Barr stepped from the shadows into the street.

Tapping the horse, Clay maneuvere'd the carriage into the centre of the street and towards Barr, who was now walking to meet it. As the carriage slowly drove passed, Barr pulled open the door and stepped inside. Sitting back as the door closed he dropped the items he had stolen onto the seat opposite, reached for his cloak and wrapped it around him. The temperature had dropped considerably and he hadn't realised just how cold he had become.

The first snow of winter began to fall as the carriage made its way through the streets to Barr's home.

Chapter 16

Barr had been sitting in his library since they're return. His secret bookcase exposed and many of its volumes piled next to him. He had made many notes as he translated the pages taken from the church, some had been in Latin, others in Old English. They now covered most of his desk and some of the floor around it.

A tray of food prepared by Clay lay untouched under a scattering of papers he had already translated. The books cover had been discarded and were now sat at the corner of the desk, empty now their pages had been removed. Upon them sat the mask he had found at the entrance to the church, its weight indenting the soft covers, the remaining leather strap hanging from the table edge.

Barr had found himself subconsciously staring at it many times over the time he had been seated. Each time he couldn't recall exactly when he had stopped working and had begun gazing at it, nor how long he had spent doing so.

Clay knocked twice on the door and entered, "Sir, everything is ready."

Barr sat holding one of the pages in his right hand as he flicked back and forth through a book with the other. He answered without looking up, "Are they all here?"

Clay had noticed the untouched food and had retrieved it from underneath the pages, "Yes Sir," he said placing the straightened papers back on the desk.

Barr closed the book he had been reading, "Do they know what we are about to do?"

"Sir," answered Clay picking up the tray, "I don't know what we are about to do!"

Barr smiled as he stood, "Does the name Erebus mean anything to you?" he asked.

Clay thought for a moment, "No Sir, it doesn't."

"Excellent," Barr laughed, moving to leave the room.

Clay placed the tray on the desk and picked up the mask, "What is this?" he asked.

Barr took the mask from him turning it over in his hands, "I'm not exactly sure yet, but if I've translated the text correctly it seems it could be of great use to us," he said replacing it. "Now, shall we change? I imagine our brothers are anxious to find out why they have been summoned."

Clay picked up the tray and followed Barr out of the room.

Both men stood naked in the anti-chamber hidden below Barr's house, their clothes neatly folded and stacked on a small table. No longer master and servant, all formalities had been dropped as they undressed. They were now equals in their religion, both admired and feared by their followers. Barr's knowledge of both dark arts and ancient ceremony's, along with Clay's knowledge of potions and magic had made them a formidable force.

Known throughout Europe, both men were welcomed wherever they travelled. Guests of some of the wealthiest and most powerful families. Their influence now stretched far and wide.

Barr took a red robe that had lay folded next to their clothes and gave it to Clay, he passed it over his head and as Clay straightened it Barr took a similar one and did the same.

Standing for a moment both men admired each other, "Shall we begin?" Barr asked indicating for Clay to move into the next room.

As they left, both men lifted the large hood that hung from the robe and pulled it down hiding their faces.

Clay entered the chamber. The room was dark, lit only by candles. Five hooded figures stood in the room, each at the point of a large pentagram painted on the floor. At its centre was a bowl, within it burnt shavings of both Ash and Cedar. The first wood to protect, the second to induce visions. The air in the room was heavy with both its smoke and odour.

Clay passed the silent figures and made his way to a small altar. Lighting two black candles he placed one at each end, he then pulled a cord that hung to his left. A curtain opened in front of him revealing a dead goat suspended by its legs above the altar, its throat had been slit, its thickened blood matting its hair and pooling in a silver cup that had been placed under it.

Barr entered the room and sat at the centre of the pentagram, he bent and placed his hood over the embers. He breathed the smoke in deeply and sat upright.

'*Erebus, Erebus, O te videamus,*' he shouted, before bending over once again to inhale the smoke. The five followers immediately began chanting the same phrase. Clay picked up the blood-filled cup and circled the followers rotating the cup behind each of them.

Barr sat up again, '*Erebus, Erebus, O te videamus,*' he began to sway. Clay now stood directly behind him. Barr breathed the smoke in for a third time, this time as he rose Clay passed him the blood-filled cup. Red rivulets ran down the sides of his mouth as he drank, taking his fill he poured what was left onto the smoking embers. More smoke rose from the bowl as Barr bent over for the final time.

The chanting around him quietened to a whisper, as he raised his head from the smoke, he fell back into Clay's waiting arms. Clay lowered him to the floor, his face was white, a thin wisp of smoke rose from his lips. Barr had entered a trance, he was beginning his vision.

Barr's conscious hung in the air above the city, a fog clung to the darkened streets below. In his mind's eye he could see the people, the buildings and their rooftops. Focusing his mind on the Tower of Westminster in the distance, its bold outline easily recognizable, his mind was instantly transported there. The city below passed as a blur.

Focusing on the dome of St. Paul's he once again felt his consciousness move over the city. From his vantage point he could see and hear the people moving below, with his mind he found he was able to tune in to an individual person if he so wished and listen to their conversation.

He focused on a nearby rooftop. From his vantage point Barr could scan the skyline of the city, he knew that whatever had been let loose from the churchyard was using the rooftops, as it had been mentioned in both the reports. Looking for its silhouette he scanned the horizon, nothing.

Barr leapt across the city focusing his vision from rooftop to rooftop, from church spire to monument. Using tall trees in parks, leaping south of the river then back again.

As he paused over Tower Bridge he became aware of something in the distance to the East. He focused on a nearby warehouse, once there he noticed that whatever it was that he had glimpsed, had also moved.

Choosing a building he judged to be between them he leapt, when he stopped he could clearly see it was a large figure and that it too had moved to a building nearer to him. Barr slowly realized that whatever it was knew he was there.

'But how could it?' he thought.

He marvelled at the power it must have, if it too could sense his presence.

Barr focused on a large chimney that emerged from a rooftop near the figure. He paused hoping its stack hid him.

Slowly he focused his way around the edge of the brickwork, he found it difficult to control the small movements needed. Miscalculating he leapt further than he had wanted and found himself hanging in the space above the street. He focused his mind to turn back to the rooftop, instantly returning, his vision cleared.

The Beast stood before him. His mind reeled from the sight of it, long hands reached out and needle like fingers gripped at his consciousness. It let out a piercing cry and forced itself upon the mind of Barr. His body shook as he desperately tried to end the vision. He could feel the Beast probing him. Darkness fell upon him, he suddenly felt relaxed, quiet.

Feeling that there was something in the darkness that he needed to see, he allowed his mind to be led by it. He began to perceive buildings and then heat! Barr had entered a vision state many times, but this was the first time he had sensed anything physical. The buildings around him were alight, the city was burning. Hordes of people ran screaming through the streets towards him, trampling both the living and the dead. There was no order only panic and chaos.

Through the crowds he caught a glimpse of a huge fire. As he neared it he could make out more bodies. Bodies piled upon bodies. All burning, some were still alive, the burning mass writhing, their screams mixing with those who ran, trying to escape their fate.

The streets filled with them, the writhing mass reached high above the buildings. One giant pyre, the city's population a burning tower. He felt his mind being forced to look up, to look upon the peak of the human tower

For a moment Barr was confused, the top of the pyre was in darkness. Where bright flames should have been licking the night sky, there was nothing but a deep all-consuming blackness.

He felt himself rising, being lifted from the ground. Past the screaming burning bodies, up to the darkness above. He felt the heat but could do nothing to protect himself from it, his mind screamed in pain.

From above he could hear a piercing cry, it came from within the darkness. As he neared, he could see the one true Beast, Satan, Lucifer. The desolate one sat atop the pyre on a throne made from the burnt and charred limbs of the dead. The flames around it dying as they reached the darkness that surrounded him.

Barr let out a deafening scream, he could feel his lungs burning. Clay and their followers had surrounded his convulsing body. "What's happening?" they asked.

Clay had no answer, "I don't know, nothing like this has ever happened before."

Barr lay below him, his body shaking violently. He screamed again, Clay slapped him across his face, "Maximillian," he cried, "Maximillian."

Clay hit him hard, hard enough to leave a red hand print across his cheek.

Barr began to emerge from the trance, his body calmed. He opened his eyes, "I have seen the future," he muttered.

Clay turned to the group of hooded followers gathering around them, "Mark, get him some water!" he said lifting Barr's head and placing it in his lap. "It's over now Maximillian," he comforted him, "it's over now."

Sitting up Barr turned to face Clay, "That's the problem," he replied, "this isn't over," his face was ashen, serious. "It's just the beginning."

Struggling, he tried to stand but found he couldn't, "I'm fine," he said, hoping to reassure the group. "I just need a minute," taking his hood in his hands he pushed it back. Everyone in the room gasped, Barr's once black hair had turned pure white.

Shocked, Clay turned once again to Mark, "I said get some water," he spat.

Mark ran passed Barr as he sat disoriented on the floor, but as he left the meeting a smile played on his lips. *'It seems,'* he thought, *'the master isn't as powerful as he has always made out.'*

Chapter 17

The night had been long and sleep had eluded Barr, the vision he witnessed haunted him. Nothing he had ever experienced throughout his life, could have prepared him for what he had seen.

As he sat back in the chair Clay shaved his head, his white hair fell in clumps to the floor. Those who had been present at the ceremony had been shocked not only at the sight of his hair colour, but at the unmistakable look of fear they had seen in his eyes when he woke from the trance.

They had witnessed many ceremonies at which Barr had had visions, some had even balked at the graphic way he had explained them later. However none had witnessed anything like that evening's events.

Barr had become fearful since the end of the ceremony, although he trusted the few chosen members Clay had requested to be present, he was unsure as to how any information of his weakness would be received by the lower ranks. Those who had no influence or power that was useful to him but had none the less declared their allegiance to him.

He ruled over them with fear and could not risk them seeing or hearing about anything that would show him to be vulnerable. The colour of his hair showed weakness, he had encountered a force and power of which he had never seen before.

He knew that the writings he had taken from the church held the key to its control, they had once before beaten it, he needed to know how?

During breakfast he had explained to Clay the vision he had witnessed. The city aflame, its population frightened and panicking, chaos reigned. Finally, he told him of the vision of Satan he had witnessed, how he had seen him atop the tower of burning bodies, how his servant had invaded his mind allowing him a vision of the future. He had decided, that together they would discover its purpose, its plans, and most of all a way to pre-empt it before finally taking control of it, before the future he had seen came to pass.

Barr had taken great interest in the article written in the *London Evening Star*. The author had reported on the first incident involving Lucy Strong, having then made a connection to the second involving the prostitute, he had then written the follow up article Barr was now reading.

In it he had surmised that a connection could be made between the two, this had piqued Barr's interest, as he himself had known not only of their connection, but he knew that they had not been the first and if he was correct, would not be the last. Barr had decided that it may be beneficial for both parties if they met. A plan to use the reporter was beginning to form.

"Clay?" he said, as his hair continued to fall around him.

"Sir?" answered Clay stepping back.

"No, no continue, no point stopping half way through," Clay did so.

"I want you to invite Mr. William English to a meeting later today, say three o clock. Leave the invite at the offices of the *London Evening Star*, I'm sure he'll pick it up there."

Clay finished shaving and washed the cutthroat, Barr wiped the remaining soap from his head and peered at his reflection in the mirror. "I like it," he said turning his bald head from left to right, "I like it a lot."

As Clay finished Barr stopped him, "There is one other point I wish to make," he said.

"Sir?"

"I know," Barr began, "that I have allowed you complete control over both the employment of staff and the choice of . . . " he paused thinking of the correct word, "of members you feel are worthy of entering the inner circle. But I question your choice of the boy."

"Sir," Clay replied, "with all due respect Mark is no longer a boy, he has become a most trusted member of not only our household, but has proven himself as one of your most loyal followers."

"There is something about him I don't like," interjected Barr, "he's immature and naïve."

"I feel he is ready," Clay replied, "I have tutored him personally and I would now trust him with my life."

Barr lent forward staring into the mirror, "And I am trusting you with mine!"

Chapter 18

Will laughed as he left Kingsley's office, they had been discussing his wife Sarah and the imminent arrival of their child. "I'll tell her," he shouted back still smiling.

Sitting at his desk he picked up the report he had written and was about to read it through, picking up any mistakes in both spelling and grammar when he noticed an envelope laying partly hidden under a folded newspaper. He picked up both.

The newspaper was one of their own and had been folded in such a way as to show the article Will had written a few days previously on the connection between the two 'Springheel Jack' attacks.

Placing the paper back onto his desk, he mused over the envelope, "Pip?" he shouted, knowing that his friend was somewhere about. "Pip?" he turned the envelope over in his hand, on the back was a deep red seal and on the front in beautiful handwriting, was his name.

Pip's face appeared at the door to the newsroom, "What is it?" he asked.

Will held up both the letter and the newspaper so that Pip could see them, "Any idea who delivered these?" he asked.

Pip walked over to the desk to look at the items Will held, "No," he answered, "I've been about all morning and I ain't seen anyone come in here except you and the Boss," he said, holding his hand out to take the envelope, "Whose it from?"

Will took it out of reach before Pip had chance to grab it, "Let's find out shall we, it is addressed to me."

Breaking the seal, he reached inside and took out a thick card. "Nice paper," Pip observed, "what does it say?"

Will read the card to himself then announced to Pip, "I've been invited to lunch with Maximillian Barr at three o' clock."

Pip stood back, an astonished look on his face, "What does he want to see you about? Is that all it says?"

Will looked down at the invitation, "Yes, that and his address. Grosvenor Square," he turned the card over, "nothing more."

"Well I'll be," Pip mused, "have you heard this Boss?" he shouted into Kingsley's office. "Will 'ere has only gone and been invited to lunch with one of the richest blokes in London."

Kingsley slid his chair back and leaving his office asked, "Who's this then?"

Will held the invitation up so Kingsley could read it, "Maximillian Barr," smiled Will as the editor took the card and like Will read it then turned it over.

"Doesn't say why?" he puzzled handing it back to Will. "What you going to do?"

"I'm not going to disappoint him," he said returning the card to the envelope. Will held up the newspaper and pointed to his article, "I'm thinking it's about this."

Kingsley took the paper from him and scanned the folded page. Picking up his coat Will crossed to the door, as he left the room he shouted, "I'll give you a full report later."

Kingsley passed the paper to Pip, "Nice for some!" he said returning to his office.

Will stood on the steps to Barr's home, he had smiled to himself as he told the cabby the address. He had never had cause to be in this part of town before with its beautiful tree lined avenues and bright white fronted town houses.

As the cab left he stood looking up at the black painted door, it shimmered in the sunlight. Taking hold of the large lions' head knocker he gave the door three loud taps.

The door opened and Clay stood looking down at Will. He was slim and impeccably dressed, and from where Will stood on the steps, he seemed impossibly tall. "Yes?" enquired Clay, "May I help you?"

Will held out the invitation he had received earlier, "I've been invited to lunch," he blurted out. Reaching down Clay took the card from Will's outstretched hand, "My name is Will." he smiled, "Sorry. William English."

Clay inspected the card, then looked Will up and down, he was toying with him, knowing full well he had been invited to lunch. He had been the one that had written the card out and surreptitiously hand delivered it. Smiling he opened the door wide and indicated for Will to enter, "This way Sir."

Will entered the building; the hallway floor was beautifully tiled in a green and white chequered pattern. At the end of the hallway a staircase led up to a large stained-glass window. Its coloured light dappled the stairs.

"If you could wait in the Library, I'll inform Sir of your early arrival," Clay smirked knowing how uncomfortable he was making their guest feel. He opened the library door and once Will had entered, closed it behind him.

Will was surrounded by books on three sides, he had assumed that it was just a name for a room that Barr would read in, but this really was a library, he couldn't imagine reading these many books, never mind owning them. The fourth wall had two large floor to ceiling windows, the light from which illuminated the whole room, between them stood a large desk. Will walked around the desk, he looked down at the chair tucked underneath it, it looked very comfortable and he imagined Barr sat at it for hours studying.

On the desk sat a sturdy wooden bookstand. Will looked over the book that rested upon it. He could tell that it was very old, its loose pages were very worn and tattered. He couldn't read any of it as it was in a language he was unfamiliar with.

The door opened and Barr walked in, "I thought the invitation was for three o' clock!" Barr said as he took out his pocket watch and held it up, "it's twenty-five off!"

Will looked at the watch dangling in front of him, he knew he was early, "With all due respect Sir, when the richest man in London asks you to luncheon with him at his home you don't wait about." An uncomfortable silence fell between them, Will was sure he was being sized up. "We at the Star don't just wait for a story, we make one happen," he continued, giving Barr the line Kingsley had given him as he set out on his first assignment, "I believe that you Sir, are about to make one happen."

Barr stood staring at him for what seemed an eternity, "Point taken," he said finally, smiling as he returned his pocket watch. He passed Will and sat at his desk, "Please, sit," he said, indicating that Will should sit facing him. Lifting one of the nearby chairs, Will placed it at the opposite side of the desk and sat.

"If you don't mind me asking Sir, but what happened to your hair?" Will had been conscious of Barr's baldness since he had entered the room but was unsure at first whether to mention it.

Barr ran his hands over his head, "I decided on a new image. Makes me look a little more . . . ruthless. Don't you think?" he laughed, stood and made his way to a small drinks cabinet next to the door, "Would you like a drink?" he asked holding up a bottle of clear liquid. Will declined. Barr shrugged his shoulders as he poured himself a large vodka and returned to his seat.

"I like your article," he said sliding a copy of the Star across the table.

Will looked down at it, "And?" he asked.

Barr sipped his drink, "And I'm interested in what makes you think the two attacks are connected?"

Picking up the newspaper Will answered, "It's all here," he said, pointing to his piece, "I've highlighted the connections and I had hoped that I'd made quite a valid argument."

Leaning over Barr took the paper from him, "You have, but these are just words. I want to know your gut feeling, the things you cannot report, those feelings you get that you can't quite explain."

Will sat thoughtful, there had been things he had wanted to say, both in the article and to the police, but he had decided that it would be best not to say something that others may not understand. "I've reported on many things," he began, "and although I'm still relatively young

I believe I've gained a nose for things. When somethings not quite right, or there's something just bubbling under the surface, I can usually spot it. I will stake my reputation that these attacks are connected and that whatever evil has perpetrated these crimes is not going to stop."

Barr sat with his elbows on the table, his palms pressed together listening, "You're a clever man Mr. English and what's more, I believe you."

Will sat shocked, he hadn't expected to be agreed with, "You do? Why? The police didn't."

"Mr. English," Barr spoke softly, "unfortunately, our police force has a blinkered view of the world. They think they know what is happening, or should we say, what is happened in their local area. They have no interest in the bigger picture. Would it shock you to learn the Lucy Strong was not the first victim of your so called Evil that night?" Barr held his hand up as Will was about to speak, "Please, let me finish. That very same evening three man had been killed and mutilated at a small derelict church in the same area, their bodies found the next morning."

"That's preposterous!" shouted Will, "how could that have happened and no one know about it?"

Barr stood and faced one of the windows, "Calm yourself, it is not preposterous, it happens all the time. Money talks Mr. English, someone of influence doesn't want a certain incident to become public knowledge. Speak to the correct person and that can easily be achieved."

Will sat, astounded by Barr's revelation, "When I went to the police they knew nothing about these three men, I'm sure if they had done, they would now be investigating it, there would be a city-wide search for their killer."

"You are correct Mr. English, but you are an honest hard-working man. Because of your profession, your interest is city wide, you also believe in justice and that that justice is always fair. But when one police force prefers to keep certain information secret, how can another, one that may be many miles away across the city learn of that incident? How could they then perhaps make a connection to something that has happened within their own jurisdiction?" Barr turned and sat back at the desk, "Please, come here. I'd like you to see this." Barr tapped the book in front of him.

Will did as he was told, he stood peering over Barr's shoulder, looking down at the book. It was the one he had been looking at as Barr entered the room, it still made no sense to him.

"These are the parish records from St. Augustine's Church," Barr turned the pages as he spoke, "although when these records were written, the church had been known as St. John's. It had been built by the Knights of St. John on their return from the Crusades in the thirteenth century. They must have seen it as some form of penance for their actions during that unholy time." Barr paused for a moment before continuing, "The book records the events of that area between the year's fourteen hundred and fourteen o nine."

Will watched as Barr carefully turned the loose pages over, "Where did you get them from?" he asked.

Barr smiled, "Let us just agree and say that I have acquired them. Can you read any of it?"

Will shook his head, laughing out loud Barr continued, "I don't suppose there is much call for Latin at the London news?"

Turning the page Barr stopped, drawing his finger across the words, "This page tells of four killings, well to be literal three killings and a drowning."

Will peered at the pages trying to distinguish any of the words, "A drowning?"

Barr continued, "Yes, it seems that the first victim was drowned by the local villagers before anyone could intervene. The records state that she was driven mad by possession and they were trying to drive the Demon from her. Sound familiar? You could say that Lucy Strong was driven mad, only modern medicine has saved her from the ducking stool."

Will returned to his seat, "I don't understand. This all happened nearly five hundred years ago? What bearing could this have on what's happening now?"

Barr closed the book, 'Fourteen hundred and two too be precise, and believe me, I do understand your scepticism. It is as you say nearly five hundred years old, but I have been translating these pages diligently, and I believe that these recent events are echoes of what happened then. These pages tell of four attacks, four very different attacks. The first two correspond with the two that you yourself have reported on, and that you yourself believe to be connected." Barr could see the disbelief on Wills face, "Mark my words, a third and then a fourth killing will take place."

"I just don't understand how writings that are at least five hundred years old could predict events that are happening now. Or are you telling me that whoever killed these poor unfortunates is now back, and killing again?" Will folded his arms across his chest, "After five hundred years?"

Barr sat for a moment calming himself, "I have only recently come across this book. Who can say how many individuals have read and translated these pages? Maybe in the past few months some unhinged individual has translated it, deciding to recreate the killings. Look at the Whitechapel murders a few years ago. This is not beyond feasibility."

"I do see your point, but why would someone do such a thing?" asked Will

"Why? Is something that we may never find out, but the fact remains that someone may be recreating the incidents detailed in this book?" Barr rested his hand on its cover, "and if that is true, then we have a good chance of predicting the locations of the next two killings, it seems that the author of the text discovered a pattern and managed to stop the perpetrator at the last. We can't be sure which one will be first, but between us we can observe the two sites in question."

"What?" Will asked surprised, "Try to find the murderer? Us? Are you mad?"

Barr stood becoming a little annoyed at the way he was being spoken too, "No Mr. English I can assure you that I am not mad, you yourself have already been to see the police, have tried to convince them that your theories are correct. They don't think they're connected. You and I are the only ones who think . . . no . . . the only ones who know that they are connected. Who know that not only have there been killings before these two incidents, but who now know that there will be further killings? We two together must prove them wrong. Now listen to what I have to say."

Barr sat back at his desk. He was about to speak when two taps at the door sounded, Clay entered, "Luncheon is served Sir."

Barr once again stood, "Thank you, Clay. We will be along presently."

Clay closed the door as he left the room, Barr looked over at Will, "We can talk whilst we eat, the Dining room is this way."

Will followed as he left the library. He was no longer happy that he had accepted the invitation.

Clay stood in the hallway as the two men ate. He could hear the hushed conversation and once or twice a raised voice. He had already been briefed by Barr as to what was going to be told to the reported and although he hadn't totally agreed with the plan he kept silent.

As the two men exited the dining room Clay entered and began to clear away the service. He could hear the passing of pleasantries as Barr bid farewell to his guest. Entering the hallway Clay found Barr watching from the front window, "Forgive me sir," he asked, "but I'm at a loss as to why you've chosen him. A reporter?"

Barr continued to watch from the window, "Because my dear friend, when the real trouble begins we will need someone to take the blame. He's a good citizen, one who I'm sure now feels he's in over his head. He'll go straight to the police and try to convince them again." Both men watched as Will called a cab and climbed in, "See, there he goes now."

"But won't he mention you Sir and what you've told him? The book? Those three murders?"

"I doubt it very much Clay, that he has the courage to involve me. As for the book? I don't think he made any sense of it. He may tell them that a reliable source has given him new information about the killing of the three men. The police will waste valuable time checking it out and when they find it is true they will perhaps begin to suspect Mr. English. When a man in his position is seen to know too much they'll want to make sure they know exactly how he came by such information and where he is every moment of the day."

Chapter 19

As Barr had suspected Will made his way to see
the police. He was convinced that with the new
information he had gained, they would now have to
take his claims that the cases were connected seriously.
He was anxious to arrive; his mind swam with Barr's
words.

*'Could there really be someone living in the city that would commit
such crimes as Barr had intimated?'* he thought.

He still wasn't convinced that there was someone
recreating a series of crimes perpetrated five hundred
years ago.

*What would be the point? Who would recognize the connection
except someone else who had also read the text?'* Will's mind swam
with both questions and suspicion.

He wondered at how Barr had so conveniently come
across the records. Will suspected there was still much
that he was not being told. His nose was telling him there
were certain things he should be concerned about now
that he had become involved with Barr, the rumours of
black magic and his connection to the dark arts had not
escaped him.

'What if the things he said turned out to be true?' Will thought, his story could become a countrywide sensation, *'had that not been true a few years earlier with the Ripper case?'* he smiled.

'I would be at the thick of it,' he thought, *'I would be able to take my pick of the newspapers, work for any of them.'* As he sat in the back of the cab, he dreamed of a better life for himself, Sarah and the baby.

The Hansom came to a stand at the front of the Leman Street station, Will paid the driver as he stepped down onto the pavement. It appeared to be a lot quieter than the last time he had stood in front of the building. He made his way up the steps and in through the doors.

On entering, he observed two men now sat on the bench where he had waited a few days before, they sat quietly leaning against each other, eyes closed. Will stared at them for a few moments, he suspected that they were drunk and had been left there to sleep it off.

Noticing that he himself was under observation he stepped over to the desk. The officer he had spoken to the last time he had been here had been replaced by a younger man. "I'd like to speak to either Detective Rutherford or Bolton please, " requested Will, speaking before the young officer could open his mouth.

"You would, would you?" said the officer, "whom should I say is requesting to see them, and what would it be about Sir?"

"My name is William English and it's about the killing of the prostitute at the docks a few nights ago, I've already spoken to Detective Bolton about the incident, but I have new information that they must hear."

"New information eh?" the officer looked Will up and down, "Wait here, I'll see if one of them is available," he added, before he disappeared through the door behind him, Will considered taking a seat next to the two sleeping men but decided against it.

Detective Bolton entered the room, closely followed by the young officer, "Ah, Mr English," he said, seeing Will stood at the desk, "I believe you have some additional information that you feel I should hear?"

"Yes," answered Will, "It's unbelievable, is there somewhere we can discuss it? You won't be able to so easily dismiss me this time, not when you've heard what I've got to say," Will said. Not waiting for the invitation, he made his way around the desk and through the door.

"Please," Bolton said, smiling as Will passed him, "this way."

Chapter 20

Will had left the police station more furious that he had been on his last visit. Bolton had taken no interest in the information he had given. He had listened patiently to what he had to say and then began once again to find fault in his statement.

Will fumed at the disinterest given to what he had told him attaining to the deaths of the three men in the churchyard. Bolton had pointed out the impossibility of such a crime not only going unreported by the newspapers, but also actually taking offence at the intimation that the local police could be silenced by bribery.

He reminded Will that all police officers, from the lowest rank to the highest had sworn an oath and that they were there to serve the public, not to be ruled upon by individuals just because of their privileged social standing. The rich had no sway over them.

There was still, in his opinion, no connection between the two cases and that the new information Will had given, was either an invention of someone's furtive imagination, or an embellishment of some small incident with the sole objective of making a fool of

Will and a mockery of the police. As well as adding that Will's reluctance to expose his source, only confirmed in Bolton's eyes that it was most likely untrue.

Will had stormed out of the room and left the police station.

Bolton's disinterest had made him so angry that he was now more determined to expose the killer and to prove the police wrong. Barr had been right; his plan was the only way, Will's mind was now made up. He would consent to help him.

Over their lunch Barr had instructed him as to what to do and where to be. He did impress on him that he couldn't be sure of the exact date of the next attack, but he was sure on the two locations and had agreed that Will should observe one whilst Barr spent his time observing the other.

He was certain that they wouldn't have to wait long. The attacks detailed in the records had taken place over a few short weeks. A few uncomfortable ights observation and they would have their killer. Will now thought that Barr's promise was worth the sleepless nights.

Sarah welcomed him as he arrived home, her smile brightened his day. She was, as always happy when he was home, she loved to hear him talk about his day as she prepared his evening meal.

Will held her in his arms, "I need you to listen very carefully to what I have to say," he began.

"What about your meal? I was preparing a little meat," Sarah felt his mood change and was becoming a little anxious.

"It's fine, there's a lot I need to tell you and only a short time for me to tell it in," he said leading her over to the table and sitting her in one of the chairs, once she was sat Will took the other.

Sarah sat silent as Will told her of his day. The invitation and the newspaper left on his desk, the meeting with Barr and all he had said. Sarah was visibly upset at the killings Barr had spoken about. He told her of Barr's suspicion, that they had been deliberately kept from being reported on and his plan to capture the perpetrator based on the information translated from the ancient parish records.

Will went on to tell her of his visit to the police station, that he had spoken to one of the officers involved in the murder of the prostitute and of their disbelief in what he had to say. He told her how angry the Detective had become at his accusation of a cover up and the intimation that the police were corrupt. Finally, he told her of his decision to help Barr in executing his plan.

Sarah put her head in her hands and began to cry. He knew this would happen, he also knew that if he didn't keep his resolve he would allow her tears to sway his judgement, his determination to be involved in Barr's plan would falter. He couldn't let that happen.

Will stood fighting every urge in his body to take hold of his wife, to lift her into his arms and tell her that things would be alright, that he would detach himself from Barr and the killings and stay home with her. He looked down at her sobbing, her back stooped. She seemed so small and helpless. Standing, Will stared out of the window, afraid to look at her. The street below had begun to empty of people, the sky above darkened.

"Please, Will," Sarah sobbed, "I don't want you to go. Please don't get involved"

Will turned his gaze from the street. Knowing that the sight of her face would sway him, he looked down at the floor, "I have too, please Sarah, ou have to believe me when I say that." He slowly walked towards the door collecting his coat as he did so. "The police don't believe me," he said, "what if Barr's right, what if someone is out there copying the killings? I know it's a long shot Sarah, but I could never forgive myself if someone died and I had known that there was a way to have prevented it."

"You should have told the police about Barr!" Sarah shouted angrily at him.

"How could I do that? What could I say? A rich successful business man, whom I have no connection with contacts me and wants to include me in his plans to capture a killer?" said Will lifting his bowler from the stand and placing it on his head, "It sounds implausible as it is, without adding Barr in to the mix. I'm sorry my love but this is something I must do."

Sarah stood and ran to him as he opened the door, "Please Will," she pleaded placing herself between her husband and the door, "please don't go, what if something happens to you?"

"It won't," Will held her as she sobbed into his chest, "Don't worry."

"I can't help it," she cried, her tears dampened his jacket. Turning his head away from her he struggled to hold back his own tears. He could no longer look at her beautiful face.

Irrationally he began to feel an anger rise in him, angry at Sarah for making him feel so bad, angry at Barr for involving him, but most of all anger at himself for allowing himself to be manipulated into a hopeless situation.

"I don't want to bring up our child alone," Sarah cried.

"Alone, with your mother?" the moment the words had been spoken, Will regretted them. He had allowed his anger to momentarily take over him, he had said something that he knew he could never take back. He couldn't even remember thinking the words, they were just there.

Sarah pushed herself away from him shocked, he had never spoken to her in such a way. She beat at his chest as she began to cry uncontrollably. Will held both her wrists until she calmed and became limp, slowly she fell to the floor.

Sarah sat crouched at his feet crying. Will hated himself for what he was about to do. With steely determination he turned his back on her and closed the door behind him.

Tears welled in his eyes as he walked along the corridor and down the stairs to the front door.

'Why have I done and said those things?' he thought as he opened the front door, stepping out into the cold night.

Seeing Will exit his home Detective Rutherford slipped back into the shadow of a doorway. He had been watching his house since Will had arrived home, Bolton's description of him was spot on and he had recognised him immediately. Luckily for him he had taken a Hansom and had managed to find a spot from where he could observe the house, before Will had returned.

At some point, although Rutherford couldn't say exactly when, a fog had begun to drift over the city and it now lay thick on the ground.

He had discussed the case with Detective Bolton as soon as Will had left the station. Rutherford had listened to the new information and was of the opinion that if what Will had told them about the killing of the three men was correct, *Then Mr. English and his contact would be of great interest to us.'* Being unknown to him it was decided that Rutherford should keep a close eye on Will whilst

Bolton would travel across town and discover if there was any truth in the allegations made. Rutherford had hoped that his colleague would have returned before Will left his home. Two men could follow someone much easier that one.

The Detective watched as Will stood in the street looking up at the window above. He stood silently in the fog for a few moments, the light from the window casting a long shadow across the street, then turning his collar up around his neck he walked passed the doorway Rutherford was observing him from and down the street. Rutherford waited until the fog had blurred his silhouette before emerging from the shadows, cautiously he followed him.

Will walked quickly through the streets, he knew where he had to be and had quite a way to go before he got there. The night was cold and the fog around him was beginning to thicken, he hoped that it wasn't going to become one of London's famous pea soupers. If that happened, he feared that even if he was standing next to the killer he would be unable to see him.

Leaving Sarah in the way he had hurt him greatly. Never, since the day they had met had he treated her in such a way.

'What had come over him?' he thought, *'Why had he said the things he did?'*

Will felt that since his meeting with Barr earlier that day, his mind had not been his own. He hadn't wanted to agree to Barr's plan, had intended as he left, to take the cab home but instead found himself instructing the cabby to take him to the station. He had wanted to tell Bolton about Barr, the book and the plan he had for the capture of the killer, but he had not. He had instead invented a story about a contact.

Plus his treatment of Sarah. His heart sank as he thought of his beautiful wife clinging to him pleading for him not to leave her. He told himself that he should return home, to take her in his arms and apologise, agree that she was right and that he had been a fool. Even though the thoughts raced through his head, he continued to walk toward the place Barr had asked him to observe.

'Had he been asked?' the thought flashed in his head, *'had he? Or had Barr told him where to be and he was just complying with his demand. Had he become a puppet?'* Will's train of thought was interrupted as a man stepped out from a doorway on his left. Both the shadows and the thick fog had conspired to hide him.

"Fancy showing me a good time?" the man blurted out as Will passed. Although startled, Will managed to take hold of the man as he stumbled and fell towards him.

"I'm sorry," he replied and pushed the drunk back towards the doorway from which he had emerged, "I don't think so."

The man fell back against the door, as his knees gave way he slowly slid down to a sitting position on the floor.

Will, seeing the man was now in a safer position continued on.

"I only wanted a good time," the man mumbled to himself as he sat in the darkness, "that's all, nothing more," his head slumped onto his chest as his eyes closed.

Rutherford had glimpsed the incident as he followed, he watched from the darkness and when he was sure Will had left, made his way over.

Crouching down next to the man he grabbed his hair, lifting his face. He could smell the alcohol on his breath. The man's mouth opened then closed, Rutherford let the hair slowly slip through his fingers and the man's head rested again on his chest. A sound came from him, but it was incoherent. Rutherford looked up at the direction Will had gone, he could no longer see him. Jumping up he left the drunken man and rushed into the fog hoping to catch a glimpse of him in the distance. Nothing, Will was lost to the night.

Coming upon a junction Rutherford stopped and listened for footsteps, any sound that would indicate to him in which direction Will had gone. The world around him had fallen silent. Again nothing. The Detective cursed himself for such an error. The fog around him was thick in all directions. He took a few steps to his left then stopped, retraced them and made his way to the right. Again, after only a few steps Rutherford stopped. "Damn!" he cried. Will could have been standing only meters away from him in any of the three directions, however Rutherford would not have known.

Will had left the man, turned right at the junction and was almost at his destination. The air was still thick with fog, Will walked with his hands stuffed deep into his pockets. He crossed the street knowing that he was nearing the location Barr had given him. It would have been very easy to miss it from his position on the other side.

As he turned into the street he looked up at the brickwork for the street sign. He could just make out the black lettering. 'Ship Alley', it read. He suspected that if this had indeed once been an alley, it was quite a while since it had been extended, expanded and more houses built upon it.

This was the place Barr had wanted him to observe. He was certain that the attack was going to take place here, or on one of the narrow alleys and passageways leading from it to the courtyards behind.

As Will made his way passed the houses he began to realise that this was way too much for one person. There were passageways between every two or three houses and alleys running behind them. Although the cold and fog had kept some streets relatively quiet, Will was in a densely populated area and shadowy figures rushed passed him that a moment before he couldn't see. He could the hear footsteps of people out of sight and in the distance the distinct sound of a horse and cart.

Will stopped and listened for suspicious movement around him, he became aware of a sound behind him, as he turned he noticed that he was standing at the entrance to one of the passageways. Will listened, sure that someone was hiding in the darkness between the houses. Slowly step by step Will moved further into the passage. Halting, he heard a grunt followed by a scraping sound. As his eyes became accustomed to the darkness he spied movement, something white was moving back and forth quickly, it was close to the ground. Bending forward Will took a closer look.

"Hey, A little privacy here!" a gruff voice shouted from the darkness, "It's not a fucking peep show."

Will realised that the white he could see was a petticoat and above it, the thrusting of a man's exposed buttocks. Will made a hasty retreat, "I'm really sorry," he apologised. With each step back he apologised again and again, "Sorry, so sorry," he repeated, until finally he exited the passage and stood safely back on the street.

"I've nearly finished," the gruff voice called from the darkness, "you can have her then if you want?"

Followed almost immediately by a female voice, "Just give me a moment love and I'll be right with you."

Will stared into the passage, "This is too much!" he answered, "I'm leaving now." Turning his back on the passage and the couple hiding within, Will retraced his steps back along the street, making his way home.

Sarah was in bed and asleep by the time Will returned home. She had undressed, tucked herself in and cried until tiredness overcame her and her eyes eventually closed. Her world had altered, and it seemed Will, the centre of her world had altered the most.

He looked down at her sleeping, *'How could I have urt one so innocent and beautiful?'* he thought. Taking the pillow from his side of the bed he sat in the armchair, placing it behind his head he stared at her until eventually he entered a fitful frightening sleep. He dreamed of fog, in the fog buildings burnt and people screamed. No matter which direction Will moved, the fog never cleared, nor did he get any closer to either the people or the burning buildings.

Will had already left when Sarah woke. Seeing that he had returned and taken a pillow to sleep on the chair, upset her again. She sat in the same chair holding the pillow he had used close to her bosom, his scent lingered on it, again she began to cry.

Chapter 21

Will had risen early, he had watched Sarah sleeping, standing over her as she did. After the way he had treated her the night before, he knew that he could not face her, deciding to leave before she awoke. He would spend the day clearing his head, planning just how he should apologise to her.

He found himself walking the same streets he had walked the night before. Eventually he found the passage where he had come across the couple having sex, he wanted desperately to find humour in the situation but couldn't.

Now that the fog had lifted he could see the area he would have had to cover. On each side of the street there were four passages, the two outermost on each side led to an alley running parallel with the street, the innermost two on each side led to small courtyards. The whole area was filled with people busying themselves with their daily toil. Women washed, children played, babies cried and men worked.

'How could anyone think that they could get away with murder in a place that housed so many people?' he thought.

Unbeknown to Will, since he had emerged from his home he had been followed. Rutherford had managed a few hours' sleep before being woken by Bolton banging at his door. Bolton had had more success with his investigation of the three alleged killings. As Will had described there had been an incident at the church, as he had described three men had been killed. He had briefed Rutherford and now both men followed at a distance. Will had become their main suspect.

Unbeknown to both Rutherford and Bolton, they too were being watched. Clay had managed to spot them before it was discovered that he too was following Will. He had had a momentary panic when it seemed that the two detectives had stumbled upon him. Barr had suspected that the police would be involved and had warned Clay to be on the lookout, he concluded, they had been too interested in their quarry to notice him.

Barr's vigil the night before had also been fruitless, he had sent Clay out with the instruction that Will should be followed. He doubted that he had had any success either but wanted to be sure that no matter what had happened, he was back in Ship Alley that night.

The sun had set, the sky dark blue as Will returned home. He hadn't meant to stay away all day, just enough time for both of them to clear their heads. He had tried fruitlessly to plan what he was going to say to her, his mind wondered constantly back to Barr.

All of the people he had passed in the street and those around him seemed to stare in his direction, he had a feeling that there had been a presence at his shoulder throughout the day, felt he was being watched. By evening he had become sure of it. His head spun with the faces of those he suspected, everyone seemed to be watching him.

He had also picked up on a nervousness preading through the air and the people around him, although they had been going about their daily routine, they felt wrong to him. There was a tension in the air. The city seemed to him to have become a powder keg.

Will opened the door onto an empty room, he knew as he climbed the stairs that she wasn't home. He could usually feel a warmth radiating from her, knowing instantly when she was near. There was no warmth as he opened the door.

The room was cold, she hadn't been at home all day. He regretted leaving her that morning more than he regretted leaving her the night before. His chance at reconciliation had gone and he hadn't even seen it pass. He sat in the same chair he had slept in that night, put his head in his hands and wept.

The Detectives secreted themselves into the same doorway Rutherford had occupied the night before. They both hoped that Will would not disappoint them and once again leave the house that night. They were both determined that he would not so easily disappear into the night, as he had done when Rutherford had followed him alone.

Clay watched both the house and the Detectives from his vantage point further along the street. He took from his pocket a fine silver chain, on the end hung a small silver ball. It had beautifully carved filigree. He snapped the lid open and lit the wooden shavings enclosed.

The ball swayed back and forth, smoke rising from it. Clay stood with his eyes closed, his mouth moved quickly as he whispered an enchantment. His mind reached out to that of Will's, willing him to leave. Again and again Clay whispered the words. The city around him became dark.

Will slowly became aware that the room around him had become very gloomy, he stood and lit a lamp. His head ached and his mouth was dry, he hadn't realised that he had fallen asleep.

The room around him had been filled with a faint aroma, it wasn't unpleasant, a sweet burning smell. Sarah had not returned. Without thinking Will found himself at the door.

'When had he decided to go out again? Back to Ship Alley?' Will was convinced that his memory was playing tricks on him. Still, he took his overcoat, bowler hat and left.

Clay observed Will leaving his house, then moments later, watched as the two detectives began to follow. Leaving his vantage point he made his way to the main street. Once there he hailed a cab back to Barr's address. Both he and his master had their own agenda for the evening. Clay had a feeling that he would be reading about the events of Will's evening over the next few days.

Will subconsciously walked the same route he had on the previous night, even as far as crossing the streets at the same point.

Although dark, the fog that had held the city throughout the night and most of the day had now lifted. Visibility was good, Rutherford and Bolton had no trouble keeping up with him.

Both men watched as Will entered Ship Alley. As Bolton stepped into the road to cross Rutherford gripped his arm and pulled him back, "Watch out sir!"

Bolton stepped back to the pavement in time to see a dray and horses pass close to them, followed immediately by another. "Thanks," he said brushing his coat nervously before crossing to the corner.

Looking along the street both men failed to spot Will, "We can't have lost him again," Rutherford said, looking back along the street they had just crossed, "could he have doubled back?"

"I doubt it," replied Bolton, "he couldn't have known he was being followed. He must have made his way into one of these passages."

The two men looked at the shadowy entrances along both sides of the street. "Look, you take that side and I'll take this," suggested Bolton, "he couldn't have gotten to the end before we came around the corner, so that's where he'll be. I'll meet you at the bottom. Call out if you see him."

Rutherford crossed the street and entered the first passage, it led to an alley. Bolton did the same.

Once Will had turned onto Ship Alley he had made the decision to walk to the far end and make his way back up the street to where he now stood. He had had no idea that he was being followed, but the strange feeling that niggled him throughout the day prevailed. He didn't want to spend any more time in this area than was necessary.

Crossing the street, he noticed that the area had become eerily quiet. By the time he had reached the passage near the far end, he was the only one in the street left outdoors. He looked back hoping to see some sign of movement, he didn't.

The passage he stood before was dark, it seemed to him to be endless. As he stepped inside the darkness enveloped him. Had he lingered a few moments longer before entering, he would have seen both Rutherford and Bolton turn the corner and pause before splitting up.

Will became aware that his footsteps made hardly any sound. The floor was stone, but somehow the enclosed space had deadened the noise. Seeing a change in the darkness ahead, he was sure he was coming to the end of the passage and that it would lead into a courtyard.

As with most courtyards in the East End, they were overlooked by many windows, but Will was conscious that he could see no light in the windows above, not even the dim glow of a distant candle. The darkness around him felt heavy.

He felt the space open around him and surmised that he was now standing in the courtyard. Lifting both arms, he tried to feel for one of the surrounding walls. When he couldn't he stepped to his left. When he still couldn't he stepped again. Eventually after two more steps he felt the cold brickwork of a wall under his fingers.

The courtyard was deceptively large. He stepped forward, ensuring his fingers never left the wall, its roughness scrapping his fingertips.

A few feet in front of him he glimpsed something white. His mind returned to the previous night and the couple having sex.

'Have I in-avertedly walked straight into the same situation?' he thought. Realising he could make a discrete exit by crossing diagonally to where he had entered, he took a step away from the wall and towards the centre of the courtyard. He immediately stumbled into a large wooden crate.

A piercing cry filled the air, deafening him as he rose to his feet. He covered both his ears with his hands. Around him the darkness, which only moments before had seemed impenetrable, began to clear.

Before him stood the Beast. Its huge mouth gaping, its long black tongue flicking at the air. Beneath it lay a woman, her clothes ripped apart, her body exposed to the night. Will froze leaning against the crate, his hands dropped from his ears and slipped behind him, he gripped the crates edge.

The Beast crouched down to the woman that lay at its feet, its black eyes never leaving Will's. The woman murmured something as its long arm found her head, its fingers slipped through her hair holding her head in a vice like grip. Realising it had her she began to struggle, kicking out with her legs, striking at it with her arms. Her screams muffled by its palm pressing firm against her face. It stood to its full height, lifting her by her head.

Still fixing Will in its gaze it twisted its arm, Will heard her neck snap and the woman's body fell limp. Holding her up, Will stared at the woman suspended between them, the Beast gripped her shoulders with the long fingers of its free hand and Will could see its broken talons piercing her white flesh. It bit down savagely on the exposed skin of her neck, its fingers entered the open wound and tore her head from her body.

"Oh my God!" Will finally managed. He wanted to scream, but each time he tried it died in his throat. Fighting his fear, he managed to move from where he stood against the crate, to the entrance of the passage. The Beast stepped towards him holding the woman's head at arm's length. Will felt the edge of the brickwork against his back. He tried to turn away from the sight and run into the darkness, but the Beast still held his gaze.

It bent holding the woman's head next to its own. Will watched as its tongue slipped out of its mouth and licked at the blood dripping from her neck, he tried to close his eyes but felt compelled to watch.

Its tongue lapped at the hanging flesh, found the opening to her throat and forced its way in. Finally, as her mouth opened and the tip of its tongue popped out, Will managed to release a scream. Drawing breath, he screamed again. The Beast joined him, letting out a piercing cry. The night air filled with their horrific duet.

It leapt first onto the right wall then to the left, the head still held firm in its grasp. Will subconsciously stepped forward into the courtyard as it leapt from the wall to the rooftop directly above him. He turned looking up expecting to see it looking down at him, but it was gone. He scanned the length of the buildings for it, but to no avail.

Rutherford had walked the length of the alley from one end of the street to the other and had just stepped back onto the street, when he heard Will's first scream, Bolton had emerged from the opposite side as Will screamed out a second time. Both men arrived at the passage on Rutherford's side of the street as the Beast let out its piercing cry, the Detectives stopped dead in their tracks. The dark passage loomed ahead of them, the cry ended. The silence became deafening.

"Come on Rutherford, get in there!" Bolton nudged his colleague, "our man's in there," he pointed towards the darkness.

"Thanks Sir," Rutherford said sarcastically, slowly stepping into the passage. Bolton followed. "English?" whispered Rutherford, "English?" both men slowly past through the darkness and entered the courtyard.

Candlelight began to appear in the windows overlooking the courtyard, illuminating it a little.

Faces peered down, "Who's there?" one shouted, "What's going on?" added another.

Will stood with his back to the passage, looking down at the headless corpse, his mind reeled. He was unaware that the two Detectives had entered the courtyard and were now stood behind him. He hadn't heard them calling to him.

"English? Can you hear me?" Rutherford shouted at him. Both men walked over to him and stared down at what was holding Will's gaze. "Sweet Jesus!" cried Rutherford holding his hand over his mouth, balking at the sight of the dead woman.

Bolton slapped Will across the face, "English, snap out of it."

Will stared at Bolton, his mouth moving but his words lost before he uttered them.

Rutherford turned and quickly left the courtyard blowing his whistle.

Will began to sway back and forth as his mind closed in on itself from the horror he had witnessed, he fell back into Bolton's arms, but his weight was too much for the Detective to hold and Bolton let him fall to the floor.

Reaching the street Rutherford continued to blow his whistle, he could now hear footsteps running towards his location, knowing that some of them would not be police officers he waited at the entrance, ensuring no one could enter the courtyard unless they passed him.

As the first officer appeared Rutherford instructed him to guard the entrance, "Keep the public away," he told him, before re-entering the courtyard.

Once in the courtyard, Rutherford observed Bolton kneeling between Will and the dead woman, "What happened to him?" he asked.

"He's just fainted. Get a carriage here and instruct uniform to get him to the station when it does," said Bolton standing, "he'll be fine."

Looking around he became aware of the faces staring down at them from above, "Can you all please keep away from the windows," he shouted up at them, "this is police business, unless you witnessed what happened here I don't want to see any of you looking down on this courtyard! Is that clear?"

Two officers enter the courtyard, Rutherford turned to them, "One of you get a carriage," he called to them, "We need to get him out of here," he said pointing to Will laying on the floor. "The other get a cart, we need to get her to the morgue."

The two officers turned and made their way back to the street. Rutherford followed them. As more officers arrived he directed each of them to start a door to door inquiry. The officers dispersed around the street knocking on doors.

Bolton called from the courtyard, "Rutherford, don't let anyone else in here until the carriage arrives. Understand? And get me a lamp."

Rutherford shouted a confirmation into the darkness of the alley before continuing to give orders to each officer as they arrived.

People began to crowd around the entrance to the passage, some from the houses on the street, others following the responding police as they ran towards the area. Five officers surround the entrance holding the onlookers back.

Leaning forward Rutherford whispered to the nearest officer, "When the Carriage arrives I want two of you to carry the suspect out, unless that is, we can arouse him before then," he then turned to an arriving officer taking the lamp he was holding from him before returning to the courtyard.

The sound of the arriving carriage echoed through the passage as it turned the corner, the two officers Rutherford had instructed with removing Will's unconscious body were already lifting him as it slowed to a stop. The small crowd of people were moved away from the entrance giving the officers a clear passage.

Bolton turned on the lamp Rutherford had handed him and shone it across the courtyard. As it illuminated the officers lifting Will he halted, "Just a minute," he asked them. Both officers looked over at him whilst holding Will's limp body above the ground, Bolton made his way over to them and stared at him in the lamplight.

The two officers watch Bolton slowly pass the beam of light from his head to his feet then back again. Satisfied he nodded to the officers, allowing them to continue.

"He didn't do it," he stated, breaking the silence.

"What?" Rutherford stood aghast at Bolton's revelation, "how can you say that? We caught him standing over the body." Bolton continued to cast his light over the area. "We know no one else was here," Rutherford added.

"Do we?" Bolton asked, bringing the light to rest on Rutherford's face, "do we really? We know no one left by that passage," he stated, turning his wrist slightly the lamplight illuminating the dark entrance. "But what about the blood?"

Bolton held the lamp above the body allowing Rutherford to move closer so both men could examine the scene.

The woman's left leg was bent under the right, her white stockings speckled with dark bloody spots. The right shoe stood alone a few inches from her foot. Her torso bent slightly to the left, both arms reaching out in the same direction. What was once a green heavy fabric dress had now turned black with blood, pools of it coagulated in the folds of fabric. The white collar of her blouse was torn and blood soaked around the ripped flesh of her neck and throat. Her head was missing. Blood pooled around the body, colouring the stone floor.

Rutherford looked to the wall behind her and at the arcs of her blood that had sprayed across it as she fell. He felt a sickening movement in the pit of his stomach. Although an experienced officer he had never been unfortunate enough to have witnessed such a brutal killing first hand.

"It's a right mess Sir, that's for sure."

"Exactly," answered Bolton, "so, if this whole area is in such a state then answer me this. Why wasn't English covered in blood? I just examined him, not even a spot. Whatever happened her either happened seconds before he arrived, or he witnessed it from a short distance away. Either way he didn't do it."

Bolton stepped passed Rutherford, who was still stood staring down at the body. "He must have seen them then?" he said to Bolton turning, "but what about the head?"

"You might want to get an officer on to the roof," Bolton answered holding the lamp up, illuminating the edge of the rooftop.

"Why?" asked Rutherford.

Bolton slowly passed the light from the roof to the top of the passage arch. Rutherford could clearly see lines of blood running down the brickwork. It had slowed as it descended and hadn't yet made it all the way to the arch.

"Whoever did this," said Bolton, "managed to get onto the roof, and fast. They must have paused just over the arch and then disappeared without anyone seeing them."

Both men stood silently looking up at the rooftops.

Chapter 22

Will stood in the small cell leaning against the door. He had shared the cell for the past six hours with three other men, one of whom was led asleep on a small wooden bench, he had been the only occupant when Will had arrived.

He had been led, as he was now, with his back to the door asleep on the only seat when Will was pushed in and he hadn't moved since. His huge frame impossibly balanced on the narrow wooden seat. Will's only reminder that the man was there and alive, was the intermittent sound and smell of wind escaping him.

The other two men had arrived shortly after. They had been dragged in fighting and once the door was closed and locked, had continued to do so. Will had tried to stay away from them but in the cramped cell he'd found it difficult. He himself had managed to connect with a few stray blows during their conflict and was sure that there would be some bruises on his ribs come the morning. They too, now sat sleeping, their backs against the wall facing each other. Both men had faces that were bruised and battered.

Will had not slept. At first, he was in shock. He struggled to process the events he had just witnessed. He had experienced something monstrous, something from a nightmare. If he had awoken in the night with his beloved Sarah beside him he would have shook the dream off and returned to sleep. Standing in a police station amongst those you would normally regard as criminals, it was harder to deny what had happened.

Then the two men had arrived, they're fighting had distracted him for a few hours. Once they had quietened, Will had begun to feel safer and his mind wondered back to the horrors he had witnessed, frightening thoughts entered his mind. He brought himself back to normality by concentrating on the two men and their argument. Throughout the whole battle they had not mentioned what one had done to the other. There had been lots of name calling, many threats made, but no actual intimation of the cause of it all. They had fought, sat, stared at each other and then finally slept.

Will's thoughts then passed to the man sleeping on the bench. He had not moved, nor shown any signs of waking from his sleep during any of the commotion. Will had reached the conclusion that he was either extremely drunk or that he may have been brought from an opium den, and was perhaps still heavily under its influence.

As the night passed his mind did eventually return to what he had witnessed and then more worryingly, at what was going to happen to him? He thought of Sarah, their unborn child. Her disappointment and horror at just what he had become involved in.

Will almost fell as the door opened behind him, lost in his thoughts he hadn't heard the guard's footsteps on the corridor, nor the sound of the key unlocking the door.

"English?" the guard shouted as Will steadied himself, his ears ringing with the sudden sound. He was pushed aside as the guard entered the cell, "Hey," he tapped the sleeping man to Will's left, "you're name English?"

"It's me," Will replied as the battered face of the man looked up in confusion at the guard.

Turning, the guard lifted his truncheon, "Right then, you follow me," he said, then pushed past Will, forcing him against the doorway. He held the door as Will left the cell, "Wait there!" he instructed, pointing to the floor with his truncheon. Will stood whilst the door was shut and locked, the guard peered through the observation hatch, then made his way along the corridor, "This way," Will followed.

He was led to a small locked room, similar to the one he had first been interviewed in, as he entered he was told to sit. The guard made it clear that Will should stay sitting until instructed otherwise. He then left the room, Will heard the key enter the keyhole and the deadlock slip into place.

A rush of emotions ran through his body. He placed his head in his hands and wept.

Will was in the same position thirty minutes later when the door opened and Rutherford entered. He was angry, deprived of sleep his tiredness had lowered his tolerance to the situation. He banged his fists on the table, "Right, I want to know just what is happening. I want to know how you knew where to be and I want to know now!" he shouted at the bewildered Will.

Will looked up at him, his eyes red and swollen from the tears, "I . . . I . . . I," he stuttered, "I don't know." Tears formed in his eyes, his bottom lip began to shake.

Rutherford's anger rose, he again banged his fists on the table, "I don't know!" he bellowed, "I don't know! Is that it? Is that your answer to all this?" he turned from Will and began to pace the room. "I'll tell you what I don't know should I?" he shouted from behind Will, "I don't know why I spent the night wandering the streets following you! I don't know why I have a headless corpse! I don't know why there is a trail of blood reaching to the roof!" As he spoke he moved around the table to face Will, he lent over, their faces only inches apart, "Here's the cracker," he spat at Will, "I don't know why I can't find the head!!"

"I . . . I . . . I . . ." the words stuck in Will's throat.

Ignoring him, Rutherford continued, "We looked all over the rooftops, all over. Police everywhere. We searched the whole area. Nothing."

There was a knock at the door.

Both men stared at each other, Will's tearful scared eyes looked up at Rutherford's burning gaze. "I know you know what happened. And you are going to tell me!"

The knocking sounded again, this time a little harder, "What is it?" Rutherford barked.

The door opened, and a young officer entered, "Sir, Detective Bolton wishes to see you in his office."

"I was with him five minutes ago; did he say why?" Rutherford turned to the officer.

"No Sir," he answered, "But the Commissioner has arrived Sir and he's in with Detective Bolton."

Rutherford looked down at Will sitting across from him and sighed, "Thank you, I'll be along presently," he said rubbing the stubble of his chin as the officer closed the door. "I haven't finished with you yet!" he said to Will as he turned to leave the room, once he did the door was locked.

As Will sat in the cold silence; his thoughts returned to Sarah. Tears fell from his swollen eyes.

Rutherford entered Bolton's office tapping on the door as he opened it, "Sir, you wish to see me?"

Bolton stood nervously behind his desk. He nodded to his right, "Yes Greg, Commissioner Collins has taken particular interest in this case, he . . . err . . . he has a request."

Rutherford looked over to the man on his left as he closed the door. Commissioner Collins stood at the window with his back to the room. As he turned to face Rutherford he spoke, "I want you to let William English go."

Surprised Rutherford answered, "What? But I've . . ."

Collins held up his hand stopping Rutherford mid-sentence, "No arguments. Just let him go."

"I can't do that Sir."

"What?" Collins' anger and impatience began to rise, nervously he rotated a gold ring he wore on his little finger. Both Rutherford and Bolton noticed him doing so. "Not only can you do it, you will do it!"

"But Sir,' pleaded Rutherford, "he's our only witness to . . ."

"Are you listening to me?" interrupted Collins, "he's an insignificant little man. We all know he didn't do it, we don't need him. Apologise to him and let him go. Do you understand?" Collins stared at Rutherford willing him to continue, "This conversation is over," he finally added.

Rutherford stood for a moment thinking, none of this made any sense to him. Looking across from Collins to Bolton, he felt that something had happened between the two men, a conversation had obviously taken place that he had not been privy to. Realising there was nothing he could say or do to alter the situation he turned, cursing to himself as he left the room.

Collins continued to rotate the gold ring stopping upon each rotation and rubbing a small black stone mounted on it. Turning back towards the window he basked as the rising sun warmed him. "Would you come her a moment please Bolton?"

Bolton crossed the room joining him at the window.

"You see that man?" Collins asked, pointing to a private carriage parked in the street outside the station, "do you recognise him?"

Bolton looked down at the street, next to the open carriage door stood a tall bald man, "No, I don't think so," he answered, "why?"

"That man," continued Collins, "Is Maximillian Barr."

"The millionaire?" interrupted Bolton.

"The very same. I was awoken quite early this morning by Maximillian Barr, with him was the Chief Justice. I was told about a suspect you had in custody. Mr. William English. I was asked, in no uncertain terms to facilitate his release. They waited whilst I dressed, then marched me through the streets down here to ensure this happened. All three of us walked ahead of that carriage. I felt like I was being paraded," he said, turning to Bolton, "what's going on?" he asked.

"I don't know Sir," answered Bolton, "the whole cities become a powder keg. The Ripper killings, the broken promises the government made to clear the slums around here. The continuing hatred towards the police," he said pausing, thinking, "if we don't solve these murders the whole place is going to explode."

"Is that him?" Collins watched as Will left the station, made his way down the steps and approached Barr waiting by his carriage.

"Yes, Sir it is," Bolton answered.

Will couldn't believe what had just happened. He had been playing the events over in his mind when the door opened and Rutherford re-entered the room. It was clear to Will that his mood had not improved, in fact the look on his face indicated that it had become decidedly darker. Will prepared himself for the worst. To his surprise Rutherford had apologised to him for his arrest and his uncomfortable night in the cell, before declaring that he was free to leave. Although Will was all too aware that it was said through gritted teeth, he didn't hesitate in accepting the apology and had left the building.

Emerging into the street he felt a sense of relief, a lifting from his shoulders of not only the night's events but the expectant feeling of doom that had entered his mind during the time spent in the cell. He briefly tried to imagine what it must feel like to be a man released from a lengthy unjustified incarceration. His train of thought was broken by the sight of Barr standing a short distance away.

Will's anger rose, "What the hell have you gotten me into?" he shouted quickening his pace, "you knew, you knew, didn't you?"

Hearing Will's voice Barr turned to face him. He was now only a few feet away, the anger showing on his face. "Not now William," said Barr, hoping to calm the situation, "this is neither the time nor the place."

As Will reached him, Barr placed his arm around his shoulder drawing him closer, "We need to stay calm," he whispered with determination, "there are too many eyes watching, too many ears listening." Barr scanned the area looking for any familiar faces. He had seen both the Commissioner and the Detective staring from the window, but they posed no real threat to him. "Did you see it?"

"Oh yes," Will answered, "I seen it alright."

Barr turned Will towards the carriage before he could say more, "Get in," the arm around Will's shoulders tensed and he felt himself forced onto the step. His mind swam as he entered the darkened interior and sat, this side of Barr frightened him.

Barr glanced back towards the station, the window where he had observed the two men watching from was now vacant.

He placed his foot on the carriage step, but as his weight transferred to it he was pushed out of the way by a small grey-haired woman who seemed to rise from the very pavement in front of him.

"Right you," she shouted into the carriage, "just what in God's name do you think you're playing at?"

Will knew it was his mother in law Annie's voice without looking at her. He had been on the receiving end of her tongue on many occasions.

"Get out here now!" she screamed at him.

Sarah stood at her shoulder crying, "William, oh William."

After being physically moved away Barr composed himself and addressed the woman, "Excuse me madam," he began.

"Don't you excuse me," replied Annie turning to face him, "this is nothing to do with you. The only people this concerns is my Sarah and her husband," she spat, the final word focused directly at Will, who was still sat bemused in the carriage. "What's all this about you getting arrested?"

"I haven't been arrested," he answered.

"Haven't been arrested? Well you tell me why, when Sarah arrived home this morning she was barred from entering her own home by the police? Who I might say, stated that you had been arrested!"

"Mother please," pleaded Sarah.

"Is that any way for a father to act?"

"Please, it's alright now. Will's safe," Sarah pushed passed her mother, and standing on the step took Will's hands in her own.

"Safe!" Annie exclaimed, "not if I've got anything to do with it. Did he sit up with you all night whilst you cried yourself to sleep? Did he have to walk all this way with you?" she turned to Barr finally acknowledging him, "do you know how far it is from Bethnal Green? Just look at her."

Barr did look at her, he noticed that she was pregnant, heavily pregnant, "Did you say Bethnal Green?" he asked.

"I did," replied Annie directing her anger back at Will. Sarah sat holding onto him, her head buried in his chest. "Do you think that all this walking is good for Sarah? For the child? I've had seven children you know, four survived. Brought them all up on my own. I never had occasion to set off walking all over London. My husband was never arrested," she turned to Barr and crossed herself, "God bless his soul."

Sarah lifted her head and turned to face her mother. Her eyes were red with tears, "Mother, I think we should leave."

Annie moved away from the doorway allowing Sarah to stand, "Leave? well your probably right," turning she gripped Barr's hand, "It's been nice talking to you," she said shaking it. Her grip was firm. "It'll be nice to get you back home," she looked passed Sarah to where Will still sat. "Hopefully to stay this time. Gallivanting all over London, at night . . . we all know what men want you know?"

"Mother! Will's not like that and you know it," Sarah defended.

Barr stepped forward and took Sarah's hand, holding it as she stepped down to the pavement, "Do you mind if I make a suggestion?" he asked, "I do know how far it is from Bethnal green and I personally believe it would be a better option to return there than to make your way back to your own home," he focused his attention at Sarah, "as you have already stated there is a police presence at your own home and it may be beneficial to you both if you avoid the area. Until at the very least the gossip has died down," Annie nodded in agreement as Barr spoke. "A lady in your condition would benefit from a little relaxation."

Both Annie and Sarah agreed with his suggestion, "Please allow me to offer you all a ride home."

"That's very kind of you," Annie agreed climbing into the carriage, "don't mind if you do."

Sarah smiled at her mother as she positioned herself across from Will. Barr once again held Sarah's hand as she returned to her seat, "I'll just speak to my man," he smiled.

"Tell him it's Church Row," Annie shouted as Barr moved forward to speak to Clay. "Behind the workhouse."

"I heard the address Sir," said Clay leaning down so that his voice couldn't be heard by anyone but Barr, "she's pregnant!"

"Yes, she is," replied Barr, "Very pregnant. Ensure they get home safely."

"Yes Sir, I will. Would you like me to return for you?"

"No," answered Barr looking back at the station, "I believe Collins will be waiting to speak to me. I suspect he will be wanting to leave our little group."

"Will you let him?"

Barr looked at his watch, noted the time then slipped it back into his pocket, "I'm not sure yet," he paused thinking, "When you've finished with these I want you to arrange a meeting for tonight. Only two members, not Mark. I'll have decided by then."

"I'll attend to it Sir," said Clay, lifting the reigns.

"Oh, and Clay."

"Sir?"

"Make sure you take them to their door," smiled Barr as he stepped away from the carriage.

Clay snapped the reigns and as the two horses moved forward he steered them into the road. "I will Sir," he called back.

Barr stood watching them leave. The street around him had become busy, he too began to feel a tension in the air. He was aware that the commissioner stood watching him from the station steps behind him.

"Commissioner Collins," he spoke, turning to face him, "the Chief Justice had to leave but I'm sure he would have liked to have thanked you personally for . . ."

Collins cut him off mid-sentence, he was angry, "Don't ever ask me to do anything like that again," he spat at Barr, "we agreed, in the business world we don't know each other. You've put me in an impossible position!"

"And I'm grateful," admitted Barr calmly. He was aware that the Commissioners anger could attracting unwanted attention.

"Well I'm not," said Collins as he slipped the black ring from his finger and placed it in Barr's hand, "I think this brings our friendship to an end, don't you?"

Barr glanced at the ring before placing it into his pocket, "If that's how you feel, then I will abide by your wishes," Collins turned to walk away, "I just hope that the rest of the group accept your abandonment as graciously as I," Barr added.

Collins turned, "Are you threatening me?" he snapped back.

"Certainly not Commissioner," Barr stared at him, eyes wide.

Collins' anger subsided, his mouth became dry. He could feel a churning in his stomach, the world around him lost clarity, quieted. Barr had power over him and both men knew it. He feared him.

Holding him in his gaze Barr watched a nervousness rise through the Commissioner's body. Collins began to blink faster, his eyes lost focus. Finally, Barr leaned slightly forward closing the gap between the two men, "Good day

Commissioner," he whispered. Then suddenly he turned, and without looking back walked away.

Collins let out the breath he hadn't realised he had been holding. He became aware of movement around him, people passing by him. Bolton watched the exchange from his office window.

'How long had he been there?' Collins thought, he began to feel vulnerable, exposed. The streets around him felt dangerous. He lifted his hand and called an approaching cab, "White's please, St. James Street."

Collins sat back as the Hansom pulled away. His heart pounded in his chest. Barr's threat was palpable, almost final.

The gentlemen's club he had been a member of since taking the position of Commissioner was the safest place he felt he could go. Barr had influence all over the city, every level of class could be called upon. Collins knew a few members of their group having met them by chance. Barr had made it clear to all of them that secrecy was paramount, identities must be guarded, even from other members. He couldn't be sure if any of the group were members of the club, but up to now he hadn't become aware of any that were.

Chapter 23

Barr knew as he walked away that Collins, if he felt threatened enough, would retreat to his club. He hadn't made up his mind just what to do with him but knowing where he would be would make that decision a little easier.

It had become common knowledge in certain circles that if you needed to speak to the Commissioner, you stood a fair chance of doing so if you passed by White's Gentlemen's Club. Barr's intuition had paid off.

Clay had arranged a meeting for that evening and Barr had finally come to a decision. The group met as they had done on previous evenings, at Barr's home. Dressed in the same robes, they recreated the ceremony that had culminated with Barr psyche coming face to face with that of the Beast.

He had realised that any attempt to take control of the Beast without further knowledge, would be futile. It was powerful, very powerful. Barr suspected that what he had seen was only a small example of what it was capable of.

However he could control Collins, he could use his psyche to influence the hopefully drunk Commissioner and steer him to where Barr needed him to be.

During his out of body experience Barr ad realised that as he closed in on the Beast it had somehow sensed his presence. It came to him, perhaps more out of curiosity than anything else, but Barr now hoped to exploit this curiosity. If he could use his psychic presence to attract the Beast, lure it to a position where he was also able to steer Collins, he could eliminate one problem whilst making observations on the other.

He had successfully slipped into a trance and his psyche was now hovering above the entrance to White's. He had tried to focus himself into the club, he had secretly been a member since arriving in England and knew the layout and each of the rooms, but for some reason unclear to him it wouldn't work.

It was difficult for Barr to remain in this position. The street was busy and well used, if he became distracted and focused on movement from either direction he would be rushed to that point. He could quite easily focus on the club again and he would just as easily be there, but the distractions were weakening him, each time he moved his mind slipped a little further back, nearer to his reality and the trance threatened to lift.

He was unsure how long he had left before the link would be broken completely and his psyche returned to his body, if that happened he knew there would not be another opportunity like this. He concentrated his focus.

Collins stumbled through the door as it was opened for him, the doorman gripped him firmly, stopping him from stumbling down the steps.

Barr watched, the slurred words passed between Collins and the doorman echoed around him, each word rising and falling in volume, pitch and tone. He could pick out a few, but most were lost in a cacophony that threatened to break his concentration. He focused on a point further down the street and willed Collins to follow.

He staggered past the doorman and had managed to get safely down the steps to the street. Collins now lent against the railings that ran along the front of the club. His mind spun, he hadn't meant to leave the club so late, but the company was good, the gin was free and he felt safe. The memory of the events of that morning had slowly slipped away in equal measure to the measure of gin he had consumed.

He decided to walk right, pushing himself up from his leaning position he staggered a few steps . . . stopped, almost leant back against the railings then staggered a few steps more.

Barr observed Collins' comedic drunken movement. Although he had chosen to walk in the right direction, Barr was conscious that at the rate he moved there wouldn't be enough time to complete the plan. He would have to find somewhere safe for Collins and hope to induce sleep upon him whilst Barr attempted to lure the Beast to him.

He knew the area, it was rich. Barr felt certain that if he could get him off the streets he would be able to abandon him without the fear of molestation. The lower classes stayed away from the areas frequented by the rich, they stood out, were open to questioning and arrest. It was much easier for them to stay comfortable, stay within the confines of their class, at least in the slums their business was their own and never questioned.

Collins had now reached the corner of St. James Street and Piccadilly, Barr urged him again this time to the left, if he could get him to Green Park there was a chance he could find a secluded place to leave him.

Barr focused on a point at the corner of Green Park and Piccadilly. Collins staggered after him. He had found a sort of drunken rhythm. Stagger . . . stop . . . stagger . . . rest . . . repeat.

Cabs passed him as he made his way along Piccadilly, Barr observed as one stopped close to Collins and offered their services. He willed the driver the move on.

The park lay below him dark and quiet. Lamps had been lit along its pathways but as far as Barr could see, it was empty. There was a chance that there were those in the park who also wanted to be lost in the shadows, lovers or thieves. However, leaving Collins was a risk he had to take. He knew that he needed to find a secluded area away from the web of paths in which Collins could be safely left.

As Collins stepped onto the path and into the darkness of the park, Barr left him and focused his mind around the area. He sped across the trees looking for a secluded spot. He was aware of people below him but felt no malice from them. Eventually he came across a small clearing surrounded by rhododendron bush. They had naturally created a circle of bushes, their thick twisted branches creating a barrier in the darkness that it was impossible to see through.

Barr focused his mind on Collins and was instantly above him. He willed him to leave the path, still drunk he staggered towards the bushes leaving large footprints in the wet grass.

Collins couldn't understand quite why he had left the path, nor why his journey home had involved him passing through the park. All he knew at this moment was that he was tired and he needed to sleep. Somehow, he had known about the clearing amongst the bushes and was struggling with the small twisted branches as he tried to find a way through them.

Barr urged him onward, he was aware of the people nearby and couldn't risk the noise of Collins crashing through the undergrowth bringing them to him. Once he had reached the small grassy area he could induce sleep, would be confident that even if he didn't return, Collins wouldn't awaken 'til morning.

Finally, Collins emerged from the bushes, slipped and crumpled to the ground. The grass was wet and cool. He placed his head on his arm and closed his eyes. Barr watched from above, he could feel Collins slowly slipping into sleep, his mind becoming calm and dark. It was time to leave, time to find the Beast.

Chapter 24

It crouched at the edge of the dome looking down at the curve as it fell away from it. Letting go of the stone-work it slipped down to the bottom. Ahead were two towers, it leapt to the left one gripping the small ornate carving at its peak. Leaning out from its vantage point it watched for signs of life below.

The streets were quiet, a fog had rolled up the Thames and was now beginning to work its way into the streets.

The Beast screamed into the darkness above.

There was something in the air that disturbed it, something faint, distant. It leapt from St. Paul's to the rooftops opposite scanning the skyline as it did. It had felt the presence before, had known that other eyes were upon it, eventually it had confronted them.

Although it couldn't kill it, the Beast was confused and angered by whatever it was and that anger was rising. It knew those eyes were back.

It felt drawn along the river, leaping from rooftop to rooftop. It sensed it was nearing the disturbance. Leaping across the river it rested on a roof that curved away towards a bridge. It stared across at the darkened outline of Westminster. It was there.

The Beast leapt to the Tower of Westminster. There below it was the disturbance, the air around it flickered with light. It moved away quickly towards the Abbey. The Beast followed.

Each time the Beast closed in on it the flickering light disappeared, before reappearing a little further away. It screamed with uncontrollable rage. It leapt towards it faster and faster, using buildings, trees, anything it could to close the gap between them, it had to destroy it.

Finally, the Beast sensed it had stopped. It had leapt to a large tree and now looked down at the thing, its flickering light dimmed before collapsing in on itself. The Beast dropped from the treetop to the grass below. It crouched enclosed by a ring of bushes, across from it on the grass, vulnerable, lay a man.

It crawled spiderlike across the space between them, turning its body as it reached him. The man stank, his flesh oozed with an odour that was fowl to the Beast. It ran its long fingers across his face and the man murmured. In an instant it had gripped his throat and stood holding the man up. It waved him back and forth, wanting the flickering light to emerge, the man's limp body shook easily.

The Beast couldn't understand why the man had not awoken. It shook him again screaming at his face.

Angered, it slammed his body to the floor breaking his spine. It knelt next to him, holding his head once again firm in its grip. It massaged his hairline before slipping its talons through his skin and under his hair, in one swift motion it ripped the flesh from his face and dug its needle like fingers deep into his chest.

Releasing his head, it violently stabbed at his chest, each time ripping flesh from him. It raged, the flickering light that disturbed it had disappeared into this man, instinctively it thought it was killing it, ripping it apart and tearing it from existence. The Beast stood panting, its chest heaving as it breathed in the scent of the dead man.

Collins lay below it, the carnage laid upon him horrific, his whole body had been ripped apart, his flesh torn away leaving his organs steaming on the grass. His being now covered the whole area. The Beast let out a piercing cry and leapt into the darkness.

Slowly the flickering light once again appeared above the now unrecognisable body of the Collins. It paused for a moment before disappearing.

Chapter 25

Pip had spent the last two days searching for Will. Rumours of his arrest had reached the paper and under instruction from Kingsley to, *'Find Will,'* he had set off to locate his friend.

The murder of yet another prostitute was on the lips of the people he passed that first morning as he made his way to his home. Pip knew that Will had been found at the location of the killing, after his visit with Barr he had mentioned the location he was asked to observe to Pip and if the rumours were to be believed, he had been arrested for the murder. Knowing that Will's home was between the office and the police station where he had heard the suspect had been taken too, he decided to try there first.

It wasn't inconceivable that the rumour was false and that although Will was at the scene, he had not been arrested and was in fact asleep at home after a long and traumatic night.

Turning the corner into Jubilee Street Pip quickly realised that that would not be the case. Police outnumbered those residents who had left their homes and now stood watching in the street by three to one. They spoke to them as they gathered outside Will's home, some stood in the doorways gossiping. More alarmingly to Pip, they had cordoned off the front of one of the houses. *Will's house!* He slowly walked down the middle of the road, wanting to give the police as wide a berth as possible. Passing the line of bodies annexing Will's home he casually looked passed them and in through the open doorway. Police filled the corridor between the door and the stairs, shouts passed between those downstairs and unseen police officers upstairs. Something was handed down from one officer to another. Pip couldn't see what it was, only that it was small enough to be passed between them easily. By the time whatever it was had emerged into the street Pip had passed and was now making his way to the opposite corner, the house and the police behind him. Realising that Will's predicament was more serious than first anticipated, he decided to continue to the station Kingsley had told him the suspect had been taken too.

As he walked he realised just how busy the streets had become, unusually busy for this time of day. Crowds gathered on corners near the paperboys, who in turn had to move further into the street just to be seen and heard. Their cries filled the air, every corner seemed to herald the morning's news.

"Another Murder. Police question suspect."

"Murder. Murder. Police hold killer."

"Killing on London streets continue," they shouted.

Pip passed the groups, passed people running towards them and was in turn passed by those running away to tell others, their copy of the newspaper held aloft as they did.

As he came closer to the station the atmosphere amongst those gathered around him became more hostile. People shouted waiving the morning paper at the crowds, questioning the actions and incompetency of the police. Those nearest turned and shouted the same to anyone who was listening behind them. The crowds bulged and began to connect, whole streets became one, no order, no leader, just anger.

Pip kept ahead of them, he knew that soon a suggestion would be made to march on the police station where the suspect was being held. He needed to get there first, he had to find Will and try to get him out.

His pace quickened as entered Leman Street and the station came into view. He could now hear angry shouts coming from a few streets away and realised that his fear had become a reality. The crowd had turned into a mob and was now making its way to the same location.

Pip ran the last few hundred yards to the steps of the station. Two officers stood at the door watching the street, they too had become aware of the shouting and having realised it was becoming louder, they stood wondering from which direction the crowd would come. Pip stepped between them and seeing the desk sergeant through the open door, stepped inside. He was told that he had arrived less than thirty minutes after Will had been released and had left in Barr's carriage.

Pip left the building unsure as to what would be his next move, '*Should I continue to Barr's home address or make my way back to Kingsley letting him know that Will had at least been released,*' he thought

The whole street now filled with people, most were marching towards the station, some, who were not party to the anger and hatred emanating from the mob, but who had the misfortune to be walking along the street as the first of the protestors turned the corner, now passed the station at speed in the opposite direction. Pip followed them.

He knew that there was a story here and that Kingsley ould love to be the first newspaper in London to run it, but he himself had no intention of being caught in what he believed would soon become a full-blown riot.

He looked back once before turning the corner, watching as more police officers left the front of the station and with truncheons raised, they waited for the first acts of aggression.

Pip decided not to go back to the office of the 'Star', '*Kingsley could wait,*' he thought. He had been instructed to find Will and that was what he was going to do. He had no money for a Hansom, so he would have to walk and it was quite a way to the home of Maximillian Barr, but now he knew that Will was neither at his home nor the police station it was the only lead he had. He hoped his friend was there.

Pip had been sat across from Barr's home since he had arrived mid-afternoon. He had knocked furiously on the door when no one had answered his first two attempts, but still no one answered, he peered through the windows and listened at the door, all was silent inside. He concluded that if Barr was home then his butler definitely wasn't.

If he had even a small percentage of the wealth that Barr was rumoured to possess Pip would not lower himself to answering the door no matter who it was or how loudly they knocked. He imagined Barr sitting in his lounge, shouting for the door to be answered.

Clay arrived within an hour of Pip and even though he now knew for definite that at least one servant was home, Pip didn't return to the door. He was sure that Will was inside and given that they had no reason to hold him against his will, would at some point emerge. Pip just had to wait.

As the light began to fade a carriage arrived, Pip moved to get a better view of just who had arrived, but by the time he was in a position where he could see both the pavement and the front door, the occupants had entered and the door had been closed. He was certain that at least two men had stepped down from the carriage and entered the house, maybe three. If one of them had been a woman, then he felt sure he would have seen her, given the time it would take for her to collect her dress up and with help step down to the pavement.

Once the carriage had left Pip settled down once again and resumed his watch. A lamp lighter appeared and began to light the gas lamps along the street. Pip watched as he flicked open the small glass panels and lit the gas. The street slowly illuminated. Pip watched as he passed from one side to the other lighting each lamp in turn. By the time he had reached the far end of the street some of the houses he had passed had illuminated their own lamps inside.

The front of Barr's house remained dark, its windows black, the glass seemed to repel the dim light emitted from the streetlamps.

Pip began to feel uncomfortable, he had observed the house for hours. People had entered, no one had left. If Will was inside he was staying for the night.

Convincing himself that Barr must have offered Will a safe place to stay, he decided to leave.

'Will's home had been overrun with Police, so wouldn't that be the christen thing to do? After all, wasn't it Barr that had approached Will and included him in his plans?' Pip concluded and began to feel better about his decision to leave. His conscience

was clear. He would present himself at the office in the morning, fill Kingsley in on what he had found out, then await Will's arrival. He was convinced Will would show up in the morning, a good rest, the events forgotten, he could then resume his work with new vigour.

Happy with his thoughts Pip left the shadows outside Barr's dark house and made his way home.

Arriving at work the next morning Pip had no way of knowing just how bad things had become overnight.

His friend Will hadn't showed up, Kingsley was worried. Riots had broken out all over London. The East End had seen the worst. Fires now burned out of control on the streets. The police struggled to keep order. The docks had to be closed and the dock owners had employed gangs to protect their warehouses from looting.

As dawn broke and the smoke from the East End covered the city, the mutilated body of the Police Commissioner had been found in Green Park.

A nanny with her two charges had been taking an early morning walk through the park before breakfast. The children had heard a commotion in the bushes and realising it was the sound of several large birds calling and cawing they crept through to see what had attracted them. They emerged from the tangle of branches laughing, frightening the closest birds which took flight. They in turn startled the rest of the flock and soon the air around the children was thick with birds flapping furiously in their attempt to gain height. The children laughed as they covered their faces with their arms, feeling the light touch of the feathers as the birds passed them. Soon the birds had settled on the branches above, some still cawed at the children below.

Dropping their arms, the children first looked up at the birds amazed at their number, then they looked down at the mass of flesh that had attracted them. One large crow still sat with its head lodged firmly under the ribcage. It had a large piece of meat in its beak that it was trying to pull loose.

Both children screamed. Above, the birds once again took flight, some settling on higher branches some flying off deeper into the park. The large crow finally pulled the flesh free and flew to a nearby branch to eat. It held the flesh in its talons and ripped at it, tearing off small strips it flicked its head back and swallowed each one.

Upon hearing their screams, the nanny ran head first into the bushes and as she crashed through almost fell upon the body. She collected both screaming children in her arms and turned her back on the horrific sight. She left the scene trying desperately to hold her own composure, hoping to calm the children. Her stomach balked and she knew she was going to vomit, she swallowed hard trying hold it down. Both children were now crying uncontrollably, the nanny relieved that they had at least stopped screaming.

Spying a gentleman walking towards her on the path she approached him as calmly as she could and asked him if he would fetch the police. She began to explain what she had seen but the gentleman stopped her and marched off through the gap she had made in the bushes. She heard a muffled cry then the man emerged running towards the entrance, his composure had left him.

The police arrived shortly after and within an hour all the newspapers in London were competing to be the first to get the story to the streets.

Pip's plan, if Will hadn't showed up for work, was forgotten. London was burning, its people rioting, its leaders frightened.

Chapter 26

Maximillian Barr laughed as he read the headline of the special midday edition.

He had risen late, exhausted by the events of the previous night. Taken a late breakfast and pushing the remnants of it aside, had picked up the paper left folded next to him by Clay. The whole of the front page had been given to the murder and discovery of Collins' body.

Barr read with glee the accounts of the numerous passers-by that had been witnesses to its discovery. Their gory descriptions printed in bold letters that sensationalised each word. Barr suspected that some, not all, had been flights of fancy by the writers themselves. He himself had witnessed the carnage brought upon the body of Collins as he lay in the small clearing. Not all of what he read was close to what he had seen.

Clay entered the room, placed a silver tray on the cupboard and began to clear the table, still reading Barr turned to his right, giving him easy access to the plates he had left. Silently Clay collected them together and placed them on the tray he had left next to the door. Once the table was clear Barr laid the newspaper down flattening it as he did.

"Will that be all Sir?" asked Clay.

Barr turned the first page following the story with his finger as he did. He spoke without looking up, "Is English still in Bethnal Green?"

"He is Sir," replied Clay.

"Is his wife still with him?" Barr asked looking up, more interested in his reply.

"Yes, Sir she is and I firmly believe Mr English will insist she stays with her mother, at least for the next few nights."

Barr smiled returning to his newspaper, "That my friend, is excellent news."

Clay picked up the tray and exited the room. Barr turned shouting after him, "Clay?" he said as he rose and opened the door. Clay stood in the hall looking back, "Have you finished with the ring?"

Shifting the tray, he balanced it with one hand, "Yes Sir," he said, reaching into his pocket, he dropped a small black stone into Barr's open hand, "the gold had been reclaimed Sir, the stone has been heated and has now fractured."

Barr looked at the black stone that had once shone in the ring owned by Collins. The fracture ran the length of its oval, its sheen was gone, the stone was dull, and dead! "Good," replied Barr, "that will be all."

Barr stepped into his library. He walked holding the stone in his outstretched hand, the newspaper and its story forgotten. Reaching his desk, he opened the left-hand drawer and lifted out a small black lacquered box. Placing it on the desk he sat looking at it.

The box looked solid, the lacquer floorless. Barr picked it up and turned it over in his hands. The box rattled as if filled with beads. His fingers left greasy prints on the lacquer as he felt for the key piece.

The box had been a gift from an acquaintance he had helped whilst travelling through the orient. A box in which to hide things and a puzzle to solve. He was so impressed with the ingenious object that he commissioned a carpenter to use its design in the secret bookcase he wanted.

Barr found the key and pressed, a small piece of the lacquer lifted free allowing his fingers to slide a second piece forward, this in turn opened the lid of a small compartment. He shook the box, the rattle sounded louder. Happy, he tipped its contents onto the desk. Out fell several small black beads almost identical to the one he held. Each dull, each fractured, each dead!

Barr moved them around with his finger, not really counting them, he knew exactly how many there were. Twenty-Three. He sat back looking at them, subconsciously fingering the one given to him by Clay. Twenty-Three lives lay in front of him, twenty-three of his followers gone. Twenty-Three people he had trusted had betrayed him. His thoughts drifted back through time, remembering his first two. His mother and his father.

They had been the easiest for him to kill, as they had been the hardest for him to believe they had betrayed him. After that he had lost all signs of compassion, he had forgiven no one, if his parents could betray him then the whole world could. The world now meant nothing to him.

Over the intervening years he had concluded that those who would more than likely betray him were those with money and power, they all eventually came to the foolish conclusion that they no longer needed Barr, that they themselves had accomplished their wealth and power unaided, and with old age came a feeling that maybe it was time to redeem themselves, before it was too late. Barr resented them for their weakness and narrow mindedness. Their deaths were all they deserved.

He dropped the black stone into the box, collected the others and closed the lid. *"Twenty-four now,"* he thought. Once he had reversed the opening sequence the box again looked solid, a beautifully lacquered piece of wood.

As Clay left Barr, he noticed the door to the cellar open slightly. Waiting until his master had entered his library he quickly disposed of the tray and descended the stairs hoping to find whoever it was that had left the door open.

Knowing that the door to his left, the one that led to the ceremonial chambers was always locked Clay tried the door to his right. Not only was it unlocked, but as it opened on Barr's private study it was obvious that someone was inside.

Clay had a feeling he knew exactly who he would find secreted within the room. Mark had become more than interested in the knowledge the dark arts had bestowed upon both Barr and Clay and had on many occasions expressed an interest in becoming Clay's apprentice. Clay eventually agreed and his training had begun.

Over the intervening years it became obvious to Clay that Mark had a great talent and as his knowledge grew, he suspected that he hid the true extent of his power from him. Barr had become cautious of him after Clay had inadvertently exposed Mark's inclusion at the ceremony where Barr had collapsed.

Mark stood silently reading as Clay entered the room. "You know you shouldn't be here Mark?" he said.

Dropping the book Mark turned, "I'm sorry sir," he answered. "I didn't think you'd notice my absence."

"I didn't," answered Clay. "You left the door to the stairs ajar."

Mark smiled lowering his eyes, Clay turned and closed the study door. "You'll be the death of me," he said returning the smile.

Chapter 27

Will had spent the last two days sitting quietly in the home of his mother in law trying desperately to avoid any form of contact with her. Since his arrest and subsequent release, he had heard no end of the opinion of Annie Cooper, *'How he should behave, what he should now do and what he should have done.'* Every sentence directed at him ended with her explaining again how her husband behaved and how he had never treated her with anything but the utmost respect.

He had, overnight, realised that he now hated his mother in law. Even his beautiful Sarah seemed oblivious to the constant jibes and snide comments Annie made towards him.

He sat in a chair with his back to the window, next to him on the table was a cold plate of cabbage and potatoes. It had been placed there by Sarah some time ago, but Will couldn't quite remember when.

He had been trying to place the events of the last forty-eight hours into some sort of cohesive order. He had been able to build a skeletal time frame of what had happened to him but as of, yet, he could not place any of the specifics onto it. The lane, the yard, the dead woman. He could see them all. His arrest and subsequent release, he could also place.

However a darkness had clouded his mind. He had known fear, of that he was certain. His heart raced as he remembered stepping from the darkness of the alley into the yard, something was there, something his mind was now blocking out.

Annie stood over him as she picked up the plate, Will looked up but stared through her. Her mouth opened and closed but he heard no sound. He stared at the dark of her throat, the brown stained teeth, her yellowed tongue. He felt it reach out enveloping him, drawing him closer to her gaping maw. The teeth blackened and became elongated, her lips stretched thin over the massive sharp canines, her tongue now long and slick slavered over them leaving a sick wetness that dripped from their points. Will's mind snapped, his arm rose to his face protecting him from the vision, as it did he knocked the plate from her hand, the cold vegetables spilling to the floor as it dropped. Sarah turned as the plate hit the floor and smashed, "I'll get it mother," she said as she stood.

"I give up," cried Annie and with a piercing look turned her back on Will. "He's done nothing but sit in that chair since he got home," she said directing her anger at Sarah as she bent to clear the mess, "I've cooked for him, I've sat with him and I'm trying to understand what's going on.

I'm telling you now Sarah that if things don't change, if he doesn't pull himself together soon I'm done with him."

Sarah placed the broken pieces of the plate onto the table, "Please mother," she said looking up at her, her eyes filled with tears, "Please, somethings happened, I don't know what myself, but Will seems to be mixed up in it."

Will sat on the chair oblivious to the conversation. He was aware of the two of them around him, he was even aware of the tension between them. Although his subconscious mind had concluded that it didn't concern him. He was trying to peer into the darkness, he needed to see the shape that lay there. A shape that remained hidden.

A boy's voice from outside drifted into his mind. It called of a victim, another victim. The voice passed below their window and faded to silence as the boy turned the corner. A puzzled look came over Will's face.

'*Wasn't that yesterday?*' he thought, '*It should be yesterday.*'

He became more confused. The closeness of both his wife and his mother in law was beginning to agitate him.

'*Am I mad?*' the statement popped to the front of his mind.

'*Is this what madness feels like?*' his mind brought forth images of St. Thomas's and of the silent screams of Lucy Strong.

Sarah and her mother had cleared the mess and were both now stood at the opposite end of the room, Annie held Sarah as she cried. Neither of them had any idea of how they could help Will. Sarah cried for her husband back, cried for the life they had enjoyed only a few days before.

Will thought of Barr. He played the conversations he had had with him over in his mind. Barr had known what was happening. He had instructed Will as to where he should be if he wanted to solve the murders. He knew of the killer, he knew what it was!

Will had decided, he had to see Barr, the next location was known to him. He had already mentioned it to Will, *'Hadn't he?'* he thought, he was sure he had.

The image of the black gaping maw came to him again, its teeth inches from his face.

'Madness?' Will shook himself free from the thought. Sarah was still holding onto her mother. He looked at the door to his right. It led to the landing, to the stairs, then to the front door and out into the street. He needed to confront Barr, he was desperate for answers.

Silently he stood and crossed the room, opening the door he slipped through and closed it shut behind him. Once down the stairs he left the house and stepped out onto the street.

Will became nervous, something was wrong. He walked around the corner, unknowingly following in the footsteps of the newsboy. He could smell smoke, feel a tension around him, the city was ready to explode, the tension was palpable and Will sensed its heaviness, the air pregnant with it.

Chapter 28

James Wilson and John Castor stood across from the home of Will and Sarah as instructed. They had been there for five hours and both were very cold. Jack clasped both hands together and blew a warm breath into them, "It's bloody freezing!" he remarked.

"Yeah," replied John, "Cold enough for the bloody Thames to freeze," he added stamping his feet, trying to ease the numbness that had settled on them.

"Do you think so?" James blew through his hands again.

"Within the week, don't you?" John was now rubbing his arms with his hands, "froze over the other year, I walked across it with the missus."

"Trying to find a weak spot eh?" laughed James nudging his colleague.

Both police officers laughed, it made them feel slightly warmer. "I can't see him coming back tonight, not after what's happened."

John turned his face from the cold wind that had picked up, "You're probably right, but some people are just stupid."

Dropping his hands from his mouth James spoke as he stared across to the house opposite, "And I think he's one of the more stupid ones."

"What makes you say that James?"

Jamespointed across the street to Will who was stood unlocking his door, "Because he's there. Look!"

John turned just in time to see Will disappear into the house, "Good, I'm sick of standing in the cold, let's wait a few minutes, see if he comes back out."

Will had made his way across town and knocking on Barr's door insisted that he be allowed to see him. Reluctantly Clay had let him in.

Barr had been in a good mood after reading the newspaper and had been expecting Will to call at some point. In fact, he had been disappointed that he hadn't called the previous day, although given the events that had followed, Barr thought it fortuitous that he didn't.

Will had seen the Beast, had stood directly in its gaze. Barr was anxious to know what affect that had had on him. It became clear quite quickly that he had been deeply affected by it. He was confused, had lapses in memory. Was frightened and angry.

Barr felt that Will was now a living embodiment of the city of London. He too, like the city, had become unpredictable, dangerous, a powder keg.

Barr sat and listened to what Will had to say, he had struggled to follow his disjointed ramblings, but finally Will had told him what he wanted to hear. Barr had then revealed to him the suspected location of the last victim. Will had left elated, happy that he could now end the nightmare that had woven a web around him. Barr smiled as he watched him leave.

Will had wandered the streets formulating his plan. He now knew where to go. He would make his way home, there were a few things he would need, and it would waste a little time before making his way to where he needed to be.

He had entered the house oblivious to the two police officers who stood shivering across the street. He knew exactly what he wanted and where they were.

Opening the door to the room he shared with Sarah he was surprised by the cold. He remembered the warmth he felt whenever he returned home, his wife kissing him as he entered the room. Shrugging off the memory he picked up his only other coat, having left his other one hanging on the back of the door at his mother in laws, and closed the door behind him.

Although the room was dark he didn't bother with the gas lamp, Will crossed the room and picked up the carving knife Sarah always left next to the sink, he held it up turning it slightly in his hand, the blade shone dimly.

Slipping it into his coat pocket he found his lamp and left the room. Once downstairs he paused before leaving the building to put on his coat. He could feel the knife in his pocket, its long blade next to his leg.

Leaving the house, he glanced left along the road, a few people moved in the distance. Will dismissed them and walked off in the opposite direction.

James and John watched him from across the road, Will paid them no heed. They watched as he left the road turning right, "Come on," said James "let's go."

The night was cold, the sky clear, a frost began to form on the ground. Will was aware of a red glow that tinted the horizon, it started in the east spreading down towards the south, he suspected the fire had now crossed the river. He could smell the burning buildings and although the moon shone above him he knew that smoke laid heavy elsewhere over the city, choking the life from it.

As he walked he dug his hands deeper into his pockets hoping to keep them warm. His right hand pressed against the cold steel of the knife.

His mind flittered between the plans he had made and his conversation with Barr, but also, another thought he couldn't quite grasp hold of. He knew it was important, he knew it had something to do with what he had witnessed after he had entered the scene of the murder.

'Look up!' The thought had popped to the front of Will's mind. He tried to clear his head of all other thoughts,

wanting only to concentrate on the moments after he had disturbed the killer. Its face was still lost to him. He sensed its tallness.

'Is that why I was looking up?' he thought.

Will continued into the night, the streets around him were quiet. People were scared. Most of them hid, but there were those that had deliberately sought out the frenzy let loose around them. They too had felt a tension. Each murder had fed that tension, helped it increase in mass until eventually as it snapped the first riots had begun. The fires started soon after, they had been deliberate, calculated. The city had burned, first in the areas that had been most densely populated. The sheer number of people flooding the streets fuelled the riots and held the police back. The madness of the Beast became infectious.

Reaching the river Will turned right along its banks, following it to the heart of the city. To the left he could see the fires and the huge plumes of willowing smoke, glowing red reflecting the flames below. The firelight flickered on the Thames, Will could pick out boats moored alongside the docks and they too burned as their crews tried desperately to slip their moorings, hoping to get into the centre of the river and away from the burning buildings.

'Look up!' The words popped into his head again. Will did look up, he could see nothing but the outline of the rooftops above.

The streets that ran along the river had become busier. People displaced by the fires were making their way into the city. Their faces blank, eyes dead, their hope lost. Each carried the few possessions they had managed to save, before fear finally drove them from their homes. Will imagined that those that remained were now looting freely, the flames following them from building to building, house to house, home to home.

He passed among the dazed people still looking up. He knew it meant something, it was important. Suddenly he was stopped in his tracks, he had seen a face peering down at him from the edge of the roof. It had only been a brief view, whoever it was had looked over and almost immediately their face had disappeared back, like lightning a thought had passed through Will's mind. *The rooftops,'* the thought said, *'the rooftops.'* He remembered now that the killer had somehow gotten up onto the roof. He tried to remember if he had managed to follow him, had he himself given chase? Will stood, his face pointing towards the sky, forcing his mind to remember.

He now knew that the killer had made their escape over the roofs. Will realised that that was where he needed to be, the killer was using the roofs. The police had no chance of ever catching the killer because they were on the ground. He remembered that he himself had read that after the murder in the Limehouse Basin the witnesses had all reported the killer being seen on the warehouse roof. It was beginning to make sense to him.

Will ran along the streets heading to the location Barr had told him, he knew once there he had to get up high, he had to find some way onto the rooftops. The train of thought led him to the conclusion that he hadn't taken chase, he hadn't made his way to the roof above the backyard. He had watched the killer fade into the darkness moments before the police had arrived. Will hadn't had the time to decide what to do. This time it was going to be different, this time he would be waiting.

Both John Castor and James Williams struggled to keep up with Will. They had at one point lost him, surprised by the number of people leaving the East End, they had allowed the crowd to distract them.

Luckily, they had come across him as he stood looking up at the rooftops, but then he had run. Both James and John were heavy middle-aged men, Will's slim youth outpaced them easily. They had been fortunate that, as he turned corners left and right one of them had at least managed to get a view of him before he did.

Will now stood looking up at the single-story roof. It belonged to a small factory that ran the whole length of the street. The wall that Will faced was unbroken, he slowly walked the length of it hoping to discover some way of getting onto the roof. He was unaware of the two police officers as they turned the corner, they both skidded to a halt.

Stepping back against the wall they hoped that the shadows hid them, they were out of breath and their chests heaved as they tried to get as much air into them as they could. Both James and John hoped that the chase had ended.

"What's he doing?" asked James breathing between each word.

John leant against the wall slightly bent, "I don't know, I just hope he's found whatever it is he's looking for," he said, coughed up phlegm and spat it out.

James turned startled by the sudden noise, "Shhh!"

"I can't help it," replied John, "I'm bushed. Bloody chest is killing me."

They watched as Will stepped into the street, still looking up at the roof, he slowly walked to the end of the street and followed the wall around the corner.

"Come on," James said pulling John's arm, reluctantly he followed him along the length of the wall. As they turned the corner both were shocked to see that Will was nowhere to be seen.

"Bollocks," said James thrusting his fist against the wall, "where's he gone now?"

John stepped out into the street so he had a better view of the factory wall. It was very similar to the one they had just walked along. Brick built, no windows or doors. John assumed that the entrance would be around the next corner.

He made his way along to the centre of the street, his eyes following the lines of brickwork. Ahead of him he was aware of a dark shadow that ran from the pavement to the roof.

As the distance between him and the shadow closed he realised that it was a small alleyway, upon reaching it he could just about make out a doorway at the end of the narrow passage.

James paused at his side, both men peered down the alley into the darkness, "Do you think he's gone down there?"

They stood silent listening for any sound that would reveal Will's whereabouts. The alley, although narrow had crates stacked up against the left wall, "He could be behind those," John said pointing towards them. Stepping into the alley as silently as he could, he made his way to the crates and peered around them. Will wasn't there. He walked back to where James was, both men stepped out into the street and surveyed the area.

The street was empty and dark. The wind picked up blowing colder. Once again, they knew that they had lost him.

Will had been in the alley, fortunately for him he had climbed the crates and managed to scramble onto the roof moments before the two officers appeared at its entrance. He stood and walked towards the South side. To his right he could see the unfinished outline of Tower Bridge, he marvelled as he always did, at its design. To his left he could now see the flames from the docks, burning warehouses lit up the sky, flames licked at the walls above broken windows. The buildings on both sides of the Thames burned, South side the fire had spread almost to the new bridge.

He walked the factory perimeter, peering both between the lines of pitched northlight windows that crossed the roof, then down into the street below. Both were devoid of life. Barr had told him to be here, had even mentioned the factory by name.

But where is the killer?' he thought.

Will sat on the top of the wall dangling his feet over the edge. He took the knife from his pocket and placed it next to him on the wall, patiently he waited.

Two men arguing quietly between themselves passed beneath him. They paused near the factory entrance then crossed to the opposite pavement and walked off. Will was unaware that they were police officers or that they had been following him from the moment he had left his home.

He sat quietly thinking. He knew that the attacks had all taken place in isolated areas, but this place seemed too isolated. It felt wrong, but, he concluded, Barr had been right about the last place. Will had been there as witness to that.

'That's what got you into all this trouble,' he thought.

The cold was beginning to reach his bones, he decided to make one last circuit of the roof and if he didn't spy anyone or anything, then he would head home. Back to Sarah and her mother. A chill crept into him, he had hardly thought of Sarah since walking silently out on her earlier that day. He worried what state of mind she would be in, what thoughts would have been racing through Will's mind, if Sarah had left him? He paced around the roof peering down to the street, as he suspected he had seen no one.

Climbing off the roof Will reproached himself for being such a fool. Sarah meant more to him than the world. He questioned why he had risked that.

'Madness,' he thought

'What have I been thinking? Why was I treating her this way?' Dropping to the alley Will realised that he had left the knife. He paused wondering if he should climb back up to retrieve it.

'Sarah is more important!' he thought.

Will stepped into the street as tears began to well in his eyes, "Sarah!" he cried to the darkness.

Chapter 29

Will had set off running but at some point, his running had at first slowed to a jog and then eventually a fast walk. He now walked slowly. The people he passed were just dark figures who appeared briefly before fading into the night. The way he had treated Sarah over the past few days now weighed heavily on his mind.

'Why should she forgive him?' he questioned.

He had done nothing to deserve it.

Slowly, as he neared Bethnal Green and the home of his mother in law, he became aware of whistles. The people around him were no longer walking towards him, they were running passed him, all now travelling in the same direction he was. More whistles filled the air, one large man bumped into him as he passed at a slow run.

'No apology, no manners,' thought Will as he watched him waddle off along the street.

People were now coming from side streets and they all seemed to be following each other, following the sounds of the whistles. Will's heart began to pound, thoughts of Sarah raced through his mind.

Turning into Church St. he was jostled by the number of people passing him. The whistles were louder now, *'Police whistles,'* thought Will.

Becoming aware of a large crowd, he pushed himself into it, people filed into the street, some spoke of 'Springheel Jack'. The name passed from person to person like a virus.

Will swam into the mass becoming fearfully aware that he knew exactly where the crowd would end and the line of police would begin. A scream began to build in his throat. Will emerged at the front of the crowd, police arms held him. A scream filled his lungs. Ahead of him the police had created a human barrier across the front of a house, the house of his mother in law, the house where his beloved Sarah was! Will let go the scream, "Sarahhhhh!"

A police officer with his back to him, reacted upon hearing the piercing cry and ducked in fear. Will had inadvertently screamed directly into his ear. The officer let go of his colleague's arm and seizing his chance Will slipped through the police line and ran to the door.

"Ere, you can't go in there!" a voice shouted after him, but as it did the crowd surged forward. The officer fumbled for his colleague's arm in a desperate attempt to link up. Will slipped inside the house as the crowd pushed the police up against the door behind him.

Inside, the hall and stairway were not as he had left them. Two police officers now stood in the hallway, one at each of the downstairs doors. Notebook in hand they were deep in conversation with the occupants of the lower rooms, neither noticed Will. He leapt up the stairs taking them two at a time, his footsteps booming on the bare wood, "Sarah," he cried, "Sarah. Sarah." Turning back on himself at the top he ran down the short corridor and towards their door, it was slightly ajar. Reaching out with his hand he pushed it open as Rutherford, from inside, pulled the door wide.

He was exiting the room with three officers as Will was trying to enter. The two men clashed. Will's momentum forced Rutherford back into the room and both men stumbled to the floor.

Bolton, who had been knelt, stood up to avoid the falling bodies. Will was now scrambling over Rutherford trying desperately to stand.

"Oh, my lord," cried Bolton, "get him the hell out of here!"

Rutherford tried to grip Will's leg as he stood but failed. The two officers' downstairs had, upon hearing the commotion, ceased their interviews and were now running up the stairs. The three offices that had been leaving with Rutherford managed to get a grip of Will and held him as he struggled to get further into the room. Rutherford dragged himself clear of Will's kicking feet and managed to stand.

With one officer now holding each of his arms and the other with his arms on his chest Will fought desperately to free himself, the four of them had become wedged in the doorway. Will's screams filled the room, "Sarah, Sarah, Sarah . . ."

Rutherford stood obscuring Will's view of the room, "Come now Mr English, we need to get you out of here."

Will strained his neck from left to right in an attempt to see where Sarah was. Bolton again shouted, "Get him out."

Five officers now pushed, pulled and lifted Will out of the room and along the hallway. Rutherford followed.

They had knocked at the door at the top of the stairs when they had first arrived but when no one had answered they assumed the room to be empty. Turning the handle Rutherford put his shoulder against the wooden panel and pushed. The door popped open on an almost empty single room. Luckily the previous occupants had left the sprung iron frame from a bed in place.

As the other officers pulled the still screaming Will into the room, Rutherford took off his coat and laid it over the rusty springs, "Put him here," he told the officers as he closed the door. Will was laid on the bed, he immediately turned onto his side and shrunk into the foetal position crying. Rutherford turned to the officers instructing two of them to continue with their enquiries, two to return to help Detective Bolton, and the last to stand guard outside the door they had just come through. As they left Rutherford turned and sat on the edge of the bed, he placed his hand on Will's shoulder.

"I'm so sorry," he said, comforting the crying man, "I'm so very sorry."

Now alone Bolton stood in the centre of the room, carnage the like of which he had never before witnessed surrounded him. The whistles had started only thirty minutes before. A passer-by had claimed to see 'Springheel Jack' leap from the upper window, to the rooftops of the houses opposite, he had sought out an officer and they had both returned to the house, seeing the large broken first floor window the officer had investigated.

That officer was eventually taken away screaming. News had spread quickly through the local area and by the time Bolton had arrived with Rutherford a crowd had gathered. Bolton was thankful that at the moment the onlookers were still relatively calm.

The two officers Rutherford had given instruction to, entered the room, Bolton turned towards them. "I want one of you to fetch the photographer," he told them, as he turned back to the horrific sight that lay before him, "we need this recorded."

As one of the officers left Bolton stepped over a large bloody patch on the floor and leaned over the body of

Annie Cooper.

She was sat on the chair Will had been sat in earlier. The window behind her had been completely destroyed, its glass shattered across the floor, the wooden frame splintered and torn from the plaster.

Her head hung back over the top of the chair, her throat cut so deeply that she stared out of the broken window and into the darkness beyond. Blood had sprayed the walls on both sides of her and as Bolton investigated the wound, he could see the broken white bones of her neck peeping through the torn flesh. He followed the arterial spray to his left, across the table and up the side of the window, it almost reached the ceiling.

On the table lay her right arm. It had been ripped from her body, snapping the humerus. Thickened blood dripped from both ends of the broken bone. Her hand was open, fingers stretched fully. Her stomach had been sliced open allowing her intestines to slip out, they lay in her lap a confused mass of bloated grey flesh.

Bolton turned from the scene and walked across the room to the door of the bedroom. Luckily it had been closed when Will had burst into the room. He closed his fist around the door knob and with a deep breath he turned it, entering the room.

The grey walls, now almost black as the blood soaked slowly into the powdery decaying plaster greeted Bolton.

The body of Sarah English lay on the floor at a right angle to the bed. Her left leg broken, still half covered by the blankets.

She had been dragged from beneath the covers and ripped apart where she fell. Her face was gone exposing the smashed bones of her skull. Bolton could see her brain, a grey mass splintered with slivers of white bone. The jawbone was missing, her tongue spilled out from her torn throat, drooping against her neck. Sarah's clothes had been torn away in the frenzy. Both her breasts had been ripped from her body and thrown across the room. A bloody streak stained the plaster where they had hit the wall before sliding to the floor where they now lay.

Her sternum had been pulled up snapping the ribs on both sides. Sarah's heart, lungs and liver had been ripped out and lay in a small pile next to her body. Bolton had examined them earlier and found them to have all been bitten into. He could not locate the small parts that had been bitten off.

Numerous cuts had been made across her stomach and genitals, the latter having been completely removed. Bolton could only assume that what was left of her vagina had been covered by the intestines that now protruded through the sliced skin, they trailed from Sarah to the bed. He had concluded that the extent of what had been removed was something the coroner would find out, once his examination of the body was under way.

Underneath Sarah the floor had at some time in the past been covered with a large piece of fabric, her blood coagulated as it pooled upon it.

What was left of her skin shone china white, bereft of the life-giving liquid. Bolton's stomach heaved confronted by the sight and smell of the room, he desperately tried to keep some composure as he made notes.

'God,' he thought, *'I wish the coroner would hurry up.'*

Will's mind had snapped, he couldn't comprehend what had happened to his beloved wife and her mother in the next room. He had left them that morning and apart from their recent grievance towards him, everything had been fine.

He convinced himself that Sarah must have been absent from the home when whatever had happened, happened. Although she would be upset and knew that he would have to console her once the details of what had happened to her mother came out, he began to calm himself safe in the knowledge that Sarah was at least unhurt.

'She's just looking after herself and the baby,' he thought, sobbing.

Rutherford placed his hand back on Will's arm. He had lay silent for a few minutes, but now begun to sob again. "It's ok Will," Rutherford comforted, "you just rest."

Will was aware that someone was near him and that they were touching his arm softly.

'Sarah?' "The baby Sarah?" he mumbled, "the baby?"

Rutherford tilted his head as Will spoke, trying to understand the words. Half whispered, half mumbled, his speech was difficult to hear.

"The baby Sarah."

Rutherford sat up, *'A baby?'* he thought.

He became alarmed, during their search of the building no child had been found. "Will?" Rutherford gripped his arm and shook it, "Will, where's the child?" anxiously, he shook Will harder, "Where's the child Will?"

Will dreamt of being woken by Sarah. She stood over him holding their beautiful baby. He looked up at its smiling face, "He's beautiful."

"Who's beautiful?" Rutherford asked, "Is it your child Will, where is it?"

In his mind Will sat up and took the baby from Sarah. He sat holding their child, "I didn't know you were due yet?" he said looking up at an imaginary Sarah, "I thought you still had a month to go?"

Rutherford leapt from Will's bedside and ran to find Bolton. He burst in on him as he knelt over the remains.

"She was pregnant!" he blurted out, "Sarah, his wife, she was pregnant."

Bolton stood, "What do you mean pregnant? How do you know that?"

"English is mumbling, he's mentioned a baby. I thought he meant they had a child but he's talking about not being due, still being pregnant." Rutherford stood next to Bolton, both men looked down at the bloody carnage.

"There is no child," Bolton said, as he stepped across the body to get a view from the other side. Rutherford lifted the blankets carefully looking under the bed. Blood had soaked the covers and seeped into the darkness, but there was no sign of the child, "We can't have missed it, there is no child here."

Rutherford looked up at his superior, "What do we do now then?" he asked.

Bolton sighed, "We wait for the coroner."

Chapter 30

The Beast sat squat, high above the city, its long-emaciated legs bent. In its hands it held warm flesh. It had ripped the child from the woman as she lay dead, once it had it, it had torn the small delicate body in two. The child had kicked its tiny legs once, opened its mouth as if to let out its first scream, but had made no sound. Its neck twisted and separated from its body with the minimum of pressure from its long grasping fingers.

Dawn began to rise in the East and it stood to welcome it. The rising sun cast the Beast's long shadow from one rooftop to the next, then the next. Its shadow spreading across the city as the sun rose.

It held its hands high, blood from the unborn child's body ran down its arms. It opened its mouth and screamed. High pitched, the sound it made echoed through the streets of the city. Birds took to the air upon hearing it. Dogs began to bark. Cats hissed and cowered. Horses worried, kicking out at the carriages behind them.

Philip Griss died as the horse he was brushing kicked out and caught him square in the face, crushing his skull.

Jonathan Thirsk was attacked and killed by the dogs he

was feeding, he had trained them to fight in the pit and although he fought them off desperately, they did exactly what he had trained them for.

Caroline Lamb died as she jumped from London Bridge. She and others had been crossing when the bridge became engulfed by thousands of sewer rats. As all those on the bridge that morning did, she turned to run but unfortunately Caroline had fallen, once the sea of rats had covered her body she panicked and had leapt from the bridge hoping that the water below would save her. Unfortunately, she was unaware that part of the Thames had that night frozen, the thick ice not only broke her fall but both her legs. She died of exposure over the next hour. The rats that had been attached to her when she had made her fatal jump, fed on her as she did.

Those who found themselves awake, turned subconsciously towards the sound and without reason became afraid, couples held each other under blankets as the first rays of sunlight filtered through grime covered windows.

Maximillian Barr sat straight up in bed. His body was wet with sweat. His heart raced, something had entered his dreams and had awoken him. For the first time in his life he was afraid.

The Beast screamed again squeezing the small body it held, its undeveloped bones crushed in its powerful grip. As the echo of its cries died, the city once again became silent, everything, whether it be man or beast listened.

Above the city the tall figure dropped its arms and let the remains of the child slip from its fingers to the street below. It fell as one. A small body lost in the dirt and grime produced by the uncaring people below.

Chapter 31

Three weeks had passed since the killing of Annie Cooper and Sarah English. The body of her unborn child had never been found.

Bolton and Rutherford had worked day and night to solve the double murder, but all investigations had come to nought.

The 'Springheel Jack murders', as they had been nicknamed by the newspapers, had ended. The city should have been settling itself down for the long cold winter ahead. Instead the city burned, its people rioted, fought and died.

The Thames had frozen over for the third year in a row. Bodies lay on the thick ice from Westminster, downriver to the abandoned Tower Bridge. East of the unfinished bridge, the heat from fires that burned the warehouses and docks, prevented the ice from reaching the banks of the Thames.

At high tide, the bodies of the dead piled up against the frozen edge, some slipped under the ice only to be swept up river, their bloated decaying bodies lying in wait miles away from London, to be found come the spring thaw.

The whole of the East End burned, both the local police and fire crews had given up on the area and were now employed in creating a cordon to protect the adjoining districts. Streets were patrolled constantly in a vain attempt to not only prevent the spread of the flames, but also the rioting, looting populous.

Emergency meetings had been held in Parliament, the Prime Minister declared it a *'National Disaster'*.

All agreed that unlimited funds would be spent to bring peace back to the city and to rebuild, what was now being called, London's *'Gateway to the World'*.

The rich and powerful had also felt a need to hold meetings, Parliament couldn't be seen to favour them, so quietly and unobserved they had met to decide their fate.

They didn't hold with the promises made by the Prime Minister and had no confidence that however much Parliament wasted time and effort on the poor areas of London, the rest of the city would eventually befall a similar fate.

They had seen the streets filled with those made homeless by the fires. They died where they slept, the cold killing them as surely as the flames would have done if they had stayed within their home. Their belongings were taken and their bodies thrown to the frozen river.

Parkland that had been set aside to serve he wellbeing of the population, had become makeshift campsites for any that could manage to build shelter. Within a few days London's green areas became cess pits as the poor pissed, shit and slept wherever they could find. The rich looked down from the security of their homes and prayed that the fires would cleanse them of the poor disease.

Money had begun to leave the city. The bank vaults had been emptied by those who no longer trusted its security. They had taken everything they could and moved out to the surrounding countryside. Those rich enough, would watch and wait surrounded by their possessions safe at their country homes and private estates. The city would belong to the poor.

Although he had the opportunity, Maximillian Barr was not one of those that had left the city. He had been present at many of the private meetings held in secret at gentlemen's clubs across London. He had listened to their arguments and had sat in silence as those he despised frightened each other with tales of murder and looting.

'*Let them go,*' he thought directing his anger at those who decided to leave.

Barr had unfinished business. The Beast had not yet been caught. He had become more and more alarmed at the lack of sightings of 'Springheel Jack' being reported. After the double murder every edition of every newspaper ran stories of sightings, confrontations and even reports that he had been captured. One report turned out to be two men fighting on their rooftops, each thinking that they had 'Jack'. They had in fact been tending to their rooftop pigeon coops and had startled one another in the darkness.

Barr had both Clay and those trusted members who had not yet fled the city, out searching for any news since the killing of Sarah and her mother.

Only once had he seen Will since the murder of his wife Sarah. Barr had attended the funeral, he wanted to gauge the mental state of those living within the area, the populous were already rioting and he believed that many more were teetering on the edge, the Beast had infected the city like a virus. By paying his respects to both Sarah and her mother and passing on his condolences to Will, he could see first-hand the effects the killings had on normal people. He knew that his presence would not be appreciated but he needed to attend.

The graveside had become an ugly place once his presence had been noticed.

They were both to be buried in the grounds of St. Mathew's church. Positioned as it was on the very street that Sarah had been raised.

The family had attended mass every Sunday until the death of her father Albert Like many from the area he had been laid to rest in an unmarked pauper's grave.

After the shocking double murder, the government had decided that the only decent thing they could do, was to pay for both Sarah and Annie to be given a proper funeral and burial. The streets had been lined with thousands of onlookers, Church Row was crowded with well-wishers jostling for position as the cortege made its way slowly towards the church entrance.

Barr had made his way through the crowd and had emerged opposite Will at the graveside. He had wanted to enter the church and hear the service, but on witnessing the sea of bodies that crushed against its entrance he decided to wait for the graveside service and interment.

Will had kept his head down throughout the whole graveside service. As the priest spoke he stared at the coffin holding the body of his wife. The crowded cemetery around him stood silent in prayer.

"As we commit these two bodies to the earth, we give thanks for the life of both Sarah English and Annie Cooper. Their lives cut short, but lives well lived, they gave great joy to many . . ."

Barr watched as the two coffins laid side by side were covered with flowers, the onlookers slowly filed past crossing themselves as they each dropped two flowers. Will stood watching them as they fell, Pip at his left, Kingsley at his right.

Slowly his head lifted and his gaze fell upon Barr, standing only a few feet from him. The dark hole of the grave separating the two men.

"You Bastard!" he cried at him, lurching forward in an attempt to jump the void. Both Kingsley and Pip's reactions saved Will from an action that would have certainly ended with him falling into the grave and on top of the coffins. They caught his arms and held him as his foot landed on the edge, earth that shook loose fell amongst the flowers below. "You knew you bastard, you knew," cried Will.

Barr reactively stepped back as Will moved towards him, his exit sealed by the mass of bodies behind. "I can assure you," he lied, "that I did not."

"Horse shit," Will cried at him, struggling with his friends to release his arms, "you told me the locations, you told me you had translated that book and knew where it would attack!"

Pip struggled to keep hold of his friends' arm. Will was much stronger than he had expected. "Please," he screamed across to Barr, "leave now."

Kingsley also shouted at Barr to leave. The line of people paying their respects moved away from the graveside creating a ring around the four men.

"I'll kill you, you bastard, I'll kill you," Will's voice cracked as the words left him, tears began to flow down his cheeks.

"I made a mistake," returned Barr. Feeling a gap behind him open, he moved a step away from the graveside, "It was just a mistake."

Will's rage sored upon hearing his words, "What? You call the murder of my wife and child a mistake?"

Barr's interest piqued with mention of the child, "Is the child gone?" The police had thought it prudent not to mention the missing child to the newspapers.

In disbelief Will stayed his struggle and relaxed, "What?" his mind couldn't comprehend the question Barr had asked. "What do you mean?"

"The child," Barr repeated, "was it taken?"

Will's fury raged once more, "You sick bastard."

Luckily neither Pip nor Kingsley had let their grip of Will's arms slacken when they had felt him relax. "You fucking sick bastard."

Onlookers shocked by both the scene and language used, began to leave the cemetery. Two policemen emerged from the dispersing crowd and seeing the two men struggling with Will stepped in to help.

"Please now Sir, calm yourself," one said pulling Will away from the edge. The other officer slipped in front of Will and placing his hands on his shoulders said, "Sir if you don't calm yourself you'll be arrested."

Will's attention was drawn to the officer standing in front of him, blocking his view of Barr. "What? It's him you need to arrest," Will shifted his body left and right attempting to see past the officer, "arrest Barr!" he cried, "arrest Barr. He's the murderer."

The officer turned to see who Will had been arguing with, but Barr had slipped into the crowd and was lost. He turned to face Will, "Look son, I can't imagine how you must feel and I know it's neither my place nor my job," Will looked up at the officer's face, "but I want to give you a little advice. Whoever you think was responsible for this, whatever thoughts you might have of revenge, my advice to you, is to leave those thoughts here. Let them rest with your wife." The officer watched as a calm passed over Will's face as he looked down at the grave, "Just let them go son."

Both Pip and Kingsley relaxed their grip on him. Will dropped to his knees and sobbed. Turning to Kingsley, Pip asked, "Do you think he'll be alright now?"

Kingsley nodded his agreement. The two police officers slowly walked away asking those who had stayed to move on, leaving the three men alone.

Pip and Kingsley stood by Will as he cried. Neither left his side for over an hour. Finally, Will stood and turning to his two friends, thanked them. "I want you to stay with me," Kingsley offered, "Emily hasn't seen you for some time and would love you to be our guest."

"Thank you," replied Will, "Thank you."

Smiling Kingsley placed his arm around his friend and together they left the cemetery. Pip followed behind.

"Should we go to The Flag?" he asked, "Charlie said he would meet us there."

Kingsley laughed, "What a good idea, a drink's just what we all need."

Chapter 32

The normality of the Kingsley household had had a
calming effect on Will. At first he kept himself to himself,
not wanting to leave the small room Emily had made up
for him. However as the days passed he made more of an
effort, his friends were making a great fuss of him and he
didn't want to appear ungrateful.

Kingsley hadn't spoken to Will about the escalating
troubles in the East End and had deliberately avoided
leaving any newspapers about the house. The riots and fires
had devastated not only the area around Will's home, but
it had been reported that they had also spread to Bethnal
Green, Kingsley prayed they wouldn't make it as far as
Church Row.

Will had seemed calmer over the last few days and the
evenings they spent sat talking around the fire had been
most pleasant. He hadn't mentioned Barr for over a week,
although Kingsley was certain that the resentment and
blame still festered within him.

Will had forced himself to forget Barr when in company,
however when alone in his room he planned his revenge.
He knew Barr held the secret to what had happened.

Evidence must be present at his home. He had decided to break into Barr's Kensington home and find it.

No amount of wealth and power could save him from the gallows at Wandsworth if proof of his knowledge of the killings could be found. Each night Will fell asleep with the thoughts of Barr's body dangling from a rope at the forefront of his mind.

Will had noticed that there had been no moon the night before and made the decision to break into Barr's home that night. He would spend the day walking the streets making his way across the city to Upper Grosvenor Square, arriving just before dusk. There he could secrete himself in the gardens opposite Barr's home and await his opportunity.

He sat uncomfortably in a rhododendron bush watching the house. A light was on in the window of the library, Will remembered his first meeting with Barr in that very room. It seemed so very long ago.

The street was quiet. A lamplighter had passed on his nightly duty, paused briefly within sight of Will to light a cigarette, then he continued zig zagging between the lamps. The gates to the gardens had then been locked, from Will's position he couldn't see who had locked them but the sound of the bolt slipping into place was unmistakable.

Barr sat at his desk with his back to the library window. He wanted to be seen. He had known that retribution would come, each night since the funeral he had sat in the same position waiting for it, the library window lifted slightly allowing the cold night air in.

Clay stood each night at the darkened sitting room window watching the street from the front of the house. Whilst Barr sat, Clay watched. Night after night they set the scene, but night after night Will had not shown. Clay was beginning to question his master's confidence in the reporter.

Barr flipped the pages of the book in front of him as the clock in the hallway chimed eight times. He had been sitting in the same position now for three hours and all interest in the book and its contents had been lost. He heard the door to the sitting room open and close.

'Clay would again be certain of Will's nonattendance and soon the door to the library would open and the discussion as to whether to carry on or not would take place,' thought Barr, he was himself beginning to doubt that he would show.

The door opened and Clay stepped into the room, "He's here Sir."

Surprised Barr almost turned too looked out of the window, "Are you sure?"

"Yes Sir," said Clay, he crossed the room and closed the drapes behind Barr, deliberately forgetting to shut the window. "I thought he had entered the gardens opposite a number of hours ago but couldn't be certain. Since then I have been observing the bushes facing the house and have just witnessed him stretching his leg out, possibly cramp."

"Excellent," Barr stood closing the book, "the servants know not to approach him?"

"Yes Sir," replied Clay, as Barr slipped the volume he was reading into its space on the bookcase. "They are to remain downstairs and not to venture out."

"And Mark?"

"He is upstairs Sir and has been instructed to ensure that Mr English be prevented climbing the stairs," a worried look came over Clay's face, "are you sure about this Sir?"

Barr sighed, "I know your concerns Clay and I do understand that you think this an unnecessary risk. I can assure you that Mr. English bears me no physical harm. He is confused and like all in stressful situations he says things he doesn't really mean. In reality he is desperate to know what happened to his wife and where her killer is. He believes that I have that information. He may harbour some plan of involving the police at some later date but be reassured me friend, once he has the information we allow him, everything else will be destroyed. All he will have will be meaningless."

"I know Sir."

"And don't forget," continued Barr, "we've lost Erebus, there's been no sighting of it for some weeks now. I believe that this small insignificant man is somehow connected to it. It's seen him and let him live, it took his wife and child. It may have given up on him, it may have given up on this city, but I doubt that he's given up on it. He will search for it 'til the day he dies." Barr paused, watching Clay, "Does that satisfy you?"

Clay reprehended himself for doubting his master and mentor, "Yes Sir, it does."

"Good," Barr opened the door to the hallway, "then let's get on with it."

Will's legs had cramped. He had stretched the left one out but now the right hurt like hell. He couldn't sit for much longer hiding as he was, a frost was beginning to cover the ground around him.

The front door of Barr's home opened. Will watched as Clay left. He had seen the curtains to the library close a few minutes before, moments later the light had been extinguished.

The street was quiet, Will found that he was holding his breath, he let it out. He could hear a carriage approaching. Risking being spotted he crept forward so he could see the street corner. He smiled as Barr's carriage entered the street driven by Clay. It slowed to a stand in front of him, Will's view of the house was obscured but he heard the front door close, he could see a pair of well-polished shoes cross the pavement, then witnessed the carriage tilt, as he assumed Barr stepped into it.

Clay cracked the whip and the horse's pulled away, their hooves clipping loudly as they left.

Will waited until the carriage had turned the far corner and he could no longer hear its wheels on the cobbles. The street had once again become silent. Lights illuminated the homes opposite the garden, but Barr's was now in darkness.

Crawling from beneath the rhododendron bush, he jumped up climbing the railings easily despite his stiffness and cramp.

There was a lamp near to where he had emerged, Will crouched as he crossed the street and climbed the steps to Barr's front door. He noticed the window to the library had been left open, on a normal day Will would have been suspicious of this most opportune discovery, but his mind had become clouded by his thoughts of revenge.

Slipping over the small fence that divided the steps from the space between the street and the window, he crouched below it and forced the sash up. It moved easily and quietly. Once a gap big enough for him to fit through had been attained he hopped onto its ledge and slipped his body inside. Will dropped to the floor behind the drapes and pulled one aside peering into the darkened room.

Barr's desk stood in front of him, dark thick legs preventing him from seeing further into the room. Will stood and emerged from behind the drapes. The room was as he had remembered. A strip of light could be seen along the bottom edge of the doorway opposite. He stepped across the room and stopped with his ear at the door listening for any sound from the hallway.

Will could hear his heart beating fast as he held his ear against the cold wood. All was silent. He assumed that with their master gone the servants would stay below, taking a well-earned rest.

Placing his fingers on the door handle he slowly turned it. The door popped open slightly as the catch left its housing, producing a thick strip of light that stretched across the library floor.

Opening the door onto the hallway Will could see that the coast was clear, he stepped into the light leaving the library door slightly ajar. Silently he crossed the hallway to the door opposite. Once again, he pressed his ear to the door listening, he heard nothing.

To his right, another door was open, Will could see the large dining table where he had sat with Barr surrounded by chairs. Without entering the room, he passed it and continued along the hallway, pausing for a moment at the foot of the stairs he listened to the silent house.

Passed the stairs at the end of the hallway were two more doors. Cautiously he made his way to them and listened at both. He could make out voices from behind one and concluded that it led to either the kitchen, or a servant's area. The second he opened after listening for a long period to nothing but silence.

Stairs led down from the open door, he paused looking at them, within a few steps the stairs turned back on themselves, a light flickered dimly against the wall from below.

Suddenly, from above Will heard the unmistakable sound of footsteps on the stairs, someone was coming. He turned and looked down towards the steps ahead of him.

'Nowhere to go now,' he thought as he made his way down to the point where the steps turned back. Holding the door closed he peered around the corner slowly emerging until he was certain that anyone lingering below couldn't spy him.

The stairs led to a corridor that ran directly under the hallway. Doors on each side led to rooms that Will imagined echoed the floorplan above. The corridor was sparsely decorated, the walls were bare apart from a lit gas lamp,

'Fortunately, lit,' thought Will.

Its only other feature was a small half-moon desk against the wall between the doors on the right. As Will walked towards it he noticed a candle, its wick already burned. Rivulets of wax had melted down its surface.

He opened the small draw and found matches. Will's mind should have been screaming that something was wrong! A convenient source of light and the means to illuminate it? His suspicious journalistic nose was lost to him.

Taking both of them Will tried the door to his left, it was locked. The door next to the half-moon desk though was unlocked and turning the handle Will opened the door.

The room beyond was in darkness, he could just make out a table and some scientific equipment illuminated by the dim light of the corridor. Lighting the candle, he entered and closed the door behind him.

In the candlelight Will could see two gas lamps on the wall, with the door shut he risked lighting them.

He was in a room that Barr had obviously wanted to keep secret from visitors. As he peered at the wall cabinets filled with jars of chemicals, books, handwritten journals and experimental apparatus Will realised that he was in Barr's personal study. A long table stretched across the back wall, on it Will noticed many glass bottles filled with plants, tree bark and to his horror, small animals floating dead in a yellow liquid.

The table in the centre of the room was covered in books, Will spied the book filled with the loose papers Barr had shown him on his first visit. He was about to take it when he realised that Barr had told him that there wasn't aware of anyone alive who could translate it except for Barr. Will had to find the translated papers.

As he moved around the table he opened its two large draws. Both were filled, from what Will could see, with a collection of Knick knacks, objects Barr had picked up whilst travelling, no papers.

The only other item of interest on the table was something that Will had heard of but had never actually seen. It was an Edison Phonograph. Its huge flaring horn faced him, the deep black mouth seemed to mock him with its silence. He knew that you could record your voice onto a wax cylinder and that the Phonograph would then play it back anytime you wanted. He had even seen some cylinders for sale that had been used to record music. Will wondered what it would be like to listen to real music. He searched the room for the cylinders.

Next to the wall cabinets stood a tall cupboard that Will thought to be strangely positioned, it had been placed a few feet from the corner of the wall. He stared into the dark gap between it and the wall, the shadow of the cupboard seemed to fall wrong, it was too dark, too deep, for a moment a fear of being discovered filled his mind and he had to prevent himself from panicking. An overwhelming feeling of being watched caused him to turn back into the room, he searched for its source, the room was empty and the door was still closed.

'Calm yourself Will,' he thought, *'calm yourself.'*

Ignoring the shadows and the strange positioning of the cupboard Will opened its door, on the shelf in front of him were the cylindrical tubes he had been hoping to find. Picking up the two tubes he noticed a rolled-up map that had been resting against them, it rolled to the edge of the shelf and fell to the floor. Placing the cylinders next to the player Will retrieved the map.

Dropping it to the table he popped the lid off one of the tubes, the cylinder slid out into his hand. He placed it on the player pulling the needle forward onto the start of the recording.

The horn burst into life with a loud pop followed by a continuous hissing. Will listened as the haunting voice of Maximillian Barr filled the room.

"I have found in the parish record the testimony of Father John. The year is 1402, and chaos reigns in London. He believes a creature, whom he calls 'Erebus the Son of Chaos' is at large, he calls it the harbinger, but a harbinger of what? From his testimony I have found resemblances between the victims of then and now. I believe it is the same creature, but how? Why four main victims? Why in such precise locations? There must be a connection."

The cylinder ended and Will slid it off and replaced it in its tube. Taking out the second he once again slipped it onto the phonograph and listened. Barr's voice sounded more hurried, clearly, he was excited by what he had found.

"I now believe that the killings themselves are more symbolic than they first appear. All must be women, they are the givers of life, the reason we all exist. Attack what we must protect and you stab at the heart of mankind. The first victim does not lose her life but does lose her sanity, the ability to reason. The second her heart! The symbol of love and passion. The third, their head! The seat of both knowledge and consciousness. And the fourth? What is taken from the fourth is the ability to create life. The fourth victim in both instances had been heavily pregnant. Finally, placing the position of the last victim alongside the locations of the other victims a precise pattern becomes clear. As I have marked on the map, it is clear that collectively they are not only an attack on our humanity but also work as a subconscious attack on our religious beliefs. Slowly the city falls apart, chaos reigns."

The cylinder fell silent, Will stared at it as it rotated thinking it had finished. He noticed the map that had been kept with the recordings. As he opened it Barr's voice continued.

"He is taking everything and leaving nothing but devastation and death. I believe he will now move to another city and this whole sorry affair will begin again. Erebus exists to bring chaos. But why? What is its purpose?"

Will unrolled the map and saw that Barr had made notes and markings across it, rolling it up, he slipped it into his shirt. Taking the cylinder from the phonograph he placed it safely into its tube and pocketed both of them. Looking around the room he noticed the open cupboard door and shut it before turning out the gas lamps and leaving the room.

Barr stood quietly in the corner of the room, his face and hands blackened with the soot from burnt willow bark. He had been whispering the enchantment taught to him by Clay since before Will had entered the room. He had used it many times and his ability to *Dim'* had been a closely guarded secret that was known to only himself and Clay. Its use was so beneficial to their cause, that news of it amongst even their closest trusted members would render it useless.

Will had stood inches from him as the shadows between the cupboard and the wall absorbed his form. There had been a moment when Barr thought the enchantment was not having its usual effect. Will had stared into the shadows a little too long for his liking.

He was right when he had said that Will wanted merely to find out what had happened to his family and to see if Barr knew the location of the killer. Now he knew that Barr believed the Beast had moved on, he felt sure that Will would unwittingly help him in his search for it. Whilst Barr's loyal members continued with their investigations, he hoped that Will and his contacts would scour the newspapers for similar stories. Barr was sure that he would find Erebus and that once found, he could and would take control of it.

Chapter 33

Will left the house from the library window. He hadn't wanted to risk leaving by the front door, opening and closing it could have alerted the servants. Safer to slip away the same way he had entered.

He casually walked along the street and made his way towards speakers' corner in Hyde Park, from there he knew he could pick up a Hansom Cab. It was quite a ride back the Kingsley's house but that would give him time to reflect on what he had learnt and how he was going to procced.

The cab turned onto Spencer Street, when Will realised where he was he tapped the roof twice indicating for the driver to stop the cab. From the pavement he paid the fair, the cabby thanked him and slowly steered the horse back into the road. Will watched as the driver pulled back in further down.

'Another customer,' he smiled, *"life in London just carry's on."*

He fumbled for his door key whilst walking the short distance to Kingsley's. Reaching the door, he found it to be unlocked, as he stepped inside Emily's voice drifted from the sitting room "Is that you William?" she paused, "I've left you some supper in the kitchen."

"Thank you, Mrs Kingsley," Will replied. He had hoped they'd both be asleep by the time he had arrived back. "I'll just freshen up first . . . if you don't mind," not waiting for her reply, he took the stairs to his first-floor room.

"That's fine," she called after him unaware he had walked off, "Edward and I will be retiring soon."

Will slipped the map from under his shirt and dropped it onto the bed. Throwing his coat over the chair back, he reminded himself to take it downstairs with him and leave it on the coat stand by the door. He placed his jacket on a hanger and left it in the wardrobe, rolling up his shirt sleeves he took the pitcher and filled the basin with water.

He Unbuttoned his collar and splashed the cool water onto his face and neck. It felt refreshing. Although it was cold out, his skin was clammy with sweat. He held the towel to his face, it felt soft, comforting. As he dried himself he heard the Kingsley's climbing the stairs.

"We're turning in now," Kingsley's voice accompanied a tapping at the door, "you've been out all day," his voice dropped to almost a whisper, "are you alright Will?"

"What? Oh yes . . . yes everything is fine," Will opened the door, "I just had some errands to run, family matters. You know how it is?"

Kingsley considered his friends answer, "Yes, I know what you mean," he said and turned to join his wife, "oh," he called back, "don't forget your supper."

"I won't. Thanks," Will closed the door, dropped the towel and picked up the map. Hearing their bedroom door close he was now free to study the map at the kitchen table whilst he ate. Picking up his coat as he left the room, he made his way downstairs to the kitchen.

The lamps had been left on for him in the kitchen. Emily had placed a plate on the table, cooked meat, tomatoes and bread had been left for him. Taking a seat, Will unrolled the map securing it at the top with the plate.

The map Barr had used had been printed a few years earlier in 1889. Charles Booth's 'Map of London Poverty' it was very detailed indeed. Will amused himself with the thought that the fires now raging in the East End had made its publication almost obsolete.

Barr had drawn a large inverted cross that covered many districts in the East of London. Each of the four points coincided with the location of an attack. Lucy Strong at Bishop's Manor. Ethel Jones in the Limehouse basin behind Narrow Street. The third victim, Will himself had witnessed in the yard behind Ship Alley and finally the house of Annie Cooper, where not only had his wife and mother in law been murdered, but the sickness and depravity that now permeated the city had reached an even lower level with the disappearance of his unborn child.

Will studied the surrounding areas. The church where Barr had taken the records from had been marked, so had the Leman Street Police Station. He followed the roads leading west, another mark recorded the location of the Evening Star Office.

He ate, absorbing the places Barr had been interested in. It was obvious to Will that Barr had deliberately misled him as to the location of the final victim. He raged at the thought that Barr must have been a witness to the murders in Church Row. Will's absence had ensured the slaughter of his wife could take place.

He began to sob, holding his head in his hands he let the tears come. Anger had kept his grieving at bay and now, with proof that her death could have been easily prevented, his grief came. Tears fell from his cheeks to the map, the ink from Barr's pen spread as they soaked into the paper.

Will wept for over an hour, the map and his food forgotten. The Kingsley's slept soundly above, ignorant of his emotional breakdown. His tears eventually dried up, tiredness overcame him his head nodded as Morpheus guided him to sleep. Will slept, head in hands until Emily's hand, gently shook him from his dreams.

"Oh William," her voice gentle, "you haven't slept here all night, have you?"

Will's mind felt sluggish, he tried to remember falling asleep but couldn't, "I'm sorry Mrs Kingsley. I didn't mean to. I'll clean this mess away."

"You'll do no such thing," replied Emily, stoking the kitchen fire. "I'm putting water on to boil for Edward to wash in, I'll make sure there's enough for both of you," she said turning towards Will, "now you get yourself upstairs and changed. I'll cook you something warm whilst the water boils."

Will could feel the emotion rising within him again, "Oh, thank you Mrs Kingsley," he kissed her lightly on the cheek and left the kitchen to do as she had asked. Emily smiled to herself as Will left.

Clearing the kitchen table, she paused to examine the map Will had laid out. Holding it up she noticed that the ink had run at the centre of what had been a large cross. The street name that had been obscured by the ink could now easily be read. Jubilee Street.

'Strange,' she thought, *'that's the street William and Sarah lived on.'*

Taking the map, she folded it and placed it on top of the welsh dresser for safety. She would give it back to Will once breakfast was over and Edward had left for work.

Will took his time undressing, he emptied the cold water from the wash bowl and left the empty pitcher by his door.

A few minutes later there was a tap at the door and Emily informed him that he now had warm water.

It felt good to be washed and dressed in clean clothes. The tears of the night before had been forgotten, Will felt positive that with the evidence on the phonograph cylinders and the notes Barr had made on the map, he could ensure an investigation by the police. Although Barr could never be convicted of any of the crimes committed, his fore knowledge of the events and subsequent willingness to do nothing to avoid them taking place, would in Will's eyes be enough to convict him.

Will ate his breakfast heartily whilst Kingsley chatted. He had skilfully avoided the questions about his actions the previous day. Responding that he had been with family members he hadn't seen in quite a while and that time had run away with them. Emily hadn't mentioned the map nor the fact that she had found Will asleep at the table.

He had surveyed the kitchen when he noticed the map had been taken from where he had left it but couldn't see where Emily had hidden it.

Breakfast eaten, Kingsley kissed his wife goodbye, wished Will a fine morning and had left for work. It was just over a mile to the office of the Evening Star and Will suspected that Kingsley enjoyed his daily walk there and back.

"Mrs Kingsley," Will spoke collecting the empty plates together, "have you the map I left on the table?"

Emily dried her hands on her apron, she had been washing the breakfast pans whilst Will finished eating. "Yes dear," she said retrieving it from the dresser, "It's here," she passed it to Will. "Isn't it funny how your home was at the centre of that cross?"

Will stood shocked, "I'm sorry?"

"Jubilee Street," she continued, "It's at the centre of that cross. The one drawn on the map."

Resisting the urge to open the map there and then to confirm what Emily had said, Will laughed and agreed with her, "Yes, it is. Very funny indeed."

Will took the map to his room. Opening it on the bed he stared in horror at what Emily had noticed. With the ink gone he could clearly see she was right. The centre of the cross did indeed pass directly over the street where he and Sarah had lived.

Pip watched as Kingsley exited Spencer Street and made his way south down Goswell Road. He and Charlie had agreed not to let their boss know what they were doing. They had wanted to help their friend and both were certain that Kingsley wouldn't agree with their plans.

Tucking the newspaper he held into his armpit, he stepped into the road to better observe his boss in the distance. Happy that he was well on his way to the office, Pip crossed into Spencer Street to call on Will.

Emily answered the door. "Oh, good morning Pip," she said slightly bemused, "If you're wanting Edward then you're too late, he set off to work a few minutes ago."

"That's fine Mrs Kinglsey. I've come to see Will," he paused reaching for the newspaper, "I've come to give him this."

"He has had quite a restless night, if you let me have it I'll see that he gets it." Emily tried to take the paper from Pip, but he pulled his hand away.

"I'd rather give it to him myself," he paused feeling slightly guilty for pulling the paper out of her reach, "If you don't mind. There's something I would like him to see."

Emily moved from the doorway allowing Pip to pass, "That'll be fine Pip. If you would like to wait in the sitting room, I'll see if William is up to a visit."

Pip opened the door indicated to him. The sitting room was warm and cosy. The fire had been backed up the night before and still generated a nice heat. Placing himself in what he assumed was Kingsley's armchair Pip waited for Will to arrive.

Emily tapped on Will's bedroom door, "William, there's a visitor for you," she could hear her guest moving around the room.

"Thank you, Mrs Kingsley. I'll be down in a moment."

"He's in the sitting room. Would you like a pot of tea?" Emily wondered what he was doing. He seemed to be opening and shutting the set of draws she used for bedding.

Will opened the door, his face a little flustered, "Yes, that would be lovely, thank you," he answered, closing the door behind him. "Who is it?" Will's heart raced, he didn't want to alarm Emily, but he couldn't help feeling that having discovered the theft of the map and cylinders Barr now sat waiting for him.

Emily stepped away from him and began to descend the stairs, "It's Pip," she said turning back, "It seems that he has something for you, wouldn't leave it for me to give to you so I imagine he feels it important."

Relieved, Will followed her down the stairs, as they reached the bottom she left him and entered the kitchen. Will opened the sitting room door, Pip jumped greeting him, "Oh Will, it's so good to see you, how've you been? It's been awful quiet without you," he said and shook his hand vigorously.

"I'm fine, I'm fine Pip," Will said prizing Pip's hand from his own, "Now sit, Mrs Kingsley said that you have something for me?"

Pip sat back down, the springs of the armchair creaked slightly as he did. "Charlie and I have been doing a little investigating of our own since . . . since," he paused struggling with the next few words.

"It's fine," said Will, understanding what his friend was trying to say.

Pip took a deep breath, "Since Sarah's death," he continued. "Both of us sent telegrams to every reporter we knew across the country. Charlie knew quite a lot from his days in the North West. Anyway, we asked them for any unusual stories, strange sightings, unsolved murders, vicious attacks. Basically, anything that could be reported as unexplained."

Will's brow furrowed, "Why would you do that?"

"Well," Pip settled back into the armchair, "after the funeral I got to thinking that," his voice quietened, ". . . that bastard Barr has more to do with this that anyone knows. So, Charlie and I took it in turns to follow him, him and that servant of his."

The sitting room door opened and Emily entered with a tea tray. Will pulled the small side table over, so she could place the tray between them both. "Would you boys like me to pour?"

"No, that's fine Mrs Kingsley," answered Will, "I'll let it brew for a little while."

Emily stood for a moment looking down at them, trying to gauge just what was of such importance, she wondered if Will's wanderings yesterday and the map she had found him slumped over this morning had anything to do with it. Realising that their conversation would not continue until she had vacated the room she turned, closing the door as she left.

Pip continued, "It soon became apparent that they were looking for something, my guess is the killer. They searched everywhere, at all times of day. One day Charlie seen them calling on a lot of people. Rich people, rich powerful people. He recognised some of them, so those, he followed. They started searching. Every night for a week he followed them. Nothing," Pip paused pouring himself a cup of tea.

"So," he continued, "we got to thinking that whatever they were looking for was no longer in the city, well, with what's going on at the moment I doubt they'll be here for much longer either. Anyway, that's when we came up with the idea of the telegrams. You know yourself Will, every reporter likes to tell a tall tale. If we could find some of the more . . . obscure, then we might just get a clue to where this killer is."

Pouring his own tea, Will smiled to himself, "I take it that your investigations have uncovered some clue to its whereabouts?"

"They certainly did Will." Pip took the newspaper he had slipped beside him and opening it, turned it so Will could read the front page.'

"The Liverpool Herald," Will read. He scanned the articles on the front page.

"Turn the page Will, it's on page two."

Will did as he was asked. His eyes flicked across each headline, in the bottom right quarter was the article Pip had wanted him to see.

"There Will, there," Pip's voice rose as he became more excited, "that attack mirrors the one on Lucy Strong."

"I'm reading it now Pip," Will glanced at his friend, silencing him. As he read the details of the article, it did occur to him that it was uncannily like the attack he had first reported on. Will's skin crawled as he read the final line the reporter had written.

'Springheel Jack!'

Will slumped back into the chair, "Where did they get that name from?"

Pip pulled several newspaper cuttings from his jacket pocket, "From these," he said handing them across to Will.

Taking them, he laid them on the table and spread them out. Before him lay at least twenty articles from newspapers across the country, all of which mentioned 'Springheel Jack'. Will fingered through them.

'Fifteen sheep killed when Springheel Jack dropped through the roof of their pen.'

Will picked out another,

'Two men arrested in rooftop fight. Springheel Jack caught claims one.'

Will quickly flicked through the rest of the clippings, "Do they all mention Springheel Jack?"

"They do," replied Pip, "And look," Pip chose several of the clippings, "these can be discounted really. I'm not saying that they didn't happen, it's just a matter of geography."

Will watched as Pip arranged the rest of the clippings, "What do you mean?"

"If you place these reports together starting with the earliest and nearest one to London first and the latest one at the bottom, you can see that they run both chronologically and geographically from London to Liverpool," Pip sat back smiling, "It's him Will. He's in Liverpool."

Will stared at the line of paper. It was proof indeed that the killer had moved on to another city.

"What are you going to do Will?" Pip enquired. Will sat in silence, his eyes fixed on the reports. Pip thought that maybe he hadn't heard him and was about to repeat the question when Will spoke.

"I'm going after him," he said looking up, his eyes met Pip's gaze, "I'm going to Liverpool and I'm going to find that bastard. When I do Pip, I'm going to rip its heart out."

Pip became concerned for his friend, he was beginning to realise that his actions could now lead to his friend's death, "But Will, how?"

"Train from Euston to Liverpool, then the rest will be easy," Will collected the clippings together, "may I keep these?"

Pip nodded, "Sure, But I meant how are you going to find it?"

"Barr told me that it followed a pattern. If that was true before and it was true here then I'm certain that it's going to be true there. It'll kill again and when it does . . . I'll be waiting."

"But Will," Pip began, "just look what's happened to London? Look what's it's done to this city?"

Will stood and as he walked to the door he crumpled the cuttings into his pocket, "Come now Pip, don't worry," he said opening the door, "now if you don't mind I've plenty to do."

Pip protested as Will led him to the front door, "Please Will . . . at least don't go alone."

"I'm sorry Pip," replied Will opening the door, "I have to do this. I'm not going to endanger anyone else. Please thank Charlie for all he has done."

"But Will!" Pip couldn't think of anything else to say to him.

"Don't make this harder than it is already Pip. The only way I can thank you for what you have done is to not involve you anymore than is necessary," Will closed the door.

Pip stood in the street looking back at the house. Life continued around him. The sound of the city drowned out the sound of his sobs.

Will sighed as the door closed on his friend. He really hadn't wanted to exclude Pip, but he couldn't risk taking him. He had resigned himself to the fact, that should he ever come across the killer again he would probably not live past that meeting. Also, his meagre savings wouldn't allow a companion. Will had to do this alone.

The sweet sound of Emily's voice broke his concentration. She was singing.

'Sarah used to sing so beautifully,' he thought.

Hoping Pip would have left by the time he was dressed properly and had his suitcase packed, he climbed the stairs to begin his preparations. His plans to pass on the notes and the phonographic recordings to the police had been forgotten.

Two hours later Will stood outside Euston Station. The four huge columns of the Euston Arch towered above the sea of people that passed between them. It seemed that the whole of London was planning to leave and had decided that today would be the day.

Will knew that not only were the fires still raging but they had in fact become worse, as well as the rioters and looters having kept the whole of the metropolitan police busy day and night. People were scared, people were running.

Making his way through the crowded courtyard he was shocked at the number of people crammed into the area. Street traders had set up small stalls along its length, their cries echoed from one side to the other, business flourished, as those leaving the city haggled for any meagre provision that was offered. Will ignored them and entered the main station building.

The Great Hall echoed with the sound of a thousand voices. Family's huddled together against its walls, they sat on the steps and surrounded the statue of George Stephenson, his frozen stare gazed down at the myriad of life yet unable to leave the capital.

Will sighted a ticket office and joined the queue that snaked from its window towards him and around the Great Hall. Shouts and whistles from the platforms drifted into the hall, the sound of steam forced from the engines as they built up enough power the move the overloaded trains, temporarily drowned out the cacophony of voices. Manners were forgotten as people pushed their way passed him, desperately hoping to find a space to sit whilst other family members queued for their tickets.

Eventually he reached the front of the queue and was confronted by a small man who was quite clearly harassed, "How can I help you Sir?" he offered for the thousandth time that day.

"I need to get to Liverpool," Will shouted, realising he could hardly hear the man.

"Lime St. or Exchange station Sir?"

Will thought for a moment, he hadn't realised there was a choice of destinations. '*I don't know*,' he thought. "What's the difference?"

The man sighed, "If you want Lime St. it's direct, you'd have to change locally to get to Exchange."

Will had no intention of complicating the journey, "Direct to Lime St. please."

"I can get you there First Class today or Third-Class tomorrow."

Feeling the coins in his pocket Will asked, "Is there no more Third Class today?"

"I'm sorry sir," the man answered, "We've increased Third Class travel on all services leaving Euston and they're all full, as I said, you can leave First Class today or Third-Class tomorrow," the man watched as Will thought, "Sir, you will soon lose the option to travel tomorrow if you don't decide. The trains are filling up fast."

"I'll take a Third-Class ticket for tomorrow please. Single," decided Will as he passed over payment.

"Thank you," the man said, sliding the coins into the cash drawer before slipping the ticket across to Will, "It leaves at seven thirty-five sir, platform four."

Will took the ticket and slipped it into his coat pocket.

"And Sir," the man called as Will turned to leave, "Please don't be late, we have been instructed to resell the tickets of any late passengers."

"Don't worry," Will called back, "I won't be late," he forced a smile at the man.

'I doubt I'll be leaving the station tonight,' he thought to himself scanning the hall.

The floor was littered with the bodies of those who also wouldn't leave the station. Some willing to sleep in the cold to ensure their departure, others having no choice, their homes destroyed by the fires that raged unchecked throughout the city.

Will took out his pocket watch. Nineteen hours remained until his train left. He thought about leaving the station and returning to Kingsley's.

'It would pass the time,' he mused.

However the risk of returning in the morning late, outweighed the risk of spending an uncomfortable night on the station floor. He decided to take a stroll around the area hoping that as the trains left, more people would leave the station and by evening he would be able to find a quiet spot to hunker down in. With a little luck he would be able to rent a travel blanket from the Euston WHSmith book store.

Arriving back at the station a few hours later Will became dismayed at the amount of people still waiting for their trains. They still crowded the courtyard, they still filled the Great Hall. He bought bread from one of the hawkers in the courtyard and found a small spot against the wall, getting himself as comfortable as he could he crouched down for the night.

His request for a travel blanket at the WHSmith's had been laughed at, "We aint had any of them since this 'ere fire started," he had been told.

The stone was cold against his back, but at least he could draw a little warmth and comfort from the other misfortunates that sat on either side of him. He drew his knees up to his chin and wrapped his coat around his legs. Tearing small pieces of bread from the loaf he ate and watched as those around him began to settle down.

People passed him hoping to find shelter in the Great Hall but within minutes Will observed them re-enter the courtyard, only to circle it in the vain hope that someone had missed a sheltered spot.

By midnight the station was quiet. The trains had left and those crowded into the courtyard and Great Hall were either asleep or hoping soon to be. Still awake Will studied those around him. He wondered where they were from and more importantly, where they hoped a better life would be. He thought about Sarah and the plans he had had for them both once the baby had been born. The home he wanted for them. The future they had planned.

He blew warm air into his hands before slipping them into his pockets. He doubted sleep would come, if he had just been uncomfortable and cold there would have been a chance, but his mind raced with thoughts of both his past and future.

'If,' he thought, *'he now had one.'* Snow had begun to fall during the night, Will had noticed, but as there was nothing he could do so he just watched as it settled on his knees. Soon the bodies around him all had a light covering. Some noticed and in a futile attempt, tried to cover themselves, others didn't bother.

The sounds of the station waking filled the air. Will could hear the first trains entering the station, shortly followed by shouts as passengers rushed the platforms hoping to board and get a seat. The hands of Will's pocket watch indicated that he still had two hours to wait. He had a little bread left, so he ate it before brushing the snow off to stretch his legs, his joints and muscles complained as he laid them flat. He managed to stand without disturbing his overnight companions and made his way into the hall.

As the first trains left the crowd in the hall thinned. Will managed to wash in the W.C and although the water was cold it refreshed him, helped him feel better, more alive. By the time he left the washrooms a long queue had formed outside the door. More trains entered the station, the platforms filled with passengers holding tickets. Steam warmed the air around the hall.

Making his way to the platform, Will passed the window where he had bought the ticket, the little man was still there, the same look of harassment on his face. Will smiled, showed his ticket at the barrier and entered the platform.

His train had just arrived and Will was surprised at the lack of passengers getting off. It was obvious that the city had become an unwanted destination. Pushing his way passed the carriages Will found the third-class compartment, he had been allocated a seat within and stepped aboard. Luckily for him he had only a small case and was able to find a seat by a window.

The carriage filled as people pushed their way on, bags and suitcases used as rams. The back of the carriage had quickly become a dumping ground for their belongings. Cases slung about, filled the small storage compartment and an avalanche of bags had closed off the exit. A cage containing two chickens had been balanced on top of them, it almost touched the roof.

Will sat squashed against the side wall. The seat beneath him was wooden but at least it was warmer and more comfortable than the cold stone floor he had spent the night on. The carriage was full of relieved passengers, they chatted amongst themselves anticipating their imminent departure. Will could hear the chickens clucking behind him, also relieved he imagined, that the cage they sat in, was at least now stable.

From his position he could observe the platform despatcher whistling and displaying the right away to the guard, a second whistle sounded behind him. The train lurched forward unsettling the chickens who squawked in disapproval, they then settled back as the slack between the carriages was taken up and the train slowly left the platform.

Will sighed as they passed from beneath the station roof into the clear London sky. Dawn was breaking, the sky above glowed blood red. His journey had begun, Liverpool and Springheel Jack awaited him.

Chapter 34

Will stepped off the train and onto the platform at Lime St. Station, his journey north had taken him seven hours. The snow that had begun to fall as he waited overnight in the courtyard at Euston, had continued to fall throughout the journey. Every county the train had passed through was now covered in a thick layer of snow.

As the train trundled north Will tried to keep himself to himself by re-reading the newspaper articles given to him by Pip, memorizing the details of the first of the new attacks. When he was confident he had done he watched the world pass by his window, he had even f eigned sleep when the woman next to him attempted to draw him into the conversation she had been having with her friend.

The two women had been chatting as they boarded and to the wonder of Will, had continued nonstop for over three hours before they had attempted to involve him. Luckily, he had tuned into their conversation when it was mentioned that they should, *'Ask the gentleman next to you?'* This gave him time to close his eyes in the hope that they would believe him asleep and leave him alone. It had worked, although it did mean that he had to keep up the deception for a short while.

Fortunately, the train passed roughly over a set of points and the subsequent rocking gave him the opportunity to awaken, cough and then pardon himself before shifting his body so that more of his back was facing the two women. He sat in the same position for the remainder of the journey.

His thoughts returned to Barr and his planned revenge. He cursed himself for not being able to use the items he had stolen from his house against him, but time it seemed was not on his side. Seeing as he had now left London, Will worried over how he could lure Barr to Liverpool, once he had confirmed that the killer had indeed set up residence in the city.

He toyed with the idea of sending Barr a letter containing the clippings from the Liverpool Herald, but had dismissed the plan, given the time it would take the letter to arrive. Once he had them, Barr would still have to plan and make the journey north himself. The only other way Will could think off was to telegram Barr, but without evidence he doubted that he could be convinced to come. He had to think of a way that would guarantee Barr would follow him to Liverpool.

It was another two hours before Will finally came up with the solution. Once he was happy that Barr's involvement was necessary, he would send a telegram to Charlie asking him to run a follow up article mentioning the similarity of the attack in Liverpool, to the one that had begun the series of attacks in London and to mention the reported sightings of 'Springheel Jack' between the two cities. He prayed that with luck, within a few days Barr would be making a similar journey north.

Convinced that his plan would work a smile played on Will's lips as he had stepped from the train. In the concourse he had picked up an ordnance survey map from the station WHSmith's, and with it secured in his pocket made his way down the steps to the line of Hansom's waiting along the station front.

Behind them stood the impressive St. George's Hall. Will wondered at its construction and neoclassical style. He promised himself that during his stay, if he could find time to wander through its columns he would. The rest of the city was lost behind a thick snowfall, the nearest buildings, mere silhouettes.

Pulling his collar tight around his neck Will approached the cabby at the front of the line. "I need to find a guesthouse in Everton. Do you know one?" he asked.

Lifting his hat, the cabby stared down at Will, "Everton?" he asked.

Will nodded, "I have a map if that helps."

The cabby laughed, brushing snow from his shoulders, "No, you're alright Sir. I think I know of one that'll suit you. Climb in."

Will did as he was told, grateful to be out of the cold.

"There's one on Everton Brow," the cabby continued, "the Cox's run it, friends of mine." Will closed the door. The cabby continued to talk as he snapped the reigns and pulling the horse to the right he turned the cab, "I sometimes drink in the same boozer as Mathew, he owns the hotel."

Will stared out of the window as he passed closer to St. George's and the Walker Art Gallery, eventually he turned off to the sound of the cabby's voice. "Anyway, I goes drinking in The Fleet on occasion, that's his local, he's quite a character." The cab jerked as the horse lost its footing in the slushy snow, "Whoa lass," he called to the horse, "You ain't half picked a bad time to visit Sir . . ." he shouted back, but Will had finished listening.

The ride to the Cox's hotel had taken thirty minutes. Will thanked the cabby as he passed payment over to him. Without waiting for any acknowledgement, he turned and opened the front door of 'The Brow', the hotel the cabby had brought him to.

The décor inside couldn't have been more of a contrast to the weather Will had just left. The small reception was bright and airy. Will brushed a small amount of snow from his coat and approached the reception.

Picking up a small sign from the desk, he read, *'Please ring for attention,'* his hand hovered over the bell positioned next to the card when a voice drifted from the sitting room behind him.

"Won't be a moment," it said.

Turning in the direction of the voice, Will was surprised as a young woman entered the reception area. "Sorry about that," she apologised, straightening her apron, "I was just plumping up the cushions."

Once around the other side of the reception desk the woman took the ledger from a small shelf hidden from view, as she opened it her face lit up with a wide smile, "Now Sir, how can I help you?"

Will smiled back, he decided that he already liked the place, "Good afternoon, my name is William English, I'd like a room if you have one," he asked, "the cabby that brought me from Lime St. said you may be able to accommodate me?"

"Pleased to meet you Mr English, I'm Jean Cox," she said, flicking the open page of the ledger back and forth. It was all for show, the hotel had only one guest staying with them. "How long would you be wanting it for Sir?"

"I'm hoping to stay no more than a week, but it may stretch to two," Will smiled.

"That's fine, I can leave it open but I'll have to take a pound as deposit," said Jean, she could see Will weighing her suggestion up, "you get back the difference when you leave."

"Yes, that will be fine. Thank you," Will took out his wallet and placed a pound note on the ledger.

Jean picked up the note and slipped it into the front of her apron. She turned the ledger to face Will, "If you could just sign in? I'll sort you out a room," she asked.

Will signed his name, as Jean retrieved a key from the board behind her. "I'll put you in the top room Mr. English, the view from there is the best in the hotel," she giggled, "well, it would be if it wasn't for this weather. Now if you'd just follow me I'll show you the way."

Taking his case, Will followed her up the stairs.

After four flights Jean finally stopped and waited for Will to join her, the small landing had only one door. "This is your room," she said, unlocking it. As Will entered the room he smiled, pleased that his room was similar to the rest of the house, clean and bright. Placing his case on the bed he crossed over to the window.

Just as she had said,' he smiled, *'It would have been a great view if it wasn't for the weather.'*

"Breakfast is at eight am, dinner is at seven pm. If you won't be joining us please let me know the day before," said Jean, placing the room key on the dresser, "I'll leave your key here Mr. English."

Will thanked her as he took the map he had bought from his pocket. "I wonder if you could point out the location of 'Prince Edwin Lane' on this map?" he asked unfolding it

Jean took the map from him, "How about I take the map and mark out the Lane for you whilst you freshen up?" she smiled, "I'll leave it in reception, you can pick it up when you're ready."

"That would be most appreciated," Will answered, "thank you."

Chapter 35

As promised the map was lying on the desk at reception. Jean had neatly marked out the location Will had asked for and had even drawn the quickest route from the hotel via Watmough Street and an easier, longer route via Netherfield Road. Will hadn't really wanted to return to the bad weather, but the sooner he had concrete proof that the attacks had started again, the sooner he could get his plan in action.

As he stepped out into the cold, he realised how late the day had become. The sky that had been grey and full of snow when he had arrived, was now a lot darker. Snow still fell heavily and the glow of the recently lit gas lamps coloured it a dirty yellow.

Lifting up the folded map Will confirmed that the street across to his right was Watmough Street, he decided that the shorter route would be more sheltered so crossing the road he made his way into the quiet street.

It was a lot narrower than Everton Brow and the snow seemed to fall more slowly now it was sheltered from the wind. Will walked quickly passed the terraced houses hiding his face from the weather. At the end of the street he crossed diagonally to the left and entered a small alleyway. Hardly any snow had settled between the yard walls. Though the map showed the alley to be straight, Will couldn't see to the other end, with his hands pressed firmly into his pockets he quickened his pace.

Once his eyes had adjusted to the darkness he could make out piles of rubbish that had been left on either side, he skirted them being careful not to step into any. His nose told him that it would be better if the rubbish was left undisturbed. He imagined large rats scurrying ahead of him searching for some choice pieces amongst the detritus, their oil drop eyes staring up at him from the safety of the darkness as he passed by.

Gradually he began to perceive the end of the alley and the light of the street ahead. Exiting, he found himself standing back in the falling snow, the wind howled past him. Prince Edwin Lane disappeared into the weather in both directions.

The article that Will had read didn't mention the exact address of the victim, only the street she had lived on. Wondering what he should do, he stepped out of the snow and back into the alley, taking the map from his pocket Will studied the street he stood on. It seemed to him that the shortest distance to the end of the street lay to his right. He reasoned that if there was a public house anywhere in the area, it would almost certainly be on a corner, the corner of Prince Edwin Lane and Netherfied

Road was the nearest to where he now stood. Will left the alley and turned right.

His decision paid off. Not only was the snow at his back as he walked towards the corner, it wasn't long before he spied the unmistakable lights emanating from the windows of a pub. Crossing the street Will stood for a moment in the warm glow cast by its lights. The pub was called 'The Prince', Will smiled at the obviousness of its name. Kicking the snow from his boots he opened the door and entered.

The interior was warm and light. Several people stood at the bar in quiet conversation. Will could hear laughter from a room to his left. Taking off his overcoat, he hung it on a coat hook and crossed the short distance to the bar where he ordered a drink.

"What brings you up here?" asked the barman as he poured Will's pint.

Will stared at the man bemused.

"Your accent," laughed the barman, "It's not local." He placed the glass on the bar before Will and smiled, "I mean we always gets foreigners in here, what with the docks and that. But they're usually here from another country. You're from down south, very unusual to get southerners in here," the barman rubbed his chin, thinking, "let me guess. You must have come up on the train. And it must be something important."

Will laughed as he passed payment over, "Brilliantly deduced. But why would you say that it's something important?"

"Look at the weather!" the barman said as he placed the coin into his apron pocket, "It would have to be something pretty important to get me out travelling in this."

A voice from the other end of the bar beckoned the barman, he thanked Will and turned away. Will raised the glass to his lips and drank half the pint in one go, he then watched the barman as he served another customer.

Once he had finished, he returned to Will, "You're right," he said, "I am from the south, London to be precise and it is something important. Something in fact, that I think you may be able to help me with."

"How could I help you?" the barman asked, leaning closer.

Will also leant on the bar. He spoke quietly, "I'm a reporter for a London newspaper and I've followed a story I've been reporting on up here, to Liverpool."

The barman's eyes widened as Will spoke, "What is it? What you following?" he asked lowering his voice.

"I read," continued Will, "that a few nights ago there was an attack in this very street. An attack that left the victim in an extremely distraught state." Will looked around him at the other occupants of the bar, "And it's really important that I speak to her and her family."

The barman stood straight up and leaning back began to laugh heartily. His reaction caused Will's heart to jump in his chest. "You mean Florry?" laughed the barman, "that's no secret, it happened just down the road from here. Her fella told me he nearly caught him. They live on Ebor Street, it's the first one you come to as you walk along Prince Edwin," he said turning to speak to a man who stood leaning on the bar a few feet away, "hey Jim, what number do Mick and Florry live at, is it number nine?"

The man paused, holding his glass to his lips thinking, "Yeah, I think it is."

The barman's gaze returned to Will, "Definitely number nine. Caused a right commotion that did. People out all night looking for the bleeder. Never seen hide nor hair of him though. Was in the papers alright, read it myself."

"I read it to," said Will, "that's why I made the journey up here."

"Well that's where you'll find them, out the door, turn right and stay on this side. Like I said, first street you come to." The barman was again beckoned by another of his customers. Will finished his drink and took his coat from the hook as he left the pub.

The weather had not changed, Will walked head down into the oncoming snow. He passed a number of small alleyways before reaching his destination. As the barman had stated, Ebor Street was the first street he had come to. It was a dead end with only a few houses on each side. As he walked down Will looked for number nine. It was the last house on the opposite side. Crossing over to it, Will knocked on the door.

After waiting a few moments, he knocked again, still no one answered. Frustrated Will tried the door handle. It turned easily and the door opened. "Hello," he shouted into the darkened hallway, "Is anyone in?" cautiously Will stepped into the house, "hello?"

Suddenly the door at the end of the hallway burst open and a woman stumbled towards him. Seeing she had been bound and gagged Will rushed forward lifting the woman to her feet and removing the gag.

"He's here!" she screamed, "he's here! I've seen him!"

"Who's here?" Will shouted at her, "who?"

The woman's eyes flick around the hallway, "I've seen him," she screamed again, "he's coming for us all!"

Will became aware of heavy footsteps running down the stairs, "Ere," a man's voice shouted, "who are you?" reaching the foot of the stairs the man turned towards Will, "what are you doing in my house?"

"I'm a reporter," answered Will but was cut short as another voice sounded from above.

"Mick," a woman's voice shouted, "Mick, what's going on?" moments later she too joined the man at the foot of the stairs.

"My name is William English," Will shouted, struggling to be heard over the screams of the bound woman, "I'm here to help. I know what's going on."

Turning, the man spoke to his companion at the foot of the stairs, "Take Florry back into the kitchen, will you?" he asked. The woman past by Will and ushered the screaming woman back through the doorway and into the room from which she had come.

"Thank you," said Will, "as I said, my name's William English and I'm here to help."

The man eyed Will up and down, "How?" he asked.

After an hour Will was back in the snow. He had told the man, whom he found out was the husband everything that had and still was happening in London, everything he himself had witnessed. The man had listened without commenting on anything he said. He then told Will what had happened to his wife. How he had heard her screams and had ran out into the street just as the attacker had leapt to the rooftops. Thinking fast, he had given chase and had managed to keep the attacker in sight as he leapt from one side of Prince Edwin Lane to the other. He had followed him as far as the Hay Market but because of the size of the building, he had lost sight of him. By the time he had returned to his wife, Florence was hysterical, screaming, just as Will had seen her. He had called on her sister, Shirley to help and since then they had kept her tied up and gagged.

Will told him that unfortunately there was little they could do for his wife and that the best advice he could give, was for them to admit her to a mental hospital. Thanking the man for his time Will left and made his way down the street to see the Hay Market building himself, it was the last sighting of 'Springheel Jack' before he had made good his escape.

As the man had said, the Hay Market building was huge. Will walked its circumference. Half of it was hidden by alleyways, Will could see how easily it would be for the Beast to disappear. He was certain that the attacks were beginning again and that he could now set his plan for revenge upon Barr, in motion.

Making his way back through the streets to his hotel, Will decided that he would make his way to the telegraph office at Lime St. Station first thing in the morning.

Chapter 36

The Beast leapt across the gap between the rooftops. It had become curious about the sound coming from a large structure built onto the roof opposite. Crouching at the front of the structure, it stared into the darkness.

From behind the metal wire it could hear the faint cooing from the birds within. It ran its fingers gently across the mesh before violently sweeping its arm back, it cut through both the cage and the birds. Feeling their warm blood on its skin it lifted its hand to its face and licked at the liquid.

Joan Jenkins woke suddenly and placed her had into the space next to her that her husband should have been occupying. The sheets were still warm. "Thomas?" she called into the darkness.

"Shhh," replied Thomas, lighting a match.

The glare of the flame blinded her, she raised her hand over her eyes as he lit a candle. "What are you doing?" she whispered.

"There's someone on the roof," he answered, pointing up.

The room they had rented had been at the top of the house, in the attic. That had suited Thomas, he had always kept pigeons and now that they had space he could move his coop on to the rooftop.

The landlord had given him permission to build an access hatch to the roof, he now stood underneath it holding a candle with his foot on the first rung of the ladder.

"Someone's after me pigeons," he told his wife.

Joan turned over and covered herself with the blanket, "Why would someone be after your stupid birds in the middle of the night?"

"Prize racing pigeons these," said Thomas climbing the ladder, "you go back to sleep, I won't be a minute."

Thomas pushed up on the roof hatch as he climbed the ladder. Looking up into the darkness he stood listening for any sound from above, large snowflakes melted as they fell on his upturned face.

"Hurry up," Joan shouted from under the blankets, "It's bloody freezing."

Holding the candle close to his face Thomas turned towards the bed, "Shhh, woman. He might still be up there."

Thomas looked back towards the darkness, the Beast's long arm reached down, and with its long-emaciated fingers it encompassed his head. Lifting him clear of the ladder it twisted its hand, Thomas' neck snapped, the sound lost to the wind.

It released its grip and let Thomas drop into the room.

The limp body dropped on to the ladder, his leg slipped between two rungs flipping him over, Thomas ended his life with his head bent backward, one leg stuck fast between the rungs of the ladder the second hanging free, his foot pointing across the room to the bed where his wife lay.

Pulling back the blankets Joan leapt out of bed, knowing her husband had fallen, "Tom?" she cried into the darkness, "Tom, what's happened?"

She lit the candle on her side of the bed and cautiously took a step towards the ladder. A slight breeze brought snow in through the open hatch, Joan protected the flickering flame with her hand.

In the dim light she could see the crumpled body of her husband at the foot of the ladder, snow was beginning to settle on his nightshirt.

"Thomas?" she whispered as she walked towards him, "please Thomas, answer me." Subconsciously she realised that her husband was dead and began to cry, "Oh Thomas, please, please say something."

Kneeling at his side she found herself holding her hand over her mouth stifling a scream. In the candlelight his dead eyes stared up at her.

The Beast slipped its torso through the hatch, its long arms gripping the ladder below, holding it above the weeping woman. Its neck stretched down towards her, its wet black slimy hair hung above the woman's head hiding its face from her.

Realising that she could no longer feel the cold breeze against her skin Joan turned her head to see what had blocked the hatch. The Beasts face hung above her, its mouth open, saliva dripping from its extended tongue.

Screaming, Joan collapsed onto the floor, without looking away from its hideous face she crawled backwards towards the door, her feet struggled to purchase on the now wet wooden floor. From below she could hear the sound of doors slamming and footsteps on the stairs.

Bob and Molly Castle had been sleeping soundly when they had been woken by the sound of Thomas' body hitting the floor above them. Bob had climbed out of bed and was just lifting his braces over his shoulders when both he and his wife had heard Joan's first scream. "Come on Bob," Molly shouted to him, "go and see what's going on."

Molly stood at the door to their room watching Bob as he reached the door to the room above them. "Joan," he called, knocking on the door, "Joan, Tom . . ."

Joan's scream silenced him. He pushed against the door, it opened slightly, Bob put his shoulder against it and pushed harder, something was against the door.

Joan watched, her back against the door as the Beast climbed down the ladder and into the room. She heard the knocking and felt the door move against her back but was hypnotised by the spider like movement of her husband's murderer.

Bob again pushed at the door, it opened a little more. "Joan," he shouted through the gap, "Joan, I can't open the door, what's in front of it?" Suddenly the door opened and Bob stumbled into the room.

Joan realised she was against the door and pushing her back against it she shifted to the side. The Beast was almost upon her. With her weight now gone the door opened and her neighbour stumbled into the room, his back facing her.

She watched as the Beast rose above him. Seizing her chance, she threw herself at the open door and ran down the stairs.

Bob stood looking up at the Beast, his mouth dropped open. His mind struggled to comprehend just what stood in front of him. It lifted its arm, Bob followed its hand as it did. He blinked as its arm fell, by the time he had opened his eyes again, its hand was below him. Blood covered its broken talons.

Bob's chin rested on his chest looking down at his shattered ripped body, he died without any realisation of what had happened to him. In the time it had taken for him to blink, the Beast had sliced through his face and into his chest with such force, that not only had Bob's ribs been shattered, his heart and lungs had also been ripped through. He felt no pain as he dropped to his knees falling forward onto the cold wooden floor.

Reaching the bottom of the stairs, Joan had pushed Molly aside when she had stepped out of her doorway to see if she could help.

"What's wrong Joan?" she called after her as Joan ran for the second set of stairs, "where's Bob?" she asked. Realising she was not going to get an answer from her Molly stepped towards the stairs Joan had just run down.

The Beast filled the stairwell with its body, the plaster crumbled from the walls and ceiling as it clambered through the house after its prey. Falling back against the wall Molly held out her hands before her, hoping to defend herself she reached out towards the Beast. It bit down hard on her left hand severing it at the wrist, its strong fingers slipped into Molly's stomach, her soft flesh opened easily. As it turned to follow Joan it lifted Molly crushing her against the ceiling above. She slipped from its grip as it passed, like her husband she fell to the floor dead.

Reaching the ground floor, Joan had run into the two tenants who rented the two single rooms on the ground floor. Both Carter and Jacob were dressed and standing in the hallway. "Joan, what's going on?" asked Carter. He gripped her arms preventing her from passing him and side stepped her into his room.

Hearing the noise above Jacob stepped onto the stairs straining his neck to see if he could glimpse something of the commotion above. "You look after Joan," he called back, "I'll take a look upstairs."

Carter agreed and closed the door to his room. He shook Joan, "Come on Joan," he shouted at her, "tell me what happened?"

Joan looked at Carter and screamed.

Looking back when he heard the scream, Jacob considered returning to his room and closing his door until the house had become quiet once again.

The Beast halted behind Jacob as he stood pondering his actions, before he had chance to turn his head back it had gripped his shoulder and with its free hand ripped his head from his neck. Stepping over the dead body it paused at the bottom of the stairs. It could sense her nearby, could smell her fear.

Carter let his grip loosen on Joan's arms when he became aware of the silence outside his door. Shaking herself free from him, she stepped back into the corner of the room. "It's out there!" she cried, "It's out there!"

"Shhh," whispered Carter, "It might have gone." He tip toed over to the door and pressed his ear to the wood.

After a moment of listening he quietly gripped the door handle and began to turn it.

"Please don't," Joan pleaded with him.

"It'll be alright," Carter promised her, as the door exploded next to his face.

The Beasts fingers surrounded Carter's head, pulling him towards the hole it had made.

Joan watched as Carter's head disappeared through the hole, his feet lifting from the floor. He jerked up and down as his head was forced against the splintered wood cutting into his throat. Blood poured down the inside of the door discolouring the peeling paint. Joan cowered watching, tears streamed down her face.

Carter's body dropped to the floor, the Beast pushed his head back into the room, it rolled across the floor to where Joan sat. She screamed.

The Beast burst through the door, shattering it. It stood before her, its black skin glistening in the lamplight. In its right hand it still held Jacob's severed head. It threw it at her.

Joan screamed again as Jacob's head landed in her lap next to Carter's.

From outside she could now hear the shouts of neighbours attracted by the commotion. The Beast enveloped her with its body, its hot stinking breath on her face. It breathed heavily, its chest expanded unnaturally, blue flame played on its lips. Joan looked up at it, no longer screaming, no longer crying, her mind lost.

It forced its fingers into her chest snapping her ribcage. Joan's eyes closed as she slipped away. The Beast gripped her heart and ripped it out.

The front door of the house opened and a small crowd pushed into the hallway. Turning towards the noise the Beast left the room confronting the crowd.

"It's Springheel Jack!" screamed one woman.

The Beast bit into Joan's heart before throwing it at the face of the man nearest, it hit him hard breaking his nose. Screaming he turned and blindly ran into the people now crowding the small hallway behind him. The Beast leapt up the stairs and was gone.

The crowd returned screaming to the street calling for the police. None had any idea that six people lay slaughtered in the house behind them.

Chapter 37

Will slept well, he had returned to the hotel cold and wet but Mrs Cox had still been up and she provided him with both warm water to wash in and a warm supper. He had gone to bed smiling, knowing that his planned revenge on Barr was about to begin.

Looking out from his window the next morning Will could now see the view Mrs Cox had mentioned when he had arrived. It was, as she said, a good view over the city, now that the snow had ceased to fall, he could see the owering masts from the ships moored at the docks in the distance. Smoke drifted from chimneys into the cold air, gulls cried looking for food, which reminded Will that he was hungry. Dressing, he left his room and descended the stairs to the dining room.

Two tables had been set out for breakfast, one was already occupied by a portly red-faced gentleman. Will nodded as he entered, "Morning."

The man looked up from his paper, "Good morning, I'm Mr. Parry," he said holding out his hand, "you must have arrived yesterday."

"Yes, I did," answered Will shaking Parry's hand, "my name is William English."

Parry smiled momentarily before something behind Will caught his attention, "Ah, breakfast has arrived."

Will turned as Mrs Cox entered the room carrying a small tray, "Oh, I see you two gentlemen have met." she said, setting the tray on the table behind Will. Taking the plate and teapot, she placed them in front of a smiling Mr. Parry.

"Oh, I do enjoy your breakfast Mrs Cox," said Parry pouring his tea.

"If you take a seat Mr. English I'll have yours here in a jiffy," said Jean, as she picked up the empty tray and left the room.

Will pulled out the chair from the only other made up table and sat, "Excuse me Mr. Parry," he asked, "do you know the quickest way from here to Lime St.?"

"Your best bet," answered Parry, chewing on a full mouth of sausage, "Is to walk down to St. Anne's, at the end of the Brow," he paused, cutting another piece of meat, "from there you can catch a tram to the station."

Thanking him, Will patiently waited for his breakfast to arrive. Parry returned to his newspaper.

Will had taken Parry's advice and caught the tram from St Anne's, although it was cold he had decided to sit on the open top deck. It was a beautiful morning; the sun was shining and the sky was blue. Not even the smoke billowing from the chimneys could change Will's perception of the day.

Before leaving the hotel, Will had written out his telegram to Charlie, once sent he planned to spend the day as he had promised himself, looking around St. George's and the Walker Art Gallery, if he had time he would also take in the Public Library and Museum.

Leaving the tram at Lime St., Will walked past the huge façade of the North Western Hotel and entered the station.

Like all main stations, Lime St. was busy. Will looked around for the sign of the Telegraph Office, eventually spying it in the corner next to the Left Luggage Office.

"I'd like to send this to the offices of the London Evening Star please," he said handing over the message he had written to the clerk.

"Will there be a reply?" the clerk asked.

"No," Will answered, "No reply."

"That'll be just a penny please then Sir."

Will paid the clerk and left the office. He had an overwhelming feeling that the day was only going to get better.

That feeling began to slip away from him as the news boys calls drifted to him over the crowded station.

"Springheel Jack attack," the boy nearest him shouted, "Six dead!"

Will's heart sank, he hadn't realised that an attack would to take place so soon after the first. He had been so happy when his suspicions had been confirmed and that his plan of revenge could proceed, that he had completely forgotten about the pattern the killings would take.

He pushed his way through the crowd gathering around one of the sellers and bought a paper. The headline of the Liverpool Daily Post read the same as the boy's cries 'Springheel Jack Kills Six'. Leaning against a wall near the station entrance, Will read the article.

It listed the names of the six victims, four male and two female. Will knew, that at least one of them would have had their heart ripped out, although the newspaper hadn't reported the details of exactly how the victims had met their end. It did report that the bodies had been taken from the scene in Sun Street, to the morgue of the Royal Infirmary a few streets away.

Will Approached one of the uniformed station staff, "Excuse me," he asked, "could you direct me to the Royal Infirmary?"

"Certainly Sir," he answered, "If you turn right out of the station and follow the tramway up London Road you'll get to Pembroke Place where the tramway forks, stay right and you'll come to the Infirmary."

Thanking the man Will left the station. He hadn't wanted to ask for directions directly to Sun Street, fearing that the man might take him for a morbid onlooker and refuse his request. This way he could get to within a few streets away. Once there he knew that finding the street would be easy. During his time with the paper he had come to realise that people always flocked towards death and destruction. He would just follow them.

Chapter 38

Will's plan to spend the day admiring the sights of the city had fallen by the wayside. As he suspected he had no trouble in finding the sight of the murders. A crowd gathered at both ends of the small street and was being held back by the local police. Will could see both officers and detectives as they entered and exited the building. Police stood in doorways on both sides of the street taking statements from the residents.

The crowd around him buzzed with tales of 'Springheel Jack's' actions and the state of the victims. One woman stood in the middle of her own small crowd, conveying to them with great delight and detail, the sights she had witnessed when the bodies had been brought out. All those around her stood silent, transfixed by every word she uttered.

Will made as many notes as he could before he left the area. Having left his map in his room, he wished to return to the hotel, now he knew the locations of two attacks, he hoped he may be able to glean something from they're position on the map.

Staring at the marks he had made on the map Will realised that they really meant nothing to him, he had no idea where the next attack could take place. With his finger he traced the lines of a cross, then realised that the same lines could be drawn in the opposite direction and again in another two directions. The possibilities seemed endless.

Will was becoming angry.

'How had Barr Known?' he thought, *'how did he make the connection?'* Throwing the map and his notes against the wall Will left the hotel furious with himself. Barr's knowledge of the locations eventually led him to thoughts of Sarah and their child.

Walking the streets around the Everton Brow, Will became lost in his own world. The positive happy mood he had left in that morning was now gone. Thoughts of his murdered wife filled his mind.

He found himself standing outside a church not far from the hotel. Carved into the masonry above the door was its name, 'Church of St Mary'. Above that the small stone figure of St. Mary with her welcoming arms open wide watched down on him. Without realising what he was doing Will opened the door and stepped inside.

The cold hit him as soon as he entered, the dim interior of the church contradicted the brightness of the world outside. Will took a few steps into the Nave before taking a seat on a pew to his right. He looked toward the stained-glass window and the image of Christ on the cross.

A voice startled him, "Now I know I haven't seen you're face before," it said. So deep in thought had Will been that he hadn't noticed he had company, "I'm Father Miln," the voice continued.

"Sorry, I didn't see you," answered Will shaking the thoughts from his mind, "I was looking at that," he said pointing towards the window.

"Yes, it is beautiful," stated Father Miln, "I often find myself looking at it. Still, I must get on," he touched Will's shoulder, "just thought I'd say hello."

Will smiled up at the Father, "Please, won't you stay for a moment. I'd be glad of the company," he said, sliding along the pew a few feet creating space for the Father to sit.

"Is there something wrong?" he enquired, sitting next to Will, "you do look troubled."

Placing his head in his hands Will began to cry, "I am troubled Father," he sobbed, "my wife and child have been taken from me."

"And you're still mourning them?" asked Father Miln, placing his hand on Will's shoulder.

"Yes . . . No . . ." replied Will, "I don't know Father. I feel lost."

"The grieving process can be very long. People deal with it in different ways," said the Father, speaking softly, "I'm sure that your faith in God . . ."

"I'm sorry Father, but I'm no longer a believer in God," said Will, cutting Father Miln off mid-sentence, "I've experienced things that have taken my faith from me."

"Then there must be something that you are comforted by my son."

"There was Father," said Will lifting his head, "But she was taken from me."

"And you blame God?" questioned the Father.

Will stood and taking the newspaper from his pocket slammed it down next to Father Miln. "No," he shouted, "I blame this. I blame this . . . this . . . murdering Springheel Jack."

Father Miln picked up the newspaper as Will slumped back down on the pew sobbing. "I'm sorry but I don't understand." he said reading the headline.

"Do you believe in chaos Father?" asked Will, "I mean chaos as a tangible thing, something that exists."

Folding the newspaper, Father Miln placed it between them, "I believe that chaos could exist in the hearts and minds of men because of an absence of God."

"No," shouted Will angrily, "I don't mean in a spiritual sense. I mean this," he said, picking up the paper, "this . . . this is chaos. This killer is chaos."

Seeing Will's anger, Father Miln stood up and took a step away from the pew.

"It took my wife Father," shouted Will, "It took my unborn child."

Dropping to his knees Will gripped Father Miln's robes, "Please Sir, let me go. You're still grieving for the death of your wife. You need help."

"Then help me," Will pleaded, tears running down his face, "you and the church can help me."

"I'm sorry but the help you need is medical not spiritual," said Father Miln pulling his robe free from Will's grip before stepping out of his reach. "If you don't mind, I'd like you to leave now."

"But I need help!" cried Will.

"That I believe, but if you don't leave now I'll call for the police."

Leaving Will kneeling on the floor, Father Miln walked to the back of the church and opened the door. Holding onto the back of the pew, Will stood and slowly walked towards the open door. As he left the nave, he turned to the crucified image of Christ portrayed in the stained-glass window, "Who will give me the strength to see this through?" he asked it.

Chapter 39

Clay opened the door to Barr's bedroom and entered, "Sir, I think you should read this." he said, placing the London Evening Star on the bed next to Barr, he opened the drapes that surround the four poster. "It's a special edition printed this morning."

Taking the newspaper, Barr began to read, "so, it seems our reporter has indeed found Erebus. Has this been confirmed?"

"Confirmation is irrelevant Sir," answered Clay from the window, staring at the red glow that illuminated the horizon over the houses opposite, "there have been a number of developments overnight that have facilitated our need to leave London."

Barr looked up from the paper concerned, "Such as?" he asked.

"This morning I was visited by the Governor of the Bank of England . . ."

"How is William?" interrupted Barr.

"Worried," Clay answered turning from the window, "by Friday the bank and all its assets will have left London, he wouldn't say to where. He has already met with the heads of other banks and if they themselves haven't already begun to move their bullion, they soon will be."

Folding the newspaper Barr placed it next to him on the bed, "What's brought this on?"

"The Governor has been advised that the fires can no longer be held from the financial district," explained Clay, "they have already spread along the south bank towards Waterloo. All the bridges east of Westminster have been closed to traffic and are now manned day and night by fire watches. He spoke to the Prime Minister last night and was told in confidence that Parliament is in the process of moving north, Manchester maybe. The city is lost Sir."

"Well this is indeed a timely coincidence," said Barr holding up the newspaper, "what has been done about this news?"

"I have sent Mark to Euston," replied Clay, "He has a letter addressed to one of our followers at the station. This afternoon one of the Royal Carriages will be attached to the Euston to Liverpool service leaving at 13.30, provisions will be made for us to be on it."

"And just what will the Palace have to say about that?" asked Barr, pulling the blankets back as he rose from his bed.

"The Royal Family have already left Sir," Clay answered smiling.

"But the Standard still fly's over the Palace!" said Barr shocked by Clay's revelation.

"A ruse, they are in Balmoral and have been for some time now," Clay opened the door to Barr's private bathroom and entered, filling the sink with water. "A decision was made once it was apparent that the safety of the Royal Family could be compromised. The Queen and immediate family members were moved quietly north whilst the everyday duties of the Palace continued as normal. Or should I say they seemed to continue as normal."

Scooping water with his hands Barr washed his face, "Do we know where in Liverpool Mr. English resides?" he asked, drying his face.

"I'm afraid not," answered Clay from the bedroom as he lay a suit on the bed, taking a suitcase he began to pack the case for Barr, "I suspect he's been there a few days at least."

Throwing the wet towel to the floor Barr returned to his bedroom. Seeing the distant sky glowing red, he paused at the window, "I never thought we would have to abandon the capital. Have I been so blinded by obsession that I have neglected to see the things around me? Erebus has indeed caused chaos, could he really be the harbinger of doom?"

Clay new that his master had indeed been obsessed with his search for the Beast. But as his servant he knew when his tongue should be silent. "What extra items do we need to take with us?" he asked. Having packed Barr's case, he was now standing with it in the doorway.

"Just the mask." Barr answered. "As long as we get that on him we won't need anything else."

Twenty minutes later Barr sat at his dining table eating breakfast. Once it had been served, Clay had left to pack his own case, once that was done he placed it alongside Barr's in the hallway and made his way downstairs to Barr's private study to retrieve the mask.

Barr had had it cleaned and repaired and it was as strong now as it had been when the Priest had first used it.

Finishing his meal, Barr crossed the hallway to his Library and searched through his notes for the incantations he had copied from the Parish records. He had included many of his own phrases that he hoped would prevent the Beast from finally being entombed by the earth and would instead help him take control of it. The rite still had to be performed on holy ground, so it was imperative that as soon as they arrived he calculate the locations and find a suitable church nearby.

The door opened and Clay entered the room, "Mark has returned Sir and he has been assured that the carriage will be waiting for us at 13.30."

"Excellent," Barr answered without looking up from his notes, "have him call two Hansom's and instruct one to wait outside until we are ready. The second I want you to take and make your way to the offices of the Star, see if you can persuade them to tell you where English is staying. I want you to send Mark to the Telegraph office. Once there I want him to send this message to the Liverpool Herald, I'm asking if they have any more information on their Springheel Jack. Make sure he waits for a response"

"Very good Sir," said Clay taking the note, once folded he placed it in his pocket, as he left he closed the Library door.

"Oh, and Clay," shouted Barr.

"Yes Sir," answered Clay opening the door again.

"Ensure that the cabby knows he may be waiting here some time," he continued, "there's much we hope to accomplish before we leave and I'd prefer he was here when we needed him, rather than you searching for one when we have less time."

The cabby sat in the cold wishing that he hadn't taken what seemed like the easy option. At first, he was pleased with the fare to Euston but he had now been sat outside Barr's house for over an hour and wished he had taken the other fare they had offered, the one into London. He had been promised to be paid well for his time, but now that the cold had reached his joints and the pain had begun, he questioned just how much it was worth.

Clay had offered the cabbies a choice of fares and when the first had jumped at the chance to wait for a while before taking them to Euston both Mark and Clay had boarded the second. Once Mark had been dropped at the

Telegraph Office the cab then made its way across town to the offices the London Evening Star.

Fleet Street was deserted as Clay stepped from the Hansom. The Star was the only newspaper that had elected to stay. Some had made deals to print their paper alongside newspapers from outside London, others had just closed their doors hoping to ride out the storm.

Kingsley sat alone in his office with his back to the door when it burst open, "Can I help you?" he asked turning his chair.

"I'm sure you will," smiled Clay from the opposite side of Kingsley's desk, "I'd like to know the whereabouts of Mr. English?"

"I don't know where he is," answered Kingsley, "he was staying with me but I haven't seen hide nor hair of him in four days."

"Come, come. Let's not play this game," said Clay as he slowly moved to the side of the desk, his right fist flexing out of view, "we both know that he is in Liverpool, now I want you to tell me where he is staying."

"Liverpool!" exclaimed Kingsley, "well I never . . ."

"Look, I haven't much time so let us cut the crap," Clay closed the gap between them.

"Really, I don't know, I . . ."

Kingsley and his chair both tipped back with the force of Clay's punch. He lay on the floor still wondering what had happened when Clay knelt down beside him. Blood ran from his nose into his mouth, the editor spat it out.

Clay gripped Kingsley shirt, "As I said, I haven't got time to play these games. So, tell me where he is?"

Kingsley coughed blood and spittle onto his chin, "I told you," he said, "I don't . . ."

Clay's punch came as fast as the first, breaking Kingsley's nose, "I can only ask this question so many times before you lose consciousness, neither of us want that now answer me!"

As he stepped into the office Pip sensed that something was wrong. Hearing Clay in the editor's office, he ran into the room just in time to see Clay's second punch land, "Stop it!" he cried, gripping Clay's coat pulling him away from Kingsley, "he doesn't know anything."

Clay released his grip allowing Kingsley's head to drop to the floor, "Ah," he said turning towards Pip, "someone else to question."

Pip was shocked at the murderous look in Clay's eyes, he turned to run. "Where are you going?" said Clay, and pushed out at Pip's back as he ran.

Pip stumbled forward off balance and fell against the office door. He lifted himself up trying to scramble out of the room, but Clay was above him. He punched down on him twice, once in each side. Winded, Pip fell back to the floor. "Now," said clay turning Pip over, he held his throat, "where's English?"

"Let me go!" Pip shouted, "let me go!"

"When you tell me where he is!"

"Why?" asked Pip.

Clay punched Pip in the face, "I'm asking the questions."

Shaking his head clear he looked up at Clay, his fist hovered next to his face preparing to punch again, "He's in Liverpool."

"I know that," spat Clay, "but where?"

"Truly we don't know," Pip swallowed, the copper taste of his own blood filled his mouth. "The article I gave him had the name of the street where the attack took place, I imagine he's staying somewhere near," Clay lowered his fist, "It's all in the special edition you bought this morning."

"How do you know I bought a paper this morning?" asked Clay.

Pip swallowed, again tasting copper, "we only printed ten copies, I paid a boy to sell them near your home, he was told to ensure you got one." Clay lifted his fist, "It was Will's idea," Pip blurted out, "he wants you up there, in Liverpool."

Clay thought for a moment before he released his grip on Pip's throat. He rose and stepped over him, leaving the office, "Clean yourselves up," he shouted back, "you both look a mess."

Pip watched him leave before turning his head towards Kingsley. The editor had managed to stand with the aid of his desk. Blood ran from his face staining his white shirt, "What did you do Pip?" he asked.

"I'm sorry Sir," he replied, tears ran down his cheeks mixing with the blood, "It was Will's idea, he wants Barr. I think he's going to kill him."

Clay looked himself over before leaving the building, he didn't want to attract any attention from the police that patrolled the area. This near to the riots it would be easy for anyone to take him for one of them, if he was covered in blood.

'Should have instructed the cabby to wait,' he thought as he stepped into the smoke-filled London air.

Eventually he managed to stop a cab a few streets away from the Star's office. Sitting back as it set off he looked at his pocket watch, it was two hours before their train left Euston. *'It's going to be close,'* he thought.

Barr sat in the library reading as Clay arrived home, "Did you have any luck?" he asked.

"A little Sir," Clay replied, picking up the newspaper he had bought that morning, "he's staying somewhere near," he scanned the article that had been written just for them. "Prince Edwin Lane. I believe Sir, I fear that's the only clue about Mr. English we are going to get until we reach Liverpool."

"Any news from Mark?" asked Barr as he closed the book he had been reading.

"No Sir," replied Clay, he had hoped that Mark would be here to meet him with a reply to the telegram they had sent and was disappointed that he hadn't returned.

Barr pushed his chair back, "Then let us wake the cabby and make our way to Euston," he said.

Clay held Barr's coat out for him before collecting the cases, once outside he placed them in the Hansom. Barr turned looking up at his home, "Do you think we will see this place again Clay?" he asked.

"I'm sure the fires won't reach this far across the city Sir," he replied, knowing that Barr's question had referred to something more permanent.

In the days since Will had left for Liverpool, Euston Station had become twice as busy. The Hansom couldn't get near the station entrance, the two men had to struggle through the crowds of people wanting to leave the city.

"Sir," shouted Clay over the noise of the crowd, "we need to make our way to the station masters office."

Barr nodded his understanding and continued to push his way through the mass of bodies. Upon reaching the station masters office both men slipped inside. A warm fire and relative silence greeted them. "I won't be a moment," a voice called from the small room that led from the office.

Turning to Barr, Clay spoke, "I'll sort this out Sir, it won't take a moment." He then crossed to the doorway and entered the room from which the voice had called. Noticing a chair by the fireside Barr sat warming himself and waited.

A few minutes later Clay emerged from the small room followed by the station master. "Everything is arranged Sir; our friend here has acquired rooms for us at the Adelphi Hotel."

The small man pushed passed Clay forcing his hand into Barr's own, "Pleased to meet you Sir, it's a great honour to finally be of service to you," he said as he shook his hand, "I can't tell you how much this means to me Sir."

Barr looked down at the station master who seemed to be cowering slightly and looking up at him from over his spectacles, "I'm pleased that you could assist us in this most delicate circumstance." Barr smiled, "you will be rewarded tenfold for your service," he added releasing the station masters hand. "Now if you could point us in the direction of our carriage we have time to make ourselves comfortable before our journey begins."

"Certainly, this way Sir," he said opening the door. The noise of the crowd filled the room, "Follow me please."

Both Barr and Clay watched as the station master disappeared into the sea of people, his hand raised holding his hat above his head. Barr laughed as they left the room and followed him towards the platforms.

As promised one of the Royal Carriages had been coupled to the back of the Liverpool train. They had chosen one that had no livery that could indicate its royal connection and had closed the drapes on each of the platform side windows. Still, as Barr and Clay approached they could see that it was attracting attention. Passengers paused on their way to their own carriage trying to look in through the small gaps between the drapes.

The station master, who had now arrived at the carriage, gathered up the onlookers and ushered them along the platform to their own carriages. Seeing Barr approaching, he ran to the back of the carriage and held the door open for them. "This way Sir," he said, "I'm sure you will find everything to your satisfaction."

As Barr passed he dropped a gold ring into the small man's hand, the station master held it up studying it, mouth open wide. The gold ring he held surrounded a black stone. In his amazement he totally ignored Clay as he passed, closed the carriage door without acknowledgment and staggered away from the platform.

Inside, Barr made himself comfortable. The carriage had only one large seating compartment with one entrance, that door led to a narrow corridor from which you could leave the carriage in either direction. Barr sat surrounded by relative opulence, compared to any other seated passenger on the train.

Lifting the drape back slightly, he watched the crowds on the platform pass by.

"Was that necessary Sir?" asked Clay entering the room.

Barr looked over at him, "Was what necessary?"

"The ring? Why give him one?"

"Does it really matter?" smiled Barr, "If things go as planned we will take control of Erebus, London and its population will die. If we fail, London and its population will die. Let him have his brief moment of pleasure. Anyway, look what he's provided for us."

"Very well Sir, I'll ensure all doors are locked," said Clay as he exited the room. Nodding his acknowledgement Barr continued to watch the other passengers on the platform.

Mark ran as fast as he could into the crowded entrance hall at Euston Station. He had run all the way from Barr's home in Grosvenor Square when he had been told his Master had already left. It was imperative that he get the telegram he held to him.

As he had been instructed, Mark had waited at the Telegraph Office once his message had been sent, for any reply that came from the Liverpool Herald. Eventually he had been handed the reply. His heart raced as he read it. He left the office and had managed to flag down a passing

Hansom, Clay had insisted he leave him sufficient funds for his return journey.

Mark urged the cab on as it made its way through the crowded streets. Eventually it reached the square, Mark leapt from the door before it had time to stop, throwing the coins back at the cabby. Moments later he had burst through the front door only to be informed that he was too late, both Barr and Clay had left for Euston.

Seeing that the cab had turned and left the square, Mark decided that it would be quicker to run to the station rather than take time to seek out another cab to then make their way through the crowded streets.

He pushed at the people surrounding him trying desperately to get to the platform. Luckily the barrier had been left open and the crowd carried Mark onto the platform. The sound of a whistle filled the air around him. He could see the carriage Clay had organised for them at the back of the train about to leave. He pushed himself flat against a wall and used it to pass along to the buffers behind the train.

A second whistle sounded. Mark could hear the rush of steam as the train began to shift forward. He ran to the carriage banging on the window as it slowly moved along the platform.

"Mr. Barr!" he shouted, "Mr. Clay!"

The train began to pick up speed and Mark watched as it began to leave him. One window passed him as he ran, then another, soon the train would be gone and his message lost. Pumping his legs faster he shouted for his master. The train sounded its whistle and his voice was lost.

Suddenly he felt his feet lift from the ground, as he was pulled into the open back door of the carriage. Falling to the floor he looked up, Clay stood over him, "Well Mark," he said, "you do like to leave things to the last minute, don't you?"

Mark watched the platform speeding by and laughed. Clay bent and helped the young boy to his feet, "I take it you received a reply?"

"Yes Sir," Mark replied, brushing himself down and handing Clay the now crumpled telegram. Clay read it, the smile on his face slowly disappeared as he did. "You better make yourself comfortable Mark," he said, "It looks like you're coming to Liverpool."

As the train gathered speed Barr read the telegram. It was brief and concise.

SECOND ATTACK BY
'SPRINGHEEL JACK' CONFIRMED.
SIX DEAD.
NEWLY FORMED VIGILANTE GROUPS
NOW PATROL POVERTY
STRICKEN AREAS OF CITY.

Crumpling the paper Barr threw it to the floor, "That's two attacks in quick succession." he said to Clay, "and six dead!" Standing, he slid back the drapes and looked out onto the snowy rooftops of the city as the train sped them towards their destiny. "It seems that now the seeds of chaos have been sown Erebus is speeding up. If we don't catch it here . . ." Barr let the sentence fall away as they left the burning chaotic city behind them.

"We will Sir," said Clay, "I'm sure we will."

Chapter 40

Will sat in the dining room of the hotel waiting for his evening meal. He was glad that the only other guest, Mr. Parry was busy reading the evening paper. From his seat Will could easily read the headline 'Mystery of the Six Murders'. He imagined that the whole of the first few pages would have been reserved for the story.

That's what we would have done on the Star,' he thought.

"Unbelievable affair this," Parry said from behind the paper, "you're from London, what do you make of all this?" he dropped his paper down and looked over at Will.

"The murders?" asked Will confused.

"No, no," replied Parry, "the rioting in London." He folded the newspaper and placed it in front of him on the table, "Says here that there's rioting all over the city. That they have set alight the docks and warehouses and that now, most of London is burning uncontrollably."

Will sighed remembering how quickly it had all happened, "It's true," he said, "I've seen it with my own eyes . . ."

As he spoke Mrs Cox entered the room with a tray of food. Parry's attention turned to the plate she placed on the table in front of him. "Oh Mrs Cox," he said, "you've surpassed yourself once again."

Jean laughed as she left the room, "Oh you're a charmer Mr. Parry and that's no mistake," she smiled, "Yours won't be a moment Mr. English, I'll fetch it presently."

Will ate his meal in silence, he was annoyed at the way Parry's attention had turned so quickly from the serious events in London to his plate of food.

Once his plate was empty and had been taken away, Will bid Parry a good night and left the dining room. He returned to his room to retrieve both his coat and the map. He had marked on it as many locations as he could work out where the Beast could strike. He would have to be extremely lucky, if he was to stumble upon the location of the next killing, but that wasn't going to stop him trying. Picking one Will pocketed the map and left his room.

"Off out Mr. English?" Jean asked, as he neared the front door.

"What?" said Will consumed by his thoughts, "oh. Yes, I'm just going for a short walk," he replied, realising what she had asked him.

At the same moment Will stepped from his hotel and into the cold winter night, Barr, Clay and Mark emerged from Lime St. Station. "Mark, see if you can acquire a cab," Clay instructed.

Barr watched Mark approach the line of cabs in front of the entrance, "I'm not sure it's a good idea the boy being here," he said.

"I know Sir," replied Clay, "I'd rather he wasn't here either but what else could I do? He may prove useful in some way though."

"True," Barr thought for a moment, "when he returns ask him to purchase a map of the city from the stall inside the station will you, he can meet us at the Adelphi once he has it."

Barr left Clay at the top of the steps and walked towards the line of cabs. Mark was running back towards him.

"I've asked the driver to take you to the hotel Sir, he says it's not far," he said passing Barr and returning to where Clay stood.

Sitting in the cab, Barr waited patiently for Clay to join him. A few minutes later the men were on their way.

The driver hadn't lied to Mark when he had said it wasn't far to their hotel, the cab ride lasted just over five minutes. Clay took both cases and handed them to the waiting bellboy, then followed as the boy led him to the hotel reception.

Barr stood on the street as the cab pulled away. He looked up towards the rooftops, "Where are you?" he whispered to the darkness.

The Beast watched as the crowd left the building below.

Moments before, Williamson Square had been empty, it had leapt from one side to the other before resting above the huge columns of the building, from where it now watched the crowd emerge.

Once the production of 'The Tempest' had ended the Theatre Royal had emptied. People scurried out into the square before disappearing down the many streets that led from it, anxious to get home.

It watched as the last few theatre goers left the building. Sniffing at the air, it became interested in a couple that had turned right and had left the safety of the brightly lit square. Leaping to the roof above them, it scurried along the edge as the couple walked below. It could hear their conversation, it sensed the fear in them, fear that it had created. It watched as the couple were approached by a man walking towards them.

"I hope you two folks are on your way home," asked Harry Dixon. Having been a police officer for more than five years he had prided himself with the knowledge that nothing in the job could phase him, but the recent killings had made him very nervous. And he didn't like seeing people on the streets after dark.

"You don't want to be out on a cold night like this," he added, seeing how frightened the woman looked.

"No Sir," replied the man, "we're just on our way to Victoria Street to catch a tram."

The Beast stretched down over the edge sniffing the air, the woman's fear had increased. Its body shuddered with the scent of it.

It watched as the man bid the couple goodnight and continued along the street towards the square.

Samuel and Emma Rifkin linked arms once the police officer had left, "Did he alarm you dear?" he asked Emma.

"You know how frightened the reports in the newspaper have made me," she replied, "If we hadn't already bought the tickets, I wouldn't have agreed to come into town."

"I know my love," Samuel comforted her, "But it was an excellent production."

"Oh, it was Samuel," she agreed.

"And we're only a few streets away from the tram," he pulled her arm tightly against his side, "we'll be home before you know it," he said smiling at her.

Crossing Whitechapel, the couple entered Peter Street. On one side of the street ran the Midland Railway Receiving Warehouse. Its huge dark wall towered over the small row of terrace houses opposite. Leaping to the warehouse roof the Beast peered at the couple through the darkness waiting for them to reach its position. It poised itself waiting to strike.

"Look Emma dearest," said Samuel pointing towards the street ahead, "A tram has just passed by, only a few minutes now."

Squinting her eyes Emma looked towards the end of the street. The lights of Victoria Street shone brightly compared to the darkness they now found themselves walking through.

The Beast dropped from the warehouse roof. It landed silently in front of Samuel, inches from his face. Before his brain had time to react, it had lifted him by his throat and forced him against the warehouse wall. A whisper of a cry left his lips as the wind was crushed from his chest. Twisting its hand sharply, the Beast snapped his neck. Samuel's body fell limp to the floor as Emma screamed.

The Beast turned on her. Screaming, she turned and ran towards the safety of the light at the end of the darkened street. Her heart pounded against her chest as she ran. She slipped in the slushy snow and fell to her knees scraping both on the cobbles. The Beast walked after her, its long legs covering twice the distance Emma was making.

Another tram passed the end of the street, its lights briefly illuminating Emma's terrified face as she struggled to rise. The Beast stood over her, it watched as her feet slipped on the icy cobbles. It bent over her breathing in her fear. Realising it was above her Emma screamed again.

Harry Dixon was passing time speaking to some of the last theatre goers left in Williamson Square when he heard Emma's scream. Realising it came from the direction he himself had just come from, he concluded that it must be the young couple he had left only minutes before and he set off at a run, closely followed by the people he had been talking to.

Emma turned over and lay in the snow, her back was cold and wet. The Beast closed the gap between them, its horrifying features now only inches from her face. Its black tongue slipped from its mouth and caressed her face, thick stinking saliva covered her skin, Emma opened her mouth to scream but its tongue forced its way into her before she could make a sound. She choked as it slipped deeper into her throat. Small blue flames licked at her mouth, which reflected in its black dead eyes.

She felt its hand reaching between her legs, dragging them apart feeling for her sex. It ripped away the clothes that covered her, she felt its talons tear at her vagina. Her body shuddered with a sweet pain as it forced itself further into her body. She tried to scream feeling its long fingers rip through the flesh of her womb and slice at her intestines but its rancid tongue filled her throat. Lifting her head back she focused on the lights of the street ahead and the safety she had attempted to reach. People crossed the end of Peter Street unaware of the horror taking place only yards away from them. As the light dimmed she felt a tugging within as the Beast reached deep into her, as far as its arm could stretch.

Emma felt no pain as she slipped away. The blue flames that danced before her eyes were the last thing she looked upon, before total blackness overwhelmed her.

Harry Dixon entered Peter Street as Emma died, the whistle in his mouth sounded each time he breathed out. He was closely followed by three men. They all stopped when they sighted the Beast crouching over Emma's body. The whistle dropped from Harry Dixon's open mouth to the floor.

It turned its head staring at the four men, they all took a step back as it rose to its full height. The body of Emma Rifkin held in its powerful grip.

Dragging her body by the head, the Beast ran from the men towards the lights of Victoria Street. It leapt upon reaching the junction and landed on the roof of a small tram, it gripped at the wood with its free hand splintering it, the tram shifted with the force of its landing.

Emma's body hung at the side bouncing against the windows. Looking back, the Beast watched the four men as they reached Victoria Street, then, lifting Emma's body up it ripped her head from her neck. Blood pumped onto the roof from the open wound seeping into the tram through the splintered wood, it ran down the windows obscuring the outside world to those inside. The passengers screamed for the driver to stop but the two horses pulling the tram had panicked, he struggled with the reigns, trying to hold them back as they both bolted. The Beast threw Emma's bloody limp body back at the four men as they followed the tram along the street. It stood, screaming at those running from the tram as it hurtled along its tracks. Blue flame spat from its mouth, flickering across its body. It screamed into the night holding Emma's head aloft, her eyes fluttered in the wind, her mouth open as if calling to those that watched from the pavement.

The Beast rode the tram, those inside pounding on the blood-stained windows, pleading for the nightmare to end.

As the tram rounded a corner the Beast leapt from it to the roof of St. John's Church, and from there it jumped the short distance to St. George's Hall. The tram passed between the Hall and Lime St. Station, its passengers still pleading with the driver to stop, the horses almost colliding with a second Hansom before continuing along the track and into the distance.

The Beast stood at the edge of the building watching the chaos below, Emma's blonde hair firmly held in its grip, her head hanging at its side.

People ran from the station upon hearing the cries of concerned onlookers, anxious to catch a glimpse of whatever had caught they're attention. The Beast watched as people ran towards the Hall pointing to where it stood, they had followed the progress of the tram and had seen it leap from its roof.

Crouching, it screamed down at them, many upon hearing its piercing cry fell silent and subconsciously stepped back. Others pushed past them to get a better view, unprepared for the sight that beheld them.

The Beast leapt to the flagpole above the hall, it clung to the side waving the head out over the crowd. Blood fell like raindrops on their upturned faces.

"Springheel Jack!" the crowd cried, "Springheel Jack."

Passing Hansom's paused allowing their passengers to peer up at the Beast from the cab windows. Rumours of 'Springheel Jack' being sighted spread quickly through the local pubs as more people crowded into the streets around St. George's Hall.

Overhearing staff at the Adelphi speaking about the attack and subsequent sighting, Clay had rushed to Barr's suite. Both men now ran along Lime St. towards the mass of shouting bodies. Large lamps had been brought from the station and their powerful beams traced up and down the halls columns.

As Barr approached he could clearly see the Beast clinging to the flagpole, "It's there," he shouted to Clay.

The Beast hissed at the crowd before lifting Emma's head and forcing it down upon the flagpole, the final drips of her blood slowly ran from her torn neck discolouring the white paint. Releasing its grip, the Beast dropped from the pole and leapt over the heads of the crowd to the façade of the North Western Hotel. As one, the people below turned and followed its path through the air above them, they watched as it easily scaled the front of the hotel and disappeared from view.

Arriving Police Officers began to cordon off the area in front of the Hall, ushering the crowd back towards the station. Harry Dixon stood looking up at the head perched upon the top of the flagpole, "How the hell are we going to get that down?" he said to himself.

Chapter 41

Will had spent the evening searching the streets around the location he had marked on his map. To his disappointment, nothing had happened. As he opened the door to his room he sighed in despair, he was cold and he was tired. He had no knowledge of the events that had happened only a mile from where he had been. Dropping his coat to the floor he climbed onto his bed and quickly fell into a restless sleep.

Both Barr and Clay had returned uplifted to the Adelphi. Barr had retired to his suite where he slept soundly. Clay found Mark in the small servant's room they had managed to acquire for him and instructed him to hang around St. George's Hall for the rest of the night, to report on anything that had happened there.

As dawn broke over the city, Mark was confident that he had found out everything that had happened during the night. He had spoken to the men who had been chatting to Harry Dixon when the first screams reached them. Each of them told him of the horror they had witnessed in Peter Street, detailed the chase along Victoria Street as

'Springheel Jack' held onto the tram, how it had thrown Emma's headless body at them and finally how they had come upon it as it hung from the flagpole of St. George's Hall.

Mark himself had witnessed the outcome of that event. It had taken the police over an hour to retrieve the head from where it had been left.

Returning to the Adelphi, he sat across from Barr and Clay as they ate breakfast. His stomach rumbled as they devoured their meal, Barr laughed as Mark explained the efforts made by the police, trying to get the head from the pole.

Will slept ignorant of the night's events. He eventually woke hearing the knocking of Mrs Cox at his door. It was the third time she had knocked, "Mr. English," she called from the hallway, "are you awake? Breakfast is served."

Will managed a croaking, "Yes, thank you," before his tongue stuck to his palette, both his mouth and throat were dry. He had slept on top of the covers in the clothes he had been wearing that night. Lifting himself up, he sat on the edge of the bed and looked down at the crumpled mess they had become.

Happy that he had now answered, he heard Mrs Cox on the floor below knocking on Parry's door, "Mr. Parry," she called, "breakfast is served," Will couldn't hear his reply.

By the time Will had washed, changed and had made his way down to the dining room, Parry was already sat at his table eating. Across from him sat another man he hadn't seen before. Pausing their conversation, the man turned towards Will, "Here," he called over to him, "come and listen to this."

Feeling obliged, Will took a chair from one of the other tables and joined the two men. "I'm Mathew Cox," said the new man holding out his hand.

Realising he was the husband of Jean Cox and therefore the owner of the hotel, Will shook his hand, "William English."

"Sit, sit," Mathew told Will, "I'm just telling Parry here what happened last night."

"Oh, it's good," smiled Parry.

Will sat as Mathew continued with his tale, "I was just telling him that, last night I was in the pub when this guy runs in screaming bloody murder, in a right state he was," Mathew turned to Will, "I don't normally go into town but I fancied a change last night so I walked down the Brow to 'The grapes', anyway this guy tells everyone in there that he was on the tram home when something lands on its roof! Says the horses took off like the devil himself was chasing them, the driver couldn't control them, along it went whilst this woman's body hung from the side. Says he was right next to her as she banged against the glass." Reaching over, Mathew took Parry's tea and drained the rest of the cup, "Everyone was screaming for the driver to stop, he tells us. But he couldn't, just kept going. Anyway, he's banging on the glass shouting for help when the body disappears, must have fallen off I suppose. But he still says someone's on the roof, even over the screams he can hear them. Then the tram jerks as whoever it was up there jumps off."

"How did he end up in the pub then?" asked Parry.

"That's where the tram stopped," Mathew replied, "Horses kept going until one of 'em dropped dead from exhaustion, right outside the door," he smiled sitting back in the chair, "I wasn't so sure about this tall tale, so I goes out and there it was, just like he said, tram, dead horse and passengers, wandering round the road they were, some of 'em crying. So, I thinks, maybe it'll be worth a look into town. So, I sets off walking."

Parry leant forward, anxious to hear the rest of Mathew's tale, "What did you see?"

"Well," Mathew said lowering his voice, "as I gets near St. George's, I can tell there's something going on. Everyone was shouting, the police were pushing the crowd back, the crowd was pushing the police forward. But I seen it!"

Will's heart raced, he gripped Mathew's arm, "What did you see?" he asked shaking it.

"A head," Mathew answered, again sitting back in his chair, "It must have been that woman's, but I couldn't really tell because of where it was."

"Where was it?" Will cried.

"On top of the St. George's flagpole, that's where."

Will ran from the dining room, knocking his chair over as he did. He ran up the stairs, taking them two at a time, by the time he had reached his room he was out of breath and breathing heavy. The map lay where he had left it by the side of his bed. He picked it up and scanned the area around St. George's Hall. He had placed a mark on Victoria St. taking a pencil he traced a line across to Sun St., he then traced a line from Ebor St. down, extending it to . . . *'To where?'* thought Will, *'Where should it end?'* He had circled several possible areas, but none in the area he was now looking. After musing over it for some time he circled Oldham Place, a narrow street in a densely built up area.

"Is everything alright Mr. English?" Mathew called from the small hallway outside Will's room.

He hadn't realised the owner had followed him up the stairs. "Yes, I'm fine . . . I had something that needed urgent attention. Something I'd left in my room," Will cursed himself for such a feeble excuse. The Beast had struck again and he had been nowhere near. Throwing the map down, he grabbed his coat.

"Your breakfast is still there you know," said Mathew, concerned by his guest's behaviour.

Will had hoped he had left, "Yes. I'm coming now. Thank you!" he spat at the door. He didn't want anyone in the hotel observing him leave, he could do without them questioning his actions. With his ear pressed to the door he listened as Mathew's footsteps descended the stairs, away from Will's room.

Opening the door, he peered over the bannister. Seeing Mathew reach the foot of the stairs Will carefully and slowly descended after him. Reaching the reception area, he could hear the two men still conversing in the dining room and silently crossed to the front door and left the hotel.

Once outside he turned left, setting off down The Brow towards St. Anne's, from there he would catch a tram to the city centre.

Jean stood by the dining room door whilst her husband and Parry continued their gruesome conversation. The breakfast she had made for Will still sat on his table, it had been there for fifteen minutes now and she was concerned that her cooking was about to go to waste.

Mathew had been up to his room and had reminded Will that food had been prepared and, on his return, had told Jean that *'Mr. English would be down presently.'* She was sure that she had heard him on the stairs, but when she had looked the reception area was empty.

Annoyed she picked up the plate and crossed the room to her husband, "Here," she said setting the breakfast down before him, "you might as well have this."

"Oh, thank you my dear," Mathew said surprised, taking Parry's knife and fork, "I wonder where he got to?" he added, chewing on the cold meat.

"I'll pop up later and see if he's alright," Jean replied taking Parry's plate, "it's laundry day so I'll be changing the sheets, don't forget Mr. Parry."

"I won't Mrs Cox," Parry smiled, "I'll be out all day myself."

Jean smiled back, then turned to her husband, "Don't you be forgetting I want those errands run today."

"As soon as I've finished this my love," Mathew said scraping egg onto a piece of thick bread, "don't you worry."

Leaving the two men to finish their conversation Jean returned to the kitchen to clean the breakfast service away. By the time she had finished both men had left the hotel. She retrieved the plate her husband had left in the dining room, once that had been cleaned she took clean sheets from the linen cupboard and climbed the stairs to Parry's room.

He had been their guest now for a number of weeks, upon his arrival he had enquired as to when the linen would be changed and since then, when she entered his room every Tuesday and Friday, she found the used linen neatly folded and the bed ready for her to make up.

Leaving the dirty linen on the stairs Jean continued up the two remaining flights to Will's room. Unsure if he was in or out she knocked on his door, when no answer came she opened it and stepped inside.

The drapes had not been pulled back properly, dropping the linen on the side table Jean opened them. The bed was unmade and Will's jacket was on the floor where he had dropped it the night before. Picking it up, she placed it on a hanger before leaving it in the wardrobe.

Around the lamp on the bedside table Will had left a number of handwritten notes, collecting them together, Jean took them and the map that he had dropped to the bed when Mathew had called him earlier and carried them over to the small set of drawers by the window.

As she did so she noticed the markings that Will had made on the map. He had circled a number of areas. When he had given her the map asking for directions she had drawn the route from her hotel to Prince Edwin Street, she was sure there had not been anything else written on it.

In the bottom left hand corner, in the area of white that represented the Mersey, Will had made notes. Jean read them.

First Attack   Ebor St
Second Attack   Sun St
Third Attack   Peter St
Fourth Attack

As she read each line Jean searched the map for the corresponding street, each one had been circled. Staring open mouthed in horror, Jean realised that several other streets had been circled. She picked up and read the handwritten notes. Each page gave an account of the attacks.

At the bottom of the second page Will had written about taking the heart from the recent victim's body. Jean had read the newspaper articles and had also heard the rumours, but not once had she heard about organs being removed. She read the third page, although not as detailed as the others, at the bottom of the page Will had written that the head would be removed.

'How could he know?' she thought nervously, she slid the note aside and read the final one.

Seeing what Will had written, Jean drew breath, her hand covered her mouth. "Oh, my Lord!" the words slipped out subconsciously as she crossed herself. Tears formed as she turned away from the horrific writing and ran from the room.

Panicking she ran into the street, the linen forgotten. Her only thought was to find someone, anyone who could help her. She had been alone in the house, the thought frightened her.

Jean ran up the Brow towards Netherfield Rd., she knew that there would be more chance of finding a police officer on the busier road.

Passing the pub Will had drank in on his first night, Jean ran into the middle of the junction. She looked left into Shaw Street, then across into the small park. "The Barracks!" she screamed, "The Barracks!"

Positioned behind the small park was Rupert Lane Barracks. Jean ran through the park, "Help me!" she screamed emerging on the other side, "help me!"

At the entrance to the Barracks stood two young soldiers. As Jean approached them they stepped into the street to meet her, "Whoa Miss," said the first, as Jean fell into his arms. She was crying and out of breath.

"He's the killer," she whispered between breaths, "my guest . . . the killer."

The two soldiers walked her back to the park, "Let's just take a seat, see if we can sort out what's wrong." Once she was seated Jean began to calm herself, "Now, what's happened?" the soldiers asked.

"It's one of my guests," Jean blurted out, "I went in to change the linen and he had some notes, they were just lying there and a map . . . he's the killer. I know he is. Please help me!" she pleaded.

"Alright, let's go and have a look at this map, where do you live?"

She took the two soldiers back to the hotel and showed them what she had discovered in Will's room, "We better get the police," they agreed.

Chapter 42

Will made his way to St. George's Hall. Hundreds had now gathered to see and hear what had happened. Eye witnesses gave their accounts to eager onlookers as they listened open mouthed to the evening's events.

The police had eventually managed to cordon off the front of the Hall and were busy trying to keep the crowds from forcing their way through. Vigilante groups had appeared overnight and had taken up residence on the steps of Lime St. Station, they called for the police to take more action, threatening that if they didn't, they themselves would take action and insisting that the people of the city take arms and patrol the streets.

Will had seen the same crowds gathered in London and knew that before long their anger would escalate to violence and a riot would inevitably break out. Once that happened the police would be swamped. The final killing would take place, ignored by everyone and another city would be lost. The Beast would move on and the cycle would begin again. He wanted to take his revenge on both Barr and Sarah's killer before any of that could take place.

Skirting the crowd, Will made his way passed the station.

He wanted to survey the area around Oldham Place before nightfall. Reaching into his pocket he realised that the map wasn't there. In a panic he searched his overcoat, then again, he tried to remember his actions before leaving the hotel.

He could remember taking the pencil and circling off the area around Oldham Place. *The knock at the door,'* Will thought, he'd thrown the map onto the bed when Mathew knocked on the door.

"Damn Him," he shouted angrily, "Damn him to Hell."

Will tried desperately to remember where St. George's Hall was in relation to where he needed to be. He was certain that it was south of the station. Cursing both himself and Mathew, he left the crowd hoping he could find Oldham Place before nightfall.

Barr too stood in the crowd, by his side stood both Clay and Mark. The three men had been oblivious to the fact that Will had passed quite close to them and, as they marvelled at the spectacle before them was passing the Adelphi hotel.

The map in Barr's pocket was identical to the one bought by Will upon his arrival in Liverpool. It too had been marked with the location of the fourth victim.

Mark had been allowed to sleep once he had explained the events of the previous night. When breakfast was over Barr and Clay walked the area, familiarising themselves with the layout. The area looked promising, St. Luke's Church was quite close and if they could somehow lure the Beast there, then Barr's plan could be put in place.

As they watched the crowd fan the smouldering embers of a riot, Barr smiled.

Chapter 43

Luckily the soldiers had come across a police officer quite quickly, returning with him to the hotel. Jean had been waiting anxiously for them in reception, after explaining to the officer what she had found she let the soldiers take him up to the room. Jean had no intention of entering the room until the police had found Will and he had been arrested. She prayed silently that Mathew would return soon, the door could then be locked and it wouldn't be opened again until she was sure who it was that wanted entrance.

After reading Will's notes the officer had collected the evidence together and upon leaving, had asked the soldiers if they would stay with Jean until he could arrange for another officer to be posted at the hotel. They had agreed and within ten minutes three had arrived. Two had taken a statement and description from Jean before collecting the remainder of Will's belongings, the third waiting in reception just in case Will returned to the hotel before he could be arrested.

Once they had been assured of Jean's safety the soldiers returned to their Barracks. Mathew had returned shortly after carrying a large sack of vegetables from the market. He had listened to his wife's tale in disbelief, if it had not been for the collaboration of the officer sat in his reception he would not have believed her story.

Arriving at the police station, the officer had given both his evidence and his report to Detective Nithercott who welcomed it with open arms. Nithercott had been assigned to the case after the six murders at Sun Street and as of yet, had no leads. After the previous night's events he was beginning to feel the pressure from above.

Nithercott had called a meeting for sixteen hundred hours and sat waiting for the team he had organised to arrive. He had laid both Will's notes and the map on the table before him and had copied the notes on to the blackboard behind him. As the skies above Liverpool darkened his office filled with the team assigned to him.

"You all know why we are here," he began, "last night we had no clues as to the perpetrator of these heinous crimes. Now, we have too many. Before you on the table, are a map and several pages of handwritten notes," Nithercott paused, waiting for the officers to look over them, "I've transcribed the details written on the notes to the blackboard behind me. As you can see," he continued, turning to the blackboard, "the details written about the Sun Street case is of great interest to us. As the papers reported, there were six killings, we requested that nowhere was it to be mentioned that one victim had had their heart removed." Nithercott tapped the board, "We knew that and the killer knew that. No one else."

Ralf Bunan raised his hand, "Sir, do we think that this is the man the eyewitnesses claimed to have seen last night?" he asked.

"That's a good question Bunan," replied Nithercott, "the honest answer is, that I doubt it. I truly don't know what people saw last night, you've read the statements and none of them really make sense. But this man definitely knows something. My best guess is that they're working together," Nithercott answered, lifting up one of the notes from the table, "on this page Mr. English has been kind enough to inform us of a fourth attack, let me read it to you. I believe it will give you a feel for the type of mind we're dealing with."

Clearing his throat Nithercott read Will's final note, "The fourth victim has to be pregnant, heavily pregnant. Her death is unimportant. The unborn child must be taken. It has to be taken for chaos to reign."

The room fell silent, Nithercott continued, "The man is clearly deranged."

Placing the note back on the table he retrieved the map, folding it over the blackboard behind him he continued. "Fortunately, he has marked out the locations where he must be looking for his next victim. Unfortunately, we're going to be pressed if we are to cover them all. Also, we don't know when he will strike, although my guess is that it will be within the next few nights. Our best course of action is to patrol the streets around the locations marked on his map. Bunan and Tow, you take Everton Road. Hislop and Callan, you take Castle Street down to the docks. Mitchell and I will take Oldham Place. The description we have of him isn't very detailed I'm afraid. In this weather everyone on the streets at night will be wearing a long coat and hat, well if they have any sense they will. But we need to stop anyone we think is acting suspicious, or if you think them out of place. Remember he's from London, his accent will give him away so keep your ears peeled. It's a long shot I know, but if we're lucky we'll get him. Dismissed."

As the officers turned to file out of the room, Nithercott called after them, "Oh and think on. He's looking for a woman who's heavily pregnant, so keep a look out, she might be easier to spot than he will"

Leaving the station, the officers set off to patrol their given areas, standing in the station doorway Mitchell waited for Detective Nithercott to join him.

Nithercott stared at the open desk drawer, once alone he had collected the papers together and had sat at his desk ready to place them safely in the drawer, but now it was open and the revolver he kept there stared up at him, he wondered what to do.

'Should I take it?' he thought.

Eventually he picked it up, placing Will's map and notes in its place. Taking his overcoat, he slipped the gun into its deep pocket and left the room in search of Mitchell.

Nithercott found him still waiting at the entrance, "Come on," he told him, "I've a feeling he won't keep us waiting long." As the two men set off towards Oldham Place snow began to fall again. By the time they had reached their destination the sky was thick with it.

Chapter 44

Will had been stood on Oldham Place for over an hour, he had seen both the Sawmill and the Electric works empty whilst he waited. Hundreds had filed through the streets as they left their place of work, no one paid him any attention as they passed him by. Another face amongst many.

Snow gathered on his shoulders, he was cold and he was lonely. His mind wandered, he thought of Barr,

'Had he read the article? Had he made the journey north to Liverpool?' Will hoped that he had, he was sure that he would soon come across him in the area.

Barr and Clay stood at the entrance to the Adelphi watching the falling snow, "It'll keep a lot of people off the streets," Clay said.

"True, but destiny dictates that Erebus, the pregnant woman and we two must meet," replied Barr.

"What about Mark?"

Barr thought about the boy. He turned, seeing him sat in the hotel reception, "He has been of use so far," he mused, "yes, bring him."

Clay re-entered the hotel, Barr watched him chatting with the boy. Mark then jumped up and ran to the stairs that led to the servant's quarters. Minutes later he returned wearing his hat and coat.

"Thank you, Sir," he said to Barr, as they left the safety of the hotel and entered cold night.

"Would you like a cab Sir?" the doorman called after them.

"No thank you," Clay said turning back, the front of his coat already dappled with snow, "we fancy the walk."

Heads down, shoulders hunched, the three men set off into the night.

"Have you the mask?" asked Barr.

Clay opened his jacket to reveal the mask tucked into his inside pocket, "Yes Sir." he said, "And this," Clay pulled a revolver from his left-hand pocket.

"That won't do you any good," laughed Barr, "bullets won't stop Erebus."

"It's not for him Sir," replied Clay, "It's for English. I'm sure he'll show up sooner or later."

"Oh, I'm depending on it," laughed Barr, "he's the only other one that knows just what's going on and we may need his help."

"Then we can use it to guarantee his co-operation," said Clay, smiling.

"It really won't be necessary. When he sees we have Erebus he'll help."

"We have to get the mask on it first," replied Clay, secretly worried by the prospect of confronting the Beast.

"True," replied Barr, "the masks effect on him should help us though. It's the equivalent of you looking directly into the sun, it blinds you to everything else. We just have to get it close enough."

"We won't be able to see it approaching in this weather," said Mark looking up, "not if it sticks to the rooftops."

Both Barr and Clay burst into laughter, "And how have you come to that conclusion young Mark?" Barr asked.

"I listen Sir," he replied, "I know what's going on."

Barr lifted Mark's hat and ruffled his hair, "I believe you do Mark," he smiled. It had been the first act of kindness Barr had ever shown him, a shiver of revulsion ran down his spine., "I believe you do."

Will stamped his feet and rubbed his hands together. For the past fifteen minutes he hadn't seen a soul, the snow fell thicker, quickly covering the ground around him. The rooftops of the Sawmill and Electric Supply building that had been easily visible from where he was stood were now lost to him. He began to doubt that anything was going to happen.

If he only had the map he could check the area for a more suitable location,' he thought, cursing himself again for leaving it in his room.

He decided to explore the area before his feet froze solid to the ground. Hoping to find a warm pub on his way Will walked to the end of Oldham Place and into Roscoe Street.

Nithercott and Mitchell turned off Oldham Street, into Back Henshaw Street and finally into Oldham Place, moments after Will had left in the opposite direction. Nithercott was still laughing at the encounter Mitchell had just had with two prostitutes.

As the officers had turned into Oldham Street they had been approached by the two women. "Fancy something to warm you up lovey?" one had asked Mitchell, "that coats big enough for two, we could both be cosy in there," she smiled.

Nithercott stood back slightly, waiting to see how Mitchell was going to react. Even in the gloom of the cold winter night he could clearly see his bright red face, "I'm a police officer on official business ma'am," he said nervously, "kindly step aside."

"Ooh isn't he a gent Phyllis?" she said turning to her friend, "official police business. Well I says that's never stopped any of them before." Both girls had walked away laughing, as they passed Nithercott one of them winked.

"Excuse me?" Mitchell called after them, "are any of you pregnant?"

Nithercott tried to stifle a laugh but it caught in his throat and he coughed.

"What'd you say lovey?" said Phyllis, "pregnant? Well I never. We're good clean God-fearing girls us!"

Mitchell opened his mouth, but Nithercott grabbed him before he could form the words of his apology. "Come on," he laughed, "let's leave the ladies to their business and we'll attend to ours."

Nithercott had now been laughing at the incident for five minutes. Mitchell was beginning to feel less foolish about what he had said to the women and a lot angrier, although he would never have let his superior know that.

Oldham Place was devoid of life, although the snow was heavy it was possible for the two men to see its entire length. The footprints made by the workers returning home had gone, an hour had passed since the last straggler had left giving the weather enough time for the snow to re-cover the cobbles. Four gas lamps lit along the street cast shadows in the slight indentations the footprints had left.

Nithercott and Mitchell walked along the row of terrace houses, the few parlour lights that had been lit, illuminated the two men as they past, their long shadows stretching across the street and onto the tall dark walls of the Sawmill.

Nithercott crossed the road to its large wooden gates, finding them locked he pushed against one side and peered through the gap. Beyond lay the timber yard piled high with both the finished products and the raw materials that were used to make them. The ground around the doorway had an undisturbed covering of snow.

"We must have the wrong place," Mitchell shouted across to his superior.

Nithercott returned to his colleague and the relative cover of the terrace houses. "I think you're right," he said looking back and forth towards the gas lamps at each end of the Place, "It's been quite a while since anyone's been here, come on, let's get back to the main road." The two men turned and returned the way they had come, unaware that if they had stopped a few yards further along the pavement then they'd have spotted where Will had stood before he too had decided to leave the Place. His footprints leading in the opposite direction.

The Beast emerged from its place of sanctuary beneath the railway tunnels that lead into Lime St. Station. It watched as a train passed, the fireman's face illuminated by the open firebox as he shovelled coal, steam filled the air as the loco struggled to pull the weight of the carriages up the bank towards Edge Hill.

It leapt from the dark cutting up into the snowy sky, it landed on the empty cobbles of Copperas Hill. A combination of both bad weather and the murderous actions of 'Springheel Jack' had kept people off the streets, there were those that still lingered around St. George's Hall, but the rest of the city had become a ghost town as night fell.

Without effort it jumped to the rooftops, strange footprints left in the snow disappeared as it leapt towards the station.

Crouching above the entrance it observed the small crowd below. The bad weather had turned many away but the groups of vigilantes remained and with them the police. Fires had been lit, but they were small and controlled. People gathered round them, thankful for what little comfort they offered. Small scuffles had broken out, but the violence Will had predicted had not yet occurred.

Moving south, the Beast leapt from building to building. Snow whipped into eddy's behind it as it passed through the air. Reaching the rooftops of the Adelphi hotel it paused, lost amongst the forest of chimneys it surveyed the city.

The weather frustrated it, angered it, from its high vantage point it should have seen all of the city, that view was obscured by the falling snow. Its long piercing cry filled the air.

Will had indeed found a pub. He left Oldham Place turning right and had walked for only a minute before he sighted the lights of 'The Unicorn'. Pushing on the handle, he had opened the door only a few inches when he heard the Beast's cry. His body froze, looking up to the rooftops around him he quickly scanned them before realising that the sound came from further away.

"If you're coming in do so," called a voice from within the pub, "If you're not then don't, but don't stand there with the door open. It's bloody freezing."

Will released the handle and the door silently closed. He continued to look up at the rooftops as he crossed the street to the churchyard of St. Luke's.

Barr, Clay and Mark had almost reached Roscoe Lane when they too heard the piercing cry. "At least we know he's here," laughed Barr, "we won't need to spend another night searching the streets in this weather."

The three men reached the corner of the lane, "Let's just wait here for a moment," said Barr holding his arm out.

"Why?" Barr turned towards Mark, "We don't want to act to soon, if we interfere before Erebus claims his victim we may lose it. And that's not an option."

Nithercott watched Mitchell as he squinted, "I think it's them Sir," he said, convinced that the two figures ahead of him were the two prostitutes they had encountered earlier. Unable to locate Will, they had left Oldham Place and had arrived at the corner of Henshaw Street where

Mitchell had spotted the two figures making their way slowly towards the city centre. "It doesn't really matt . . ." Nithercott had begun to say when he was cut short by the cry of the Beast.

Both men looked up to the snow filled sky, "Where's that coming from?" asked Mitchell.

Nithercott continued to listen trying to gauge from which direction the sound was coming from. The snow and the streets acoustics were making it difficult, "I think it's coming from that direction," he said pointing along Henshaw towards the city centre.

From the corner both men could see that the two figures ahead of them had turned and were now walking towards them. Their pace quickened as they neared, Nithercott could now see that his colleague had been correct, it was the women that they had met earlier.

"I don't know what that was," said Phyllis as they approached the men, "But if I was you I'd turn around and follow us."

"Unfortunately, ma'am that's not an option," Nithercott said, his hand in his coat pocket nervously rubbing the steel of his revolver. He turned to Mitchell, "come on."

"Shit!" Mitchell whispered as Nithercott set off running towards the sound. Smiling at the two women, he followed.

Kate Ellis almost fell as she stepped from her rented room and into the backyard. Its icy cobbles were hidden under a covering of snow. Leaning against the wall she carefully placed one foot in front of the other, feeling that each was firmly planted before putting her weight down on it. She had managed to reach the gate before her next contraction took hold of her. Both hands immediately gripped her swollen belly as she bent forward, panting until the pain passed. It had been around thirty minutes since her last contraction. At that point she had decided to try and reach the Royal Infirmary, it had taken her until now just to dress herself.

She had left her home in Roby when her father had discovered that she was pregnant. He had told her that, *'No daughter of his was going to bring disgrace to his family by having a child out of wedlock!'* She left the next day.

Convinced that the father of her child was in Liverpool she had followed him to the city.

He had run when she had told him of their predicament, but not before he promised to marry her. Asking her to return home and wait for him, he had told her that he intended to speak to her father at his place of work, where he would ask for his permission to marry her.

She waited for him to return all that day, when her father came home it was obvious that he had not been approached with a request to marry his daughter.

Kate searched for the child's father over the next week, asking everyone she knew if they had seen him. Eventually his landlord had allowed her to enter his room. She found his clothes missing, the bed where he had lain with her had been stripped of its blankets.

Distraught, she had confided in her mother who had urged her to seek out an abortion. When Kate had refused, her mother explained to her that she had until she could no longer hide the pregnancy to sort something out. Once her father knew, she would be on her own.

Once Kate had made the decision to leave for Liverpool her mother had secretly given her enough money to live on for a few months. Finding cheap accommodation when she had arrived had meant that her meagre savings would now last her six months.

She had hoped that within that time she could find the child's father and convince him to take her back. Unfortunately, she had not.

Now, bent double with pain she needed her mother more than ever, cursing the day she had let him talk her into having sex with him and regretted the day she had left Roby in search of him.

As the pain eased she stood and calmed herself by breathing slowly and deeply before opening the back gate.

The alley was dark and narrow. Snow had fallen but the steep yard walls gave some protection, there was little more than a covering. Behind her a dog growled, she turned to see where it was, but the shadows hid it from view. Holding her stomach, Kate felt along with her feet, careful not to trip on any unseen obstacle in her path.

Leaving the dark alley, she entered the lamp light of Roscoe Lane as the sound of the Beast's cry reached her.

Kate's immediate reaction was to turn back thinking that the dog she had heard was running to attack her. But from what she could see, the alley was empty. The sound filled the air around her, frightening her. She crossed the lane to the lamp opposite, eager to be surrounded by its safe illumination and to be near the terrace houses and the people within.

Once again, she cursed the child's father and her decision to leave home. Four months she had been in the city and in all that time she had not made a single friend. She had fooled herself into believing she would find her lover and that he would receive her with open arms. The reality, as Kate stood cold and in pain, was that she was frightened and lonely and had been since the day she had arrived.

The Beast leapt over Roscoe Lane and into the alley Kate had emerged from. The dog once again growled at the new intruder to its domain. The Beast flicked its long arm back without looking, dismembering the dog. It uttered a small cry as its body fell in two.

Kate turned her attention back towards the alley, she was sure that this time there was something there. Subconsciously she began walking along the pavement away from the dark frightening place, her eyes never left the alley entrance.

Barr peered from the corner of the street. He had seen the woman enter the lane, watched as she crossed from darkness into light. A rush of pleasure ran through his body when he realised she was pregnant. The large coat she wore could not disguise the fact. "It's starting," he whispered to Clay, "she's here."

Clay and Mark had taken cover against the gable end of the terrace, it didn't need three of them to watch the lane and the gable offered some shelter from the falling snow.

Turning to see where she was walking, Kate missed seeing the Beast as it leapt from the shadows and onto the front of the terrace house opposite the alley, hissing when it saw her.

Kate tried to run when she heard the sound behind her, holding onto her unborn child as she did.

The Beast jumped at her, its long fingers caught her hair, spinning her into the road. Kate fell, slipping as she twirled, landing heavily on her back.

Skidding to a halt the Beast crept towards her. Kate tried to get up but the pain came again. She curled into a ball praying for it to stop. "It's too early!" she cried knowing only a few minutes had passed since the last contraction.

Barr watched the attack, urging the Beast on. It was now over her, its long oily black hair covering Kate's face.

She screamed. "Get ready," Barr warned his companions, "pass me the mask." Clay opened his coat and handed the iron mask over to Barr.

Will was still standing by St. Luke's Church when he heard Kate's scream. Realising it was close he ran along the churchyard wall towards the sound.

Kate felt the hot breath of the Beast on the side of her face, its cold putrid hair rested against her skin. The pain prevented her from moving. Her lungs and throat burned as her scream ended, before she could take another breath, the Beast bit down on her exposed neck severing her artery. Blood pumped into its mouth, it swallowed the thick rich life-giving fluid, lapping like a dog at the open wound.

"Right, let's go," Barr instructed, as he, Clay and Mark left the safety of the corner and ran towards the Beast. Barr pulled the clasps of the mask open.

Raising its arm, the Beast prepared to strike at Kate, as she died it would rip the unborn child from her.

Mark jumped at the Beast landing on its back, one arm around its neck the other holding its arm. Touching the pulsating slimy skin turned his stomach, he struggled with the urge to both let go and throw up.

Clay grabbed at its raised arm to help Mark as the Beast

tried to swipe down at Kate. It reared back screeching, standing to its full height. Clay's feet left the ground as he hung on to its arm. Mark clung to its neck trying to strangle it, his face whipped by its hair as it tried to shake him from its back.

Barr kicked at both its legs trying to bring it to the ground.

Kate's body was trampled underfoot as the Beast turned to face Barr, the snow around her head stained red with blood.

"Hold its arms!" Barr shouted.

Crossing his feet and tightening the hold his legs had around the Beasts waist, Mark released the grip he had on its neck, took its free arm and with all his strength pulled it back as it lunged at Barr. Its broken talons passing within inches of his face.

Will turned the corner into Roscoe Lane, the battle between Barr and the Beast played out before him. Seeing Kate led under the struggle he ran to her, it was obvious as he slid to her side that she was already dead.

Realising that Will had arrived, Clay shouted down to him, "For God's sake help us!" he cried out.

Will gripped both of its feet and pulled back hard. With Mark on its back and Clay hanging from its arm the Beast fell forward towards Barr.

Stepping back as it landed, Barr dropped to his knees. Gripping its hair, he lifted the Beasts head and slipped the mask beneath it, once it was in place he released its hair.

The Beasts head fell onto the iron below, before it could raise itself up again Barr took the first clasp and closed it on the buckle. The Beast screamed in pain, it lurched up throwing Mark from its back. Barr fumbled with the second clasp, "Sit on its arms," he shouted, "get it back down!"

Recovering himself Mark jumped at the arm nearest to him and pinned it to the ground. Once Clay had done the same with the other, Barr easily closed the second clasp. The Beast lurched its body back and forth, the mask smashing into the cobbles below. Screaming in pain it tried desperately to free its arms.

Looking toward the houses opposite, Barr called out, "Cowards!" he spat at them. Not once during either the attack, or the subsequent struggle, had anyone ventured from their homes. He sensed them cowering behind closed windows, convincing themselves that the sound they heard was the wind.

Will grabbed Barr's shoulder spinning him round. Before he could react, Will's punch landed square in his face. Staggering back, Barr fell against the Beast as it struggled to release both its arms and the mask. "We haven't got time for this English," said Barr, wiping blood from his nose, "Look around man, don't you see what's going on?"

Will looked down at Clay and Mark, almost riding the Beast as it released its fury.

"You want revenge for Sarah?" Barr said brushing the snow from his coat, "here is the cause of her death. Here is your revenge!"

"Will you two stop your procrastinating and, FUCKING HELP US!" Clay shouted.

The Beast tried to get to its knees, its feet slipping in the bloody snow. Both Clay and Mark had positioned themselves across its back, each pinning an arm to the floor.

"We need your help to get it to the church," pleaded Barr, "We can end this Will," he added gripping its legs, "take the arm from Mark, we can carry it."

Will knelt next to Mark, he took the Beasts arm and bent it up across its back. The three men lifted the screaming twisting monster. The cobbles beneath its face had been cracked by the force of it smashing the iron mask against them.

"Mark," called Barr, "In my pocket, here take it."

Mark reached into Barr's coat pocket as he struggled with its legs. He had positioned himself as close to its thighs as he could squeeze. With both arms around each leg it was difficult for the Beast to shake him loose.

Mark pulled out a small hessian sack, "What should I do with this?" he asked.

"Get the child," Barr instructed.

Mark turned to Kate's body lying behind them, she had been trampled by the Beast during the struggle and its sharp talons had cut through her clothes, parts of her flesh lay exposed. "How?" he asked, "I can't . . ."

"How?" spat Barr angrily, "use your bloody initiative boy. Get it and follow us to the church."

Urging his companions forward, the trio set off towards the church, the screams of the Beast echoing through the narrow lane.

Mark knelt next to the dead woman, through the blood he could see that she was hardly older than himself. He pulled her coat back exposing her bulging belly. Her smooth skin still warm to his touch. Bile rose to his throat, Mark swallowed hard, the three men had reached the corner of Roscoe Lane. As he watched them disappear towards the church he gathered a mound of snow together.

Nithercott and Mitchell arrived at the Adelphi hotel to find both the bellboy and the doorman stood in the middle of the road looking up at the hotel roof.

"What's going on?" Nithercott enquired.

"That screeching sound," the bellboy said, "It came from up there, on the roof. I heard it from inside."

"He's right," added the doorman, "I was standing right there," he pointed, "nearly deafened me."

"What was it?" asked Mitchell.

"Can't really say," the doorman answered, "I stepped into the street to get a better look, still had my hands over me ears. Then I seen it."

"Seen what?" Nithercott asked.

"The thing that killed that woman, the one that left her head over there," he answered pointing in the direction of St. George's Hall. "I seen it up there, then it was gone."

"Which way?" asked Nithercott anxiously, "Which way did it go?"

The doorman pointed down the road, back in the direction the two officers had come from, "That way I think."

Both men shared a look then set off running, back towards Oldham Place.

Sensing the church ahead, fear gripped the Beast, its strength surged. Pulling its arm free from Clay's grip it tried to pull the mask away from the burning skin of its face. Once the arm was free Clay jumped back waiting for it to swipe at him, when it didn't he stepped towards it, kicking at its ribs.

Barr and Will held on as Clay kicked it over and over, they all heard its ribs breaking as he did.

Eventually the Beast released its grip on the mask and swung at its tormentor. Clay had been waiting for it to do so, stepping out of harm's way as the arc of its swing passed him. With the strength of its swipe gone Clay could once again slip inside, and took hold of it.

As they reached the churchyard gate Mark came running towards them, the bulging sack at his side. "Open the gate Mark," Barr shouted.

Mark ran to the gate and swung it open, inside the covering of snow lay undisturbed. The three men struggled with the Beast as it entered consecrated ground. It see-sawed its body up and down violently, Barr dropped its legs and dived from it as the Beast kicked out at him. Clay and Will dragged it as far as they could, before they too had to relinquish their grip.

The Beast rolled on the ground pulling at the mask. Stepping over to it Barr pulled a small iron cross from inside his coat and slammed it into the ground at its feet. The Beast screamed in agony.

In its struggle it had managed to release one of the clasps, Clay leapt onto it, fastening the clasp over the buckle once again. Feeling his weight on its chest the Beast struck out, with one hand it held Clays head, using the other to slice and tear at his throat. With two swipes it had cut Clay to his spine. Throwing his body aside, it returned its concentration on removing the mask.

Mark watched as Clay's body smashed into a gravestone, before crumpling to the ground below it. His revolver fell from his pocket. Picking it up, Mark pocketed it.

Standing at the Beast's feet, Barr shuffled the translated papers he had brought with him, discarding some, he read whilst holding his arm out over the Beast, "*O domine obscure,*" he shouted, "*O domine lucis, imperto tuae potestati.*"

Flashes of light which emanating from the ground around the Beast struck the gravestones.

"*Ut detur mihi, tuo semo, qui,*" continued Barr.

Thunder rolled in the sky above the church. Wind whistled through the streets towards the place where Barr stood, his hand held out over the Beast. Static whipped at its skin from both the ground and the gravestones. Will leant forward against the wind as it blew stronger, holding onto one of the gravestones.

"Don't touch the stones!" Barr shouted at him, "don't interfere."

Slow to react Will was knocked to the floor as a blue charge slammed into him from the stone he had been resting against.

"Kill it," he called out, rising to his knees.

"*In nomine tuo, qui in nomine tou, regel!*" shouted Barr slamming his fist down.

Thunder rolled again above them, lightning struck both the church and the Beast, its electric blue charge covered the ground around it before dissipating to the earth.

"Kill it now!" Will called again over the deafening roar.

"*Qui ni nomine tuo negabit*!" Barr turned to Mark and shouted, "Bring me the child."

Mark threw the sack at him, Barr caught it and continued, "*O domine obscure, O domine lucis, capi hanc feram, humc filium discordia*!" Opening the sack, he threw its contents onto the Beast.

Snow covered its twisting, kicking legs. Barr turned to Mark, confused by what had just happened. He dropped the empty sack to the ground.

Mark held Clay's revolver at arm's length, "Fuck you!" he cried firing four shots at the Beast. Each one penetrating its chest.

Barr laughed, "You fool, do you know nothing?" he shouted at Mark, "you cannot kill chaos! Your bullets cannot hurt him. He is the harbinger of my new world. He is mine to keep, mine to command, I will make him my servant!"

Will leapt to his feet and ran towards Barr, "You can't do that!" he shouted.

Barr hit down on Will's back with both fists clasped together as he attacked him, he stumbled and fell hard against a gravestone, immediately his body came in contact with the stone a static charge threw him to the ground. Stunned he lay at Barr's feet unable to move.

"I can do anything I want," cried Barr, "With Erebus at my side I will conquer all." He raised both arms to the sky, thunder rolled, "I cannot be stopped!"

"This will," Mark shouted walking towards Barr. As the Barrel of the revolver touched his chest Mark fired, the bullet shattered Barr's rib and punctured a hole through his heart as it passed through his body and out the other side.

Will watched in horror as the man he hated, fell dead in front of him, "Nooooo!" he cried crawling to the corpse, "he was mine, he was mine, mine," he cried pounding the dead man's face with his fist. He turned to Mark, "you took him from me, you did, you bastard!"

Will jumped at Mark but the young man was a lot faster than he was and easily moved out of the way, "We haven't got time Will," he pleaded, "Barr never had any intention of killing the Beast, he's played you like a fool."

Will sat with his head in his hands, "What can we do now?"

"I can stop it," Mark boasted, "I have the translations Barr made of the original ceremony."

"How?" uttered Will.

"Simple," Mark explained, "Barr lost interest in his members years ago leaving their recruitment to Clay. He took me under his wing when I was a child and mentored me, I was to be his replacement. Barr never knew, but I witnessed all of his secret ceremonies. I was one of the hooded figures that looked on as he planned his domination of the Beast."

"And you can stop it?"

"I have the means here," Mark took the notes from his pocket and waved them in front of Will's face.

As he stood Will looked at Mark's young face, "How can I help?" he asked.

"You can't," replied Mark taking Barr's position at the feet of the Beast.

"*O Pater, Pater, ego, servus tuus ignorans,*" began Mark.

Thunder rolled as lightning crossed the sky.

Both Nithercott and Mitchell had heard the gunshots from where they stood in Oldham Place. As they neared St. Luke's they could see that the whole churchyard was illuminated. Lightning struck the church repeatedly, the ground beneath them shook violently. Losing his balance Mitchell fell to the floor, "What's going on Sir?" he shouted as Nithercott helped him to his feet.

"I don't know lad," he answered, "But I don't like it."

Blue lightning whipped up from the church striking the snow clouds above. The trees around its perimeter shook back and forth their branches lit by an eerie light.

"I'm not going in there without back up," shouted Nithercott blowing his whistle, the sound was lost in the wind. "You get back down to Henshaw and find help," he told Mitchell, "I'll wait here."

Mitchell left his superior and ran towards the main road. Once he had left the area immediately around the church, the strong wind dropped, he took out his whistle and blew. As he reached the corner he could hear whistles sounding a reply from both directions.

Will watched in disbelief as the earth beneath the Beast opened. Lightning struck both the church and the Beast, the ground beneath him shook from the impact.

The Beast, surrounded by blue light screamed and struggled as it rose, suspended above the hole in the earth. Balls of white light fired from the nearest gravestones struck at its writhing body.

Will listened as Mark shouted, his voice sounding clear above the wind, his body glowing with what seemed to him to be a divine light.

"*Abi, abi, abi o maium,*" he cried. The Beast rose and slammed into the earth. All the light in the churchyard followed it in to the hole. Will covered his eyes with his arm, the pain of the bright light was too much for his eyes.

The howling wind dropped and silence once again filled the air. Will felt the cold snowflakes landing on his open hand before he lowered his arm. Mark stood before him panting, the world around him had become dark again, and both the hole and the Beast were gone. "Is that it?" he asked hopefully.

"I hope so," Mark replied, "I hope so."

Will became aware of the police whistles before Mark did, "Run," he urged him.

"What?" Mark asked turning. Then he too heard the whistles. They filled the air all around the church.

"They're coming from all over Mark, I want you to run, get away from here. You're not responsible for any of this. I'll take the blame, let them know what Barr was and what he was trying to do. I'll make sure they know the Beast has been captured and the nightmare is over. For what you have done, you should be guaranteed a place in Heaven."

"No," cried Mark, "you can't let anyone know what is buried here, we can't risk anyone ever releasing this creature. This can never happen again!"

The air around them was now filled with both shouts and whistles, "They're getting closer, you better go," said Will placing his hand in Mark's, "I'll make sure no one knows what happened here tonight. Don't worry"

Mark thanked him then turned and ran from the churchyard.

Through the falling snow Will could see the first police officers entering the area, one leapt over the boundary wall and was making his way towards Will through the gravestones.

Will bent down feeling the ground at his feet, eventually

his fingers found what he had been looking for. He gripped Clay's revolver and held it up. If he was right there would be one bullet left. He was determined that the secret of 'Springheel Jack' would not be known, never again would his chaos reign over the land.

Will put the muzzle of the revolver into his mouth and closed his eyes.

"I love you Sarah," he said, then pulled the trigger.

Epilogue
Liverpool, the year of our Lord 1983.

Gaz Hughes held his ghetto blaster on his shoulder, lost in music as he walked towards the bombed-out church. He and his friends had always played amongst its ruins. It had been a ruin for as long as he could remember, his mum had told him it had happened during the Second World War and the city had decided to keep it as a reminder. She never explained to him what it reminded them of though and to be truthful Gaz had never really been that interested, it was just a cool place to play. As long as they didn't damage it, his mum had told him, they would not be bothered by anyone.

'How could they damage something that was known for being damaged?' Gaz had thought.

His mum was glad that her son and his friends had somewhere they could play, somewhere she felt they could be safe.

'Liverpool was not as safe as it was when she was a girl,' she had told him one rainy day.

She had been drinking, she always did when it rained and she had drunk herself to the reminiscing stage. Gaz had left before she got to the violent stage, that's when she would usually hit out at him.

But today the sun was shining, school was out and the long summer was theirs. He had arranged to meet Chris Holden at St. Luke's church and Chris was to bring his football, Gaz was bringing 'the sounds'.

His mum had bought him the ghetto blaster for his birthday a month ago, it was no real surprise to him as he had asked her constantly for it since he had seen it in the Kays catalogue just after Christmas. Since then he hadn't let it out of his sight, at home he played it in his bedroom using the power cable, but outside he played it using the batteries he and his friends had clubbed together to buy.

Mostly they listened to the radio but today Chris promised to bring some of his dad's tapes, they weren't originals, his dad had recorded them from albums he had borrowed from the library.

Chris was nowhere to be seen when Gaz arrived so he placed his ghetto blaster on the wall and sat next to it listening to the radio, Steve Wright in the afternoon was on, the show was famed for its characters, Mr. Angry was his favourite.

Cars passed by him as he sat waiting but he paid them no heed. Gaz was thinking that if he had owned a watch he would have been able to tell how long he had been waiting, when he spotted Si Clarkson across the road. Gaz knew Si's older brother Glenn. They attended the same remedial English class.

"Hey Si," Gaz called over to him, "What you up to?"

Si waved, then stood on the kerb looking both ways at the traffic. He had learnt about the Green Cross Code in junior school that year and he practiced it at every opportunity. Even on the empty cul-de-sac where he lived. Deciding it was safe to cross, Si stepped out into the road and still looking both ways he crossed to where Gaz sat on the wall.

"Alright Si, where's your kid?" Gaz asked him.

"He's still at home," Si answered, "he told mum to 'Fuck Off'" so dad grounded him."

Gaz burst into laughter, Si laughed too.

"I'm just off to post this," he said holding a letter up so Gaz could see it.

"What is it?"

"Some biscuits," Si replied, handing the envelope to Gaz, "Dad's always going on at me for not eating my tea, says the Cambodians are starving, says it all the time. So, I'm sending them some biscuits."

Gaz looked down at the envelope. Written in large letters in felt tip across the front were the words.

The Cambodians.

Cambodia.

"Nice one," laughed Gaz, handing the envelope back to Si, "I'm sure they'll appreciate it."

At that moment a ball landed next to the two boys and bounced into the churchyard. "Ahoy," Chris shouted from the opposite pavement.

"Fuck me," Gaz shouted, "Scared the shit out of me then, you dick."

Chris laughed as he crossed the road, "Should have been paying attention, shouldn't you!"

"Did you bring the tape?" Gaz asked.

"Sure did," replied Chris pulling it from his pocket. He placed it next to the ghetto blaster and leapt over the wall after his ball.

"You watch them roads Si," Gaz said to the small boy as he too jumped over the wall.

"I will," he said as Gaz retrieved both his Ghetto blaster and the tape.

Gaz watched as Si repeated his Green Cross Code ritual. When he had seen the boy was safely across the road, he turned to join his friend.

"What's this?" Chris shouted over to him. He was standing at the church wall looking up at a large sign.

"Dunno!" Gaz said joining him, "What's it say?"

Chris read the sign out loud, "Hanscom Construction. St. Luke's redevelopment project. Twelve Luxury Apartments. Coming May 1984."

Both boys looked up at the artist's impression of the new luxury flats, "Who the Fuck in Liverpool can afford a luxury apartment?" asked Gaz.

"Dunno . . . Ah fuck it!" Chris said, "we've got all summer before they'll knock this place down. Come on."

Chris kicked the ball up at the sign, "Put the tape in, get some tunes on."

Gaz opened the tape deck and popped the tape inside, once closed he pressed the play button. Chris bent over as the tape started, turning the volume up to maximum. The music began to play.

"What's this?" asked Gaz.

"It's the *Rolling Stones*," answered Chris, "my dad recorded it yesterday. It's called *Sympathy for the Devil*."

The Beginning?

Afterword

Well, who would have thought we'd get to the end? Yes, we both know it isn't, but that's a different story. However, an end it is. My first novel is written and has now been read, did you enjoy it? I hope you did.

My wish, as you turned each page, was that there was a familiarity about it for something now lost, something forbidden from your youth that gave you great pleasure. That first real horror story you read, the one from your collection that you kept hidden away in your bedroom, as our parents never would agree with such sensational stories.

The intention, when I began writing this, was to create a story that would happily sit amongst the many titles that sat proudly on the shelves of every book shop during the seventies, in my opinion the greatest era of British horror.

Titles that were designed to intrigue young minds, covers so horrific that they couldn't fail in guaranteeing the books purchase, and a story so graphic that the reader couldn't help but smile whilst characters were ripped limb from limb by hordes of giant... (insert your favourite here). God, I miss perusing the huge horror section, now the smallest, trying to choose my next book. There were no bad choices, only varying degrees of inventive deaths.

Alas, those days are gone, some of the authors are sadly no longer with us, others, well they grew up, and with them their stories. We now need our books to be gigantic tomes where a complex world is inhabited by complex characters who toil hard just to survive.

Where are the simple stories? The ones where the reader only needs to accept that things with giant teeth exist to enjoy it? Well, between me and you, your holding one. This is my homage to those great storytellers, those who's imagination didn't need anything more than a belief in somethings existence to create a world around it, a world where death in its most gruesome manner, stalks people like us.

Eddie Davies 2019